SHATTERED

SHATTERED

TERI TERRY

SCHOLASTIC INC.

ISBN 978-0-545-85367-5

12 11 10 9 8 7 6 5 4 3 2   15 16 17 18 19 20/0

Printed in the U.S.A.   40

First Scholastic printing, January 2015

Text set in Charter ITC Std

For my mother

1

IT DOESN'T LOOK LIKE MUCH FROM THE OUTSIDE. BUT WHAT you get outside is often like that. People, especially, can be so different from what you can see that you'd never guess what goes on in their secret places. What they are capable of. In my case, what lurked within was so well hidden even I didn't know about it.

Aiden parks the car along the side of the run-down building. He glances at me. "Don't look so scared, Kyla."

"I'm not," I start to object, but then I glance at the road, and all at once, I am. "Lorders," I hiss, and scrunch down in the seat. A black van pulls in behind us, blocking us in. Leaden dread pools in my veins, holds me still and numb even as everything inside is screaming *run*. The fear takes me back: another time, another Lorder. Coulson. The gun in his hand, pointed at me, and then—

Bang!

Katran's blood. A sea of hot red that covered us both, and took my friend away forever. So like my father's death years ago that it wrenched up that most buried memory. Both dead. Both my fault.

Aiden puts a hand over mine, one worried eye on the mirror and the van, one on me. A door opens; someone steps out. Not dressed in Lorder black? A slight figure, a woman, hat pulled down low to shield her face. She walks to the door of the building. It opens from the inside, and she disappears through it.

"Look at me, Kyla," Aiden says, his voice calm, reassuring, and I tear my eyes away from the van behind us. "There is nothing to worry about; just don't draw their attention." He twists in the driver's seat, slips his arms around me and tries to pull me close, but I'm rigid with fear. "Play along," he says, and I force my body to relax into his. He murmurs into my hair, "Just giving them a reason why we were lingering. In case they're getting curious."

I breathe in slow. *They're not after me.* They'll go away now. *They're not after me.* And then I'm clinging to Aiden, and his arms wrap around me even tighter. There are vehicle sounds behind; tires crunch on gravel. And keep going.

"They're gone," Aiden says, but he doesn't let go. And the relief is so strong that I sag against him, bury my face in his chest. His heart beats fast, drumming a *thump-thump* of safety, warmth, and something *else*.

But this is wrong. He's not Ben.

My fear is replaced by embarrassment, then anger: anger at myself. I pull away. How could I be such a total wimp and let them get to me like that? How could I cling to Aiden just because I was scared? And I remember what he said on the way earlier: Lorders come here. Lorders, government officials, and their families. People with money and power who can make others look away and keep quiet. That woman is probably a Lorder's wife. She is probably here for the same reason as me. I flush.

Aiden's blue eyes are warm, concerned. "Are you sure you can pull this off, Kyla?"

"Yes. Of course I can. And I thought you weren't supposed to call me that anymore."

"It'd be easier if you'd make up your mind what your new name is going to be."

I don't say anything, because I sort of have, but I don't want to share it yet. I'm not sure he'll like it.

"Walk in like you own the place, and no one will look at you twice. It's all anonymous."

"Okay."

"Best get going before anyone else comes."

More Lorders?

I open the car door, step out. It is cold, a gray January day. The chill is reason enough for the scarf wrapped around my head, obscuring an identity that will soon change. I square my shoulders, walk to the door. It opens, and I step inside.

My eyes widen; my feet almost falter until I remember: *Walk like I own the place.* This shiny place, with enormous, plush chairs, soft music, and a smiling nurse? A guard stands discrete in the corner. The woman we saw come out of the Lorder van moments ago is ensconced in a chair with a wineglass in one hand.

The nurse approaches, smiles. "Welcome. Do you know your number?"

"7162," I say, the number Aiden gave me earlier. Even though my name is best kept quiet, I'm not sure I like being known by a number, not after being Slated. Not after having a Levo around my wrist with my number carved into it, classifying me as a criminal for all to see. It's gone now; there are no visible marks left behind, but the scars remain.

The nurse checks a handheld screen, smiles again. "Have a seat for a moment. Your IMET consultant will be with you very soon."

I sit, startled when the chair moves, adjusts to my body. IMET:

Image Enhancement Technology. Barely whispered about, hellishly expensive, and totally illegal. I'm here courtesy of favors owed to Aiden's organization, MIA. MIA may stand for Missing in Action, but it turns out they don't just find missing people and campaign for the truth about the Lorders to be revealed. Turns out they also sneak people out of the UK who need to disappear, and others in at the same time: IMET consultants who know a good black market opportunity when they see one.

The woman in the other chair turns toward me. She is attractive, fifty or so. If the rumors are true, she'll look twenty years younger before she leaves this place. There is an inquisitive glint to her eyes, a *What are you here for?* look. I ignore her.

A door opens, and footsteps approach. She starts to get up, but the steps continue past her, and a man stops in front of me. A doctor? But not like any doctor I've seen before. He is in scrubs, but they are a bright purple shimmery fabric. It matches his streaked hair and purple eyes to perfection, unnatural shimmer and all.

He holds out both hands, helps me up, and air-kisses my cheeks. "Hello, darling. I'm Doc de Jour, but you can call me DJ. This way." His words are a lilting drawl, an unfamiliar accent: Irish?

I follow him and suppress a smirk at the indignant look on the waiting woman's face. She must wonder who I am, why I take precedence. If she only knew.

If she knew, it'd go straight to her Lorder husband.

Doc de Jour is disappointed in me. "Are you *sure* that is all you want done? Hair. In *brown*." He says it like brown hair is the ultimate crime of mediocrity. But blending in is what I need.

"Yes: brown."

He sighs. "Such lovely hair you have, and so hard to match. Like sunshine on early daffodils 12. With highlights 9." He runs his fingers through it, a measuring look in his eyes, like he is copying it for his next patient. Then he studies my face. "How about eye color?"

"No. I like them green."

"They're distinctive; it's a risk," he says, and my eyes widen. What does he know? He winks. "They *are* an interesting shade. Almost apple-green 26, but more intense," he says, then spins the chair I'm sitting in around and looks me up and down. I squirm. "Wouldn't you like to be taller?"

I raise an eyebrow. "You can do that?"

"Of course. It'll take a while, though."

I bristle. "What is wrong with my height?"

"Nothing. If you don't mind jumping to see over things."

"Just the hair."

"Brown. You know IMET is accelerated gene-tech: It is permanent. Brown hair forever. It'll grow that way; no more blondy ever again, unless you come back to see me."

He hands me a mirror, and I look in it. So weird to think next time I do this I won't see the hair I've always had. The color is okay, I guess, but it is so fine—I always wanted thicker hair. Like Amy's gorgeous dark hair, the first thing I'd noticed about my new sister when I was assigned to live with her family as a new Slated, just months ago. "Wait a minute. I wonder if . . ."

He leans down and stares into my eyes with his purple ones. They're hard not to look at. "Yes?"

"Can you make it longer? And thicker. Maybe . . . some streaks in it. Not anything weird: natural-looking."

He claps his hands. "Consider it done."

Later I'm told to lie back on a table that is like the chairs in the waiting area: It molds and grips my body. Flutters of panic fight to keep me awake. Is this how it was when I was Slated? Then, I had no choice; I saw the file photograph. I was tied to a table like any other criminal. The Lorders and their surgery stole my memories, put a chip in my brain that could've killed me before my Levo was taken off. This isn't the same. This is just hair. And it is my choice: I don't *have* to do this.

There is faint music. Everything is misty and vague, and my eyes start to close.

Just hair . . . but it is *the* hair Ben slipped his fingers through when he kissed me.

Since the Lorders took him away and erased his memory, he doesn't know who I am anymore. But what if he fights it, fights what the Lorders have done to him, and starts to remember? Starts to understand why I'm his *dream girl.* What then? He'll never find me if I look different.

I swallow, struggle to form words, to tell them to stop, I changed my mind.

Ben . . .

Faces blur in and out and vanish.

We run. Side by side in the night, but Ben's long legs beat out a slower measure than mine. It is raining, but we don't care. Up a dark hill now, he slips ahead; the narrow path cut into rock is running with water. Soon we're soaked and covered in mud. He's laughing when he reaches the top, and raises his hands to the sky as the rain pounds harder.

"Ben!" I reach up, slip my arms around him, and pull him under a tree, then burrow into his warmth.

But something isn't right.

"Ben?" I pull away a little, look into familiar eyes: brown like melted chocolate, shot through with warm glints. Puzzled eyes. "What is it?"

He shakes his head, pushes me away. "I don't understand."

"What?"

"I thought I knew you, but I don't. Do I?"

"It's me! It's . . ." My voice trails away. I panic inside, casting about for a name, not just any name, but my name. Who am I, really?

He shakes his head, walks away. Runs up the path and is gone.

I sag against the tree. What now? Should I run after him, just so he can deny me again? Or go back the other way, alone.

The sky lights up: A blinding flash dazzles my eyes, shows the trees and pounding rain. Before darkness returns, a tremendous crash shakes into my bones.

While the rest of me whirls with pain at Ben's departure, some part of my brain processes: Standing under a tree in a thunderstorm is dangerous.

But who am I, really? Until I can answer, I don't know which way to go.

2

DAYS LATER, DJ HANDS ME A MIRROR FOR THE FIRST TIME. I
stare, then reach out gingerly with my fingers. The hair—my hair—
even *feels* different, foreign. I don't look like me anymore. Of course,
that is kind of the point. A rich brown it may be, but shimmering with
golden highlights. They bring out the green of my eyes so much that
I stare at them suspiciously, wondering if DJ had been unable to resist
adding some enhancement to them as well, but decide they are still
the eyes I was born with. My hair is not, not in any respect: It's silky,
thick, halfway down my back. I wince as I turn my head: It's heavy, so
much so it hurts. It'll take some getting used to.

"Your scalp will be tender for a while." DJ holds up a small bottle.
"Painkillers, no more than two a day for a week. So . . . ?"

I tear my eyes away from the mirror, and look up at him. "So?"

"Do you like what you see?"

I smile broadly. "I like."

"One final touch is needed, I think." DJ places a finger on either
side of my chin, tilts my face up and stares at my eyes. He stares long
enough for it to be uncomfortable if it were anyone else, but somehow
it isn't with him. It is like he is measuring, and assessing—what? The
skin, the bone structure supporting it, the tissues, almost as though if
he stares long enough he can see the individual cells and the genes
inside them. He nods to himself, then turns to a cabinet with many

drawers; he opens one, then another, and draws something out, then holds it toward me. Something low-tech.

"Glasses? I don't need glasses."

"Trust me. Put them on," he says. I do, and look in the mirror. Startled, I gasp; look back at him, then again at the mirror.

The frames are a delicate silvery-gray metal and suit my face as if made for it, but that isn't what made me gasp: It's my eyes. The lenses are completely clear, yet somehow, I am changed. My eyes aren't green anymore. More a blue-gray. I turn my head side to side, take the glasses off, put them back on again. Study myself like looking at a stranger. This dark-haired girl is *other*. She looks older, too. No one would recognize her. Not just Ben; I could walk past Mum and Amy in the street, and they'd be none the wiser.

"That's amazing. You're amazing."

"Why, yes, I am." He smiles. "And this technology"—he touches the glasses—"isn't known in the UK, at least not yet. So wearing them shouldn't arouse any suspicions." He spins my chair around so we are facing each other again. "So. The green-eyed blond girl is gone, replaced by a more sophisticated version, one who can pass for the eighteen you need for ID and travel if necessary. What is next for you?" I hesitate, and he laughs. "Keep your secrets. I hope—no, I am sure—we will cross paths again."

"Thanks for everything."

He tilts his head, something in his eyes still measuring, assessing. "What is it?"

He shakes his head. "Nothing, and everything. Time for you to go." He holds the door open. As I step through it, he adds, "Tell Aiden I need to see him."

• • •

Later that day I'm in a small room hidden in the back of a factory. A dark room where new identities are forged. New lives begin.

"Name?" an unidentified man asks.

This is the moment. I'm not Lucy, the name given when I was born. I'm not Rain, the name I eventually chose for myself after I was taken by Nico and his Antigovernment Terrorists—Free UK, as he called them—and shaped to be their weapon against the Lorders. I'm not Kyla, the name picked for me at the hospital after I was caught and Slated for being an AGT terrorist.

I am who I choose to be.

"Name?" the question is repeated.

I am none of them. I am all of them.

"Riley. Riley Kain," I answer, one name that combines them all.

Soon I clutch a forged ID card in my hand: a dark-haired, gray-eyed eighteen-year-old cleared to travel and live her own life: Riley Kain.

What life do I choose to live?

3

THE BUS RATTLES DOWN CITY, THEN COUNTRY, ROADS. NO more hiding needed with my new ID and new look, and I'd insisted on traveling back from London by myself. But who could have known an AGT bomb would be found on one of the London trains today, the entire network shut down while they were all checked? So the bus was the only option. Every jar of the road reverberates through my sore head, and I have to hold my hands together to stop them from gathering my new hair up to support its weight.

Fields, farms, and villages rush past, become familiar. We're nearing the village I lived in with Mum and Amy, the one I left the day Nico and his remote-detonated AGT bomb nearly killed me. I ran away to hide at Mac's. Mac is a friend, yes, and one I trust, but he hasn't known me for long to take such a risk. He is the cousin of Amy's boyfriend, and somehow involved with Aiden and MIA. With-out knowing or insisting on knowing all that happened—what I've done, or why—he and Aiden were there, offering help. A safe place to hide. A chance at a new life. The old one with Mum and Amy ended just a short time ago, but already it feels distant, another life slipping away.

A long black car approaches from the other direction, a coffin in the back, and traffic slows to a crawl on both sides. A second black car follows the hearse. It has two occupants, arms linked: one young, with dark hair and skin, one older and pale. In a flash, they are gone. My eyes widen.

That was Mum and Amy.

The bus stops near the end of Mac's long lane, and I rush up it on foot. Most of me is grappling with what I saw: Whose funeral were they attending? A deep feeling of dread settles inside, while some other part of my mind is distracted, processing that the air and sky have that heavy chill about them that says *snow,* but I've never seen snow, and wonder why I feel this sense of expectation. While there must have been snow when I was Lucy, a child growing up in the Lake District, her memories were Slated away.

Another bend and Mac's house appears: a lone building on a lonely lane. From this vantage point, a small sliver of white over the high back gate says a van is there: Aiden's?

I'm expected. A curtain moves, and the door opens as I reach it: Mac.

"Wow. Is that really you, Kyla?"

"It's Riley now," I say, going in and wincing as I take off my hat and scarf and chuck them on a chair.

Aiden is there now and sees my face. "I told you I could have picked you up. Are you all right?"

I shrug and go past them to the computer down the hall. Skye, Ben's dog, tries to jump up and lick my face, but I give her a quick pat and push her back. Mac's computer is an illegal; it isn't government-monitored. I meant to do a general search for local news on the off chance that funeral was picked up, but something makes me go to MIA's website first.

Lucy Connor, missing from her home in Keswick since age ten.

Recently reported found: I had pushed the button on the screen myself, hoping to find a way back to who I was all those years ago, through whoever reported me missing. Now clearly marked *Deceased*. I stare at the screen, unable to process the word.

A hand touches my shoulder. "You're looking well for a dead person. I like the new hair," Mac says.

I turn; Aiden has also followed and stands next to him. There is something in his face. "You *knew*," I hiss.

He says nothing, and that says it all.

"Why deceased?"

"You are. Officially," Aiden says. "According to government records, you died when a bomb exploded at your assigned home. Lorders have reported you as dead."

"But there was no body. Lorders wouldn't be fooled. My bus went past a funeral procession on the way here; Mum and Amy were following the hearse. Was that *my* funeral?"

"I'm sorry. I didn't know it was today."

"But you *knew*. That they think I'm dead." I'm angry, but I'm also confused. "Why would the Lorders say I died?"

"Perhaps they don't want to admit they don't know what happened to you?" Mac suggests.

"I don't understand why the Lorders would do that."

Aiden tilts his head to one side. He's not sure, either; the uncertainty is in his eyes. "Perhaps they don't want to admit they failed," he says. Aiden had assumed the bomb at our house had been Lorder, as payback for my role in helping Ben cut off his Levo, and I never set him straight. He doesn't know the dangerous double game I'd played, for the Lorders and Nico's AGT. Guilt twists inside at secrets kept, for help repaid by silence. But he keeps his secrets, too.

My eyes fill with tears. "I can't leave Mum and Amy thinking I died in that explosion. I can't."

Aiden sits next to me and takes my hands in his. "You have to. It's better this way; they can't be made to tell what they don't know."

I pull my hands away. "No. *No.* I can't leave it like this. I didn't like it when I thought they thought I was missing, but this is far worse! I can't leave with them thinking I'm dead."

"You can't see them. They may be watched, in case you make contact; it's too dangerous," Aiden says.

"No one would recognize me anymore."

Aiden shakes his head. "Think this through. You've got another life waiting for you in Keswick. Don't throw it away now."

"But Mum—"

"She wouldn't want you to take the risk," he says.

And I fall silent. I know he's right. If I could take her aside and tell her the whole story and ask her what I should do, she'd say, *Stay safe.* My head throbs, and I twist my hair in my hands, flinch as it pulls, then hold it up. Who knew thick hair hurt so much? I ache to lie down, but all this needs to be dealt with now. Why did MIA list me as deceased because the Lorders said I'm dead?

"Are you okay?" Mac asks.

I shrug and flinch with that movement, also. "There're some painkillers in my bag," I say, and Mac gets it for me, and a glass of water. I take one.

"You should rest," Aiden says.

"Not yet. You have to explain something to me first. Why did you put me as deceased on MIA? Do Lorders monitor it; did you do it for them?"

Aiden and Mac exchange a glance. Mac answers. "We don't *know* they do; the links are hidden and changed frequently. But we can't make it too hard to get to, or it wouldn't be useful for those who need it. We assume Lorders monitor the website, and probably do so regularly."

"But what about when I reported myself found? Won't they know?"

Aiden shakes his head. "That doesn't appear anywhere on-screen; it notifies MIA. And as I've told you before, at length, only the individuals involved in a particular missing person case know about it, and only when they need to know. Listings get taken down when we judge it is safe to do so for all involved."

I'd quizzed Aiden on this relentlessly already, on who knows where I am now and where I'm going. And I believe him when he says it is all on a need-to-know basis only; he still hasn't even told me who reported me missing. Though I guess it is my real mother, he won't say until he judges I *need to know.* He must've thought I was extra paranoid; he didn't know the real reason for all my questions. He didn't know about Nico's plant in MIA—that I'd spotted one of MIA's drivers at the terrorist camp. I had to be sure he wouldn't know I'd reported myself found and tell Nico. I should warn Aiden about him, but how can I without telling him all the rest?

"But what happens generally when someone is found?" I ask. "If they're kids like me who were Slated, it'll never be safe for them to go back to their original lives. It's illegal."

"It doesn't usually happen like that," Aiden admits. "Though sometimes people do get in touch secretly, but keep their separate lives."

"Sometimes. What happens most of the time when someone is found?"

Aiden and Mac exchange a glance. Aiden answers. "Usually when we find out what happened to somebody . . . it's too late."

"They're dead for real, you mean." He nods. "But I'm different." Always back to *Kyla is different*.

"But you're officially dead," Aiden says. "You can't return to your life here. There are few choices. One is what you have chosen: to go back under a different identity; to find your past."

"I have to." I sigh. We've been over this before, but I never told Aiden the real reason. I never told him about my father's death, about his last words to me. *Never forget who you are!* And I did forget. I have to find out who I was, for him.

"What is your new name again?" Mac asks. I fish my ID out of my pocket and hand it to him. "Riley Kain," he says. "A little different, but I like it."

Aiden frowns. "That sounds kind of close to Kyla, doesn't it?"

"Not that close," I say. I knew he'd think that. If he knew my name with the AGT was Rain, he'd be really annoyed, but not many living know me by that name anymore.

Just Nico, a voice whispers inside. I push it away. That'd only matter if he came across my new name, and how could that ever happen? I'm not going anywhere near the AGT. This name lets me hang on to all the parts of myself. If I let go of them, what is left?

My head is fuzzy. I let Mac help me up and lead me to the sofa in the front room, and a blanket. He and Aiden are murmuring at the door.

For all my insisting it has to be done, that I have to find out who I was, I'm afraid. What will I find?

"Few choices?" I say, Aiden's earlier words filtering through. "What other choice is there?"

Aiden steps back into the room, kneels next to me. Smooths my hair away from my face.

"You know, Kyla. You could tell your story for MIA, be one of our witnesses."

"Then run away again."

"I wouldn't put it that way. We'd hide you someplace safe, or you could leave completely while the evidence is being gathered. Until we are ready."

"To expose the Lorders to the world. To make the people bring the government crashing down."

"Yes."

He's a dreamer; the Lorders will never go quietly. If at all. But it is a good dream. I smile back at Aiden, and his lips quirk.

"You're nice on painkillers."

"Shut up."

"And your new hair is gorgeous."

"It hurts."

"Take another painkiller?"

I shake my head. "Better not. Aiden, there are things I haven't told you."

"I know. Tell me when you're ready."

Aiden's eyes are warm, gentle. If he knew everything about me, all I've done, would they still smile at me this way? He is too trusting for this world; he has to know. I have to tell him.

I sigh. "There is one thing I have to tell you now, ready or not."

"What is that?"

"Your driver. The one who came when we saw Ben running at that track. Don't trust him."

Aiden's face goes serious, withdrawn; thinking. "That would

explain a few things," he says finally. "We'll look into it. But the curious thing is, how would you know anything about it?"

How nice it would be to tell Aiden *everything*. To not carry the burden alone. But before I can form a sentence, he shakes his head.

"No; don't answer that question. Not while you're silly on painkillers. Tell me your secrets when you are sure you want to." He starts to stand, but my mind is drifting back to what he said before.

"Wait. What did you mean by I could *leave completely*?"

"You could leave the country."

"I could?"

"You know MIA helps people leave when it is too dangerous to stay. To slip out of the country, over the sea. To United Ireland, or beyond."

United Ireland: a free place of whisper, not reality. Since they left the UK decades ago, their existence is never officially acknowledged. Would it be any better there than here?

Could I do that, just leave it all behind? My eyes close. There is so much Aiden doesn't know. Things I didn't tell him. I told myself it was because knowledge is dangerous, that he is better off not knowing. But is that really the whole reason? An uncomfortable twist of my guts says there is more to it: more not wanting him to know the things I've done. To look at me without that warmth in his eyes. I have so few friends; I can't risk losing another.

Willing or not to begin with, I really *was* in the AGT. I really *was* a terrorist. Even though I chose to turn my back on them and their methods in the end, how could I be a witness for MIA against the Lorders? I'm the poster child for why Slating is a good thing.

Over the sea . . .

To what and to where? To the unknown.

To run away.

I trudge up the path. Up and up, as fast as short legs can go. Soon all the streets and buildings are gone from sight. All is still, quiet. Alone at last.

I'm nervous but remember the way, though I haven't come by myself before. The walk seems longer alone, and I'm relieved when I get to the gate.

There is an eerie low mist hugging the stones. They lumber, asleep, half hidden in white. There is sunshine above; the mountains are bright sentries all around their sleeping babies. I walk across the field, into the mist, and press my hands against a stone. The sun doesn't make it through the mist; they are cold and huge close up. But when you stand back and look at the mountains, the stones are small.

Children of the mountains, Daddy calls them, and so do I, though I know from school that the stone circle was put here at Castlerigg by men and Druids, not mountains. Thousands and thousands of years ago. I start on one side, touching each one and counting.

I'm more than halfway around when a voice calls out, "I knew I'd find you here." Daddy.

I don't say anything; I keep counting the stones. The mountains had many children. I'm just one.

Daddy walks up to me. "Number?" he asks.

"Twenty-four," I say, and he walks around with me, and I count out loud as we go.

"Twenty-five."

"She's really worried."

"Twenty-six."

"She's scared something will happen to you if you are out of her sight."

I sigh. "Twenty-seven."

"I know she can be difficult."

"Twenty-eight."

"But she loves you."

"Twenty-nine."

"You shouldn't run away."

"But you do sometimes. Thirty." We stop. "And she makes me crazy."

Daddy laughs. "I'll let you in on a secret." He looks both ways. "Sometimes, she makes me crazy, too. Let's go home and be crazy together."

"Finish first?" I say.

"Of course."

We keep counting, both out loud now, until we get to forty.

"Done," I say, and we walk across to the gate. I look back. The mist is starting to bleed away. The stone children will be happy when they wake up in the sunshine; they have one another to play with when we are gone.

Later, I promise never to run away again. But my fingers are crossed when I say it.

4

I WAKE EARLY, STIFF AND ALARMED AS I SEEM UNABLE TO move. Then I realize that Skye has climbed onto the sofa and is sprawled across my legs: a heavy golden retriever blanket, one disinclined to wake up and tricky to dislodge.

I pad into the kitchen to make tea, and peer out the window. The world is dipped in frost and makes my hands itch for a pencil and sketch pad: Intricate white patterns trace fence and trees, decorate cars and parts of cars in Mac's backyard, one that is more workshop than garden. No snow, at least not yet, so I had that wrong. And best of all: no white van, so Aiden is gone. That'll make today's plan easier. Once I work out what it is.

I find my sketch pad and settle back on the sofa with my tea and Skye, meaning to draw frost's delicate patterns, but instead a stone circle insists on being rendered. And a small blond girl—me, perhaps eight years old?—hands pressed against a stone. Was that dream a real place? Everything inside says *yes*. I might find it when I go to Keswick; I might touch each stone, and count the mountain's children once again. But he won't find me there, not this time. He is gone forever.

Dad died trying to rescue me from Nico and the AGT five years ago, but the memory is recent; it had been buried so deep, for so long, that when it finally came back, it felt like it just happened.

Why am I going back? Dad won't be there. I can't remember

anyone else from that life. Was it my real mother I was running away from in that dream?

She loves you, he said. Fingers crossed or not, I promised not to run away again. It wasn't my choice when I left before, but now it is: I have to go back.

But I can't leave yet, not without saying good-bye. Not this time. I have to tell Mum and Amy what really happened.

I'm pulling on boots when Mac finally emerges, bleary-eyed and yawning.

He raises an eyebrow. "So, let me guess: You're going to walk Skye. Just a short jaunt around the fields and back."

"Sure. That's it." Skye's tail thumps on the ground with the word *walk.*

"Where are you going?"

"I think you know."

"Aiden won't be happy."

"But you know I have to do this."

He stares levelly back. "I'm beginning to realize more and more that there are times when, no matter the risk, something must be done. Some things *must* be said. Is this one of those times?"

"Yes. I have to tell Mum. She's lost too many other people in her life." Mac, of all people, should understand: from the guilt he has lived with since his school bus was bombed over six years ago. For surviving, yes, but most of all, for not speaking out about other survivors, like Mum's son, Robert, who later disappeared and was Slated. Gone without a trace. Just like her parents, the first Lorder prime minister and his wife, both assassinated by an AGT bomb when she was younger than I am now. I can't leave her thinking the same happened to me.

Skye slumps back down between us, evidently having worked out that the walk isn't happening, at least not with me.

"I'll take you later," Mac promises her, then turns back to me. "I just happened to drive through your village the other day."

"You did?"

"Your house is still uninhabitable from the fire that spread after the blast. No one is living there. Where would they be?"

"Oh. I didn't think of that. They're probably staying at Aunt Stacey's." I frown. Aunt Stacey and Mum are close, and she *seems* all right. But her brother is Mum's ex—a Lorder. If Stacey sees me, would she keep it to herself? "I know: I'll try Mum's work. She goes for a walk at lunch most days. I'll lurk about and see if I can catch her coming or going."

"Sounds a bit thin."

"It's the best I've got."

"Want me to drive you?"

"No. I'm less conspicuous on my own." That is what I say out loud, but this is something I have to do alone. And despite my new hair, despite my new ID, going there is still risky. If anyone is actually watching for me, would they be fooled?

"Take my bicycle."

"Okay." I smile. "Thanks."

"All right then. But be careful. And have some breakfast first."

I'm too early for Mum's lunch break, and something makes me stop at the graveyard. I get off the bicycle and lean it against the crumbling stone wall. Frost outlines bare trees; headstones are traced in ghostly white. I step through the gate and start down the path, my breath a moving shroud around me in the cold air.

It is a small village church, and the newest grave isn't hard to find. There is no headstone yet, if there will indeed be one, but the ground is disturbed: a patch of brown in gray frost-tipped grass, with a cover of scattered flowers. Was some other unidentified girl buried here, or was the casket empty, perhaps weighted with stones so no one would notice?

I kneel down, take off my gloves, and reach out tentative fingers to a frozen lily. Is its fragile beauty preserved by cold? No. A petal shatters at my touch.

"Hello," a voice says, piercing the quiet, and I jump. A voice I know.

I stand, turn. Stare at her, unable to speak.

"Were you a friend of Kyla's?" Mum asks.

"You don't know me?"

Her brows knit together. She looks older, though it hasn't been long since I last saw her. Her eyes are tired, red. "Sorry, have we met?"

Tears well up in my eyes. I take off my glasses, sweep my dark hair to one side, wincing a little as the extra weight still hurts. "It's me. It's Kyla," I whisper.

She goes pale, shakes her head.

"Mum?" I reach a hand toward her, but then she steps back, turns, and scans the churchyard and road beyond.

"Put those glasses back on," she says, and after I do, she links an arm in mine. She pulls me down the path at the back of the church, then out the gate into the woods behind it, walking fast. The path twists, then divides, and we take the less traveled branch.

She finally stops. Wheezing a little, she turns and looks at me.

"It really *is* you. You're really okay."

My tears start again, and then hers. She pulls me in for a hug. We stand there for a long time, not moving, not speaking.

She finally pulls away. "Your hair?" She reaches out to touch it. "IMET?"

I nod.

"How? No, don't answer! Is it . . ." She hesitates. "Is it Lorders?"

I shake my head. "They don't know where I am. And it wasn't them who tried to kill me, but for some reason of their own they've said I died. I don't understand why."

"So it wasn't their bomb, then. David said it wasn't, but . . ." And she shrugs, no need to fill in the sentence. She didn't believe him. Why would she believe her estranged husband, after all he put us through?

"No. It was AGT."

She pales. "They're after you?"

I shrug. "They think I betrayed them to the Lorders."

"Did you?"

I shake my head. "Not on purpose. Lorders tracked me to them." I don't say the rest of it: that I went against Nico's plans. That I wasn't there with her and the rest of her family next to Prime Minister Gregory so Nico could detonate the bomb I unknowingly wore. That instead I left to bust out his prisoner, Dr. Lysander: my doctor. The one who invented Slating. If he finds out I'm still alive, Nico's desire for revenge would have nothing to do with logic; to him, it'd be personal.

"Then maybe it's a good thing the Lorders have said you are dead. Maybe the AGT will believe them." She reaches a hand to my cheek. "I'm so glad you're all right, but you shouldn't have come here. It's too dangerous. And how'd you know where to find me? I didn't even know I was coming. I just went for a walk, and my feet brought me."

"I didn't. I thought you'd be at work; I was going to try there. I couldn't leave with you thinking I died."

She grips me in a fierce hug. "Have you got somewhere safe to go?"

"I think so. I'll try to get word to you later."

"Don't. It's safer that way."

"What about Amy? How is she?"

"She's distraught. But I can't tell her about you. At least, not now."

My tears are starting again. Amy has been my big sister since I was assigned to her family after I was Slated. No matter that it has only been a matter of months; Amy'd never do anything to hurt me on purpose. But could she keep such a big secret from the world?

"She's safer if she doesn't know," Mum says. "I'll look after her."

"I know. All right."

"Dr. Lysander called, sent flowers. She seemed genuinely distressed about you."

Another twist of pain inside. Dr. Lysander doesn't deserve to not know the truth, but there is no safe way to tell her.

Mum stares at me so long, it's like she is memorizing my face, then kisses my cheek. "I better go. Wait awhile before you follow." She grips me tight one more time, then turns and half runs back down the path.

I lean against a tree, hugging my arms around myself.

So much pain: hers, Amy's, mine. And that whole charade of a funeral. For what? Why did the Lorders pretend I died?

After a while I trudge back through the woods. When I reach the church, I hang back by the gate, but there is no one in sight. I retrieve the bicycle and start the miles back to Mac's.

Before long, thick heavy white flakes fall from the sky, swirling gently about me. I hold my hands out to catch them as they fall; they settle on my hat, my hair, changing brown to white. Obscuring my disguise; obscuring all of me. Pedaling gets harder as the snow thickens on the ground, and after a while I get off and push the bike.

When I finally get back to the house, I'm soaked and half frozen. A relieved Mac has me sit in front of the fire.

Skye is glued to the window, her eyes darting with each snowflake. "She looks a little freaked out by the weather," I say.

"That's nothing; when there is a thunderstorm, she shakes and hides under the bed. Speaking of hiding, Aiden called while you were gone."

"And?"

"I told him you went for a walk."

Mac's face says it all. "I gather he didn't believe you, and isn't happy about it."

"How'd you guess? So, did everything go well? Did you say what you had to say?"

"Yes."

"Feeling ready to move on now?"

"Can I warm up first?"

"You've got until tomorrow morning. Aiden's coming at nine. Trains are back on, and tickets have been organized; there's a computer file for you to study tonight with details of your new life."

There is one more good-bye I need to make. Late that night, after Mac's gone to sleep, I stand on a chair in the kitchen and get the owl sculpture down from the top of the fridge. I put it on the table and run my fingers lightly across its beak, the outstretched wings. All made of scrap bits of metal, but in a brilliant synthesis: It looks and feels so real. Ben's mother made it, made it for me at his request from a drawing I did. It seems so long ago. Now she is dead, killed along with her husband by Lorders. Just for asking too many questions about what happened to Ben.

I run my fingers along the back until I feel the faint edge of paper, grip it between two fingernails, and pull. I unfold the note that holds Ben's last words to me; his last words while he was still *my Ben*.

Dear Kyla,

If you have found this, it means things have gone very wrong. I'm sorry to cause you pain. But know that this was my decision, and mine alone. No one else is to blame.

Love, Ben

Despite his words, at the time I thought it was my fault that Ben wanted to cut off his Levo, and all that followed: his seizures, his mum telling me to leave. The Lorders taking him, my not knowing if he was alive or dead. Then he was found by MIA, changed somehow by the Lorders, so he didn't even know who I was. That last time I saw Ben I tried, I really tried, to get through to him, to tell him to resist the Lorders. There was a moment when I saw something in his eyes; I thought he believed me, that he understood. All I can do for Ben now is hope.

And the other thing I worked out well after the fact was that Nico had been working on Ben to cut off his Levo, to try to provide the trauma that would trigger the return of my memories of being with Nico and the AGT. But even with that, it is still my fault. If it weren't for me, Nico wouldn't have had a reason to go near him, would he?

I stare at the note in my hands. Should I take it with me? I'm tempted. But somehow it belongs where I found it the first time, where it has been hiding ever since. I fold it up, carefully slip it inside the owl, and put the owl back on top of Mac's fridge. He'll keep it safe.

Maybe one day, Ben and I will come back for it. Together.

5

THE NEXT MORNING, SNOW IS THICK ON THE GROUND; THE lane is impassable. After a call from Aiden, Mac says he'll walk down the lane with me to meet him on the main road.

I hesitate by the door, reluctant to leave what I know for what I do not, a place where I feel safe . . . for what?

Mac meets my eye. "You'll be back."

"Will I?"

"Oh yes. Skye would be very upset if you didn't visit again." He opens the door, and Skye bounds out and off the step, then skids to a stop, startled as the snow comes almost all the way to her nose.

I step out, gather some into my gloved hands, and hold it out for her to sniff. "It's snow," I explain. I roll it into a ball and throw it. She jumps to chase it, leaping in and out of the snow instead of running through it, then looks very puzzled when the snowball is indistinguishable from the rest of the snow where it landed.

Mac laughs and insists on carrying my small duffel bag of belongings. We plunge down the lane, snow well past our knees.

"So," I say, "did Aiden still sound annoyed?"

"He is at me."

"Oh. Sorry."

Mac shrugs. "He'll get over it. Once he sees that you're all right."

When we reach the main road, thankfully plowed, Aiden's van is already there.

"Thanks for putting up with me. For everything," I say. Where would I be now without Mac's place to run to, to hide away in?

Mac gives me a hug and opens the van door, then holds Skye when she tries to jump into the van next to me. I wave through the window, blinking furiously, trying to keep myself together until they are gone from sight.

Aiden nods once when I say hello, then keeps his attention on the icy road, on keeping us on it. The silence is as frosty as the winter morning until he pulls in front of the train station.

"Aiden, I'm sorry. But I had to see Mum before I could go. Don't blame Mac; he couldn't have stopped me. Don't let us say good-bye like this."

He catches my hand in his. Face serious, his deep blue eyes stare into mine. "Kyla, please be more careful in the future. Don't let anything slip. Your life, and those of others, depends on your not getting caught."

"Don't let anything slip—like getting my name wrong?"

"Exactly."

"Like you just did? I'm Riley now, remember?"

A trace of a smile crosses his face. He reaches into a folder, then hands me a plastic card. "Here is your train ticket. Don't lose it."

I roll my eyes, tuck it in my pocket. "I'll try not to."

"Have you got your ID?"

I give him a look, but he doesn't relent. I sigh, fish into my bag, and hold out my new ID card so he can see it, then tuck it away again.

"And have you got your story straight from the file I sent? Tell me."

"I'm Riley Kain. I'm eighteen, and my birthday is September 17, 2036. I'm from Chelmsford, an only child. My parents are both schoolteachers. I'm going to Keswick and staying at some place for under-twenty-ones along Derwentwater, called Waterfall House for Girls, and I'm signing up for CAS: the Cumbrian Apprenticeship Scheme. Do I really have to do that, by the way?"

"You can't just visit; you have to be there for a reason." He smiles properly this time, and the tight knot of tension inside me eases. "I did consider a hospitality job, majoring in dish-washing; we've got a connection in a hotel there. So things could be worse."

"Thanks. But you haven't told me one kind of big bit of information."

"What is that?"

"How do I find who reported me missing?"

His lips quirk. "I've told you before: It's need-to-know."

I stare at him, indignant. "Who needs to know more than I do now! Aren't you going to tell me?"

"Can't I leave it as a surprise?"

I glare.

"Just kidding—it'll be easy to find your mother, Stella Connor. She runs Waterfall House. She knows you're coming; she knows you are her missing daughter."

My mother. My actual, real mother: the one who gave birth to me, not one assigned in a Lorder insta-family. She was the one who reported me missing, just like I thought. My mother . . . the one I can't remember.

Aiden squeezes my hand, as if he can see the thoughts that are keeping me from speaking. "Get going. Don't look like security worries you, or they'll pay extra attention. Just sail through the gate like you haven't a care in the world."

"Okay," I manage to say. But I'm still sitting in the van, and Aiden is still holding my hand.

"Kyla—Riley, I mean—take care of yourself. You know what to do if you need help, if anything goes wrong?"

I nod. Aiden's file also mentioned a certain community notice board. One where a coded note will reach his contact.

"I hope this works out for you. I hope you find what you're looking for. But if you don't . . ." His voice trails away. "Anyhow, best get going." He still holds my hand in his, some emotion too raw and private in his eyes, but I can't look away. Seconds slow and stretch until finally he lets go.

I clamber out of the van with my bag, shut the door, then turn and hold up my hand in a good-bye; a hand now empty and cold. Words are stuck in a throat that feels tight. Another friend I may never see again. I stare at him through the window, storing him up: the way he tilts his head to one side when he looks at me intently like he is now, the fiery glint of his red hair in the morning sun. Aiden has done so much for me, and all I do is make him worry and cause problems. None of this could have been easy to arrange, and I didn't even say a proper thank-you.

But like he can see what is inside me, Aiden nods his head. *It's okay. Go on,* he mouths.

I turn, square my shoulders, and walk away from his van to the front of the station. As I approach, the barriers open. Aiden's file said they detect tickets and ID anywhere on your person and operate automatically; they also scan for weapons. Guards in a booth glance my way and then back at their security screens. I'm through. An arrow coded to my ticket lights up at my feet, shows which way to go. I start to walk away from the barriers to the designated elevator, still thinking of all the things I should have said . . .

DJ! What with first me being upset about my so-called funeral, then Aiden being angry I went to see Mum, I forgot all about the IMET doctor's message—that he wants to see Aiden. I turn to look through the glass barriers, but Aiden's van is already disappearing from sight.

Too late. I hope it wasn't important.

6

THE ELEVATOR DROPS SWIFTLY, THEN OPENS TO AN UNDER-
ground platform. The train is already there; once again an arrow at
my feet is coded to my ticket and points the way to the right car of the
train and then to my seat. Other passengers move around me, following arrows of their own.

Have I ever been on a train before? If I have, I don't remember. I
put my bag into the overhead, then second thoughts have me pull it
back down to retrieve my ID and put it in my pocket with my ticket
before shoving it back up again. I can't lose my ID. Unlike most people's, mine would be quite a bother to replace.

The train is about half full; no one sits next to me. I have a window
seat, and when the train leaves moments later, a vid runs in the window: glorious countryside, or Antarctic glaciers, or a steamy jungle.
All at the flick of a switch, and I can't stop myself from trying them all.
I'm glad Aiden's file explained this, or I would have been both alarmed
and baffled. After a while I notice almost no one else uses the window
vid, and I turn mine off. I study fellow passengers instead.

A few are younger and in jeans like me, perhaps students or off on
apprenticeships, but most look like businesspeople. Both men and
women in suits, much like my assigned dad wore when he was off sup-
posedly installing and maintaining government computer systems.
Though who knows what he really did for the Lorders? He traveled all
over the country, or so he said; a nervous thought makes me check

every passenger I can see to make sure he isn't here. He did travel by car to some places, and there were buses also for short journeys, like to London, but most long-distance vehicular travel is banned now: All must travel by environment-friendly high-speed train.

The minutes tick to an hour; the train stops several times at other underground stations. At one, a harassed-looking mother with a boy about four years old gets on, his small hand clenched tight in hers. They sit a few rows in front of me. Before long his head peeks over the seat, dark eyes staring at mine. I smile and he dips down. Seconds later his head bobs up again, giggling and flashing a crooked grin this time, until his mother makes him sit down. He squirms into her lap and her arms go around him.

A mother holding her child close. Was that how things were with me and my mother? I blink hard, then stare at the window vid screen, as blank and dead as my memories of her. I close my eyes. Maybe when we see each other, it'll all come back, like I am ten years old again. Maybe we'll run to each other and she'll hold me, and I'll be *home.* I'll know who I was, who I am.

Maybe, I won't.

There is a panic inside, one that says *run.* That not knowing may be better than knowing; that things will change, and change isn't always good. I'd been desperate before to know who I was, where I came from, why I was Slated. Finding out about Nico's AGT and their plans for me didn't make anything better, did it?

Some part of me notices that while I've been thinking, the train has stopped. For much longer than at any other stop. I open my eyes; the doors are still closed. We're not at a station?

I glance about at the other passengers, and it is tangible, the growing unease. What is happening? The woman and boy get out of their seats and walk to the connecting door to the next car at the front of ours. I've seen people go in and out of it, returning with steaming cups in their hands. But this time the door won't open. They go back to their seats.

Moments later the locked door opens, and unease turns to dread. Lorders. Two of them, with steely, dead eyes. In black ops gear, vests. One has a weapon in hand, the other a small device. There is a train guard with them, a bead of sweat on his brow.

"Get your tickets and IDs out, folks," the train guard says, his voice not quite steady. And passengers shuffle, get cards out of bags and pockets. I get mine out, hand shaking. *Get a grip.* Aiden's notes said a ticket and ID check is common. That mine'll pass fine, to stay calm if it happens. But he never said anything about Lorders being involved.

The Lorder with the gun stays at the door; the other follows the guard. When they get to the first passenger, the guard scans his ticket and ID. Then the Lorder holds up the device he carries and orders the passenger to look inside it until it beeps; first with one eye, then the other.

A portable retinal scanner?

This is not a standard check. Swirls of fear turn to panic. Glasses must come off to scan retinas; they'll see my eye color is masked. If only I'd let DJ *change* them to gray permanently, not mask them; vanity to keep my eyes green might kill me. I could take them off before they get here, hope they don't notice, but then I panic further: Who knows if my retinal key will show up the wrong name, that of a dead girl, Kyla Davis? We had them done at school. And at the hospital. I glance back, but there are Lorders at the back door also. Blocking the way.

Nowhere to go. Trapped. As a Slated, seeking out my past life is completely illegal. Not to mention the IMET and traveling under a false identity. After everything, is this as far as I get? Keswick should be just minutes away now. Did my fake ID trigger some warning? Are they looking for me?

They get closer, row by row. The guard checks each ticket and ID; the Lorder operates the retinal scanner.

Something bumps my foot and I almost scream. I glance down; the small boy is crawling under the seats. Ahead they have reached his mother. Her face is beyond pale, more gray, and her shaking hand holds out her ID and ticket. The guard scans them; they pass. But the Lorder's lips curve in a small smile of satisfaction. He knows. He is certain he's found the one he looks for. *It's not me.* He holds up the retinal scanner to her eye. Instead of a beep, it buzzes. His smile widens.

His hand clamps on her shoulder, pulls her up. Pushes her into the aisle. "Walk!" he barks. They start toward the front of the car. There is a small cry behind. I don't dare turn, but she does, and her face crumples. Moments later one of the Lorders from the back of the car walks past, dragging the small boy along with him.

They disappear through the front connecting door. No one says anything; no one looks at anyone. I'm horrified, but also *relieved.* They weren't after me. Not this time. But if my seat had been before hers, and they'd scanned my retinas . . . I quake inside.

And then I'm ashamed. What will happen to them now? I'll never know if she did anything bad enough to warrant being hauled off by the Lorders like that; I'll never know what happens to her, or her son. What if everyone in this car had said, together, *No, you can't take them.* Could we have stopped it?

The answer might have been yes, for a few minutes. But they'd have reinforcements at the next station; we'd all be arrested and taken away. We'd face the same fate as she will. Is that a good enough reason to say nothing?

What if every person in the country said *no,* all at once, like Aiden thinks they will if they know what really goes on. They can't arrest every single one of us.

7

I STEP OUT OF THE DIM STATION ELEVATOR INTO DAZZLING sunshine. Keswick sunshine. It is cold, crisp; the air is so chill that breathing it in almost makes me cough. No snow on the ground here today, but above? White-peaked fells. There is a prickle on the back of my neck, my spine, but not from the cold. It is a physical reaction to being in this place, to breathing this air. I stand stock-still, gaping up at the mountains, until a whisper of sanity draws me back to here and now. *Don't draw attention.* I force my eyes to drop and look around me.

Only a few other passengers have come off here, and they are walking swiftly away. There is a Lorder van parked next to the station, blocking the view of one of the elevators; are they taking their new prisoners from the train? I walk away from any watchful eyes. Adjusting my bag on my shoulder, I find and follow the town center sign Aiden's notes said would be there. There is no recognition inside me now, of this station, or where to go. I glance back, and over the archway containing the elevators and ticket office is carved *2050.* This station didn't exist when I lived here. It's new.

Ten minutes later I've reached the center of town, and the prickling feeling of wonder, of both knowing and not knowing this place, comes back. There is a crowded pedestrian area leading up to an ancient building with a sign that says MOOT HALL. Cobblestones crumble underfoot, with a vague sense they are smaller than they should be. Because I'm bigger now?

I shake my head. Am I imagining things? There is no definite memory, only shadows that seem to mist away if I stare. Maybe it's just the *longing* to know this place.

On arrival in Keswick, I'm to go to Waterfall House. And my *mother*. I swallow; the word sounds all wrong. The house is along the shores of Derwentwater, on almost the opposite side of the lake from Keswick. I memorized maps of how to get there: about three miles to walk on footpaths. Or there is a boat across the water. Or a bus on the road.

Walking takes longest. Walk it is. Roads then paths lead out of the town center, past a ruined theater and down to the lake; paths wander through woods with views over the lake, then drop to cut down to the water. There is ice silvering out from its deep blue edges; the ground underfoot is hard frozen. There are people, some with dogs, ambling on paths in all directions, breath puffing out white around their faces. They dwindle away the farther I get from Keswick. Soon I'm alone.

My feet move slower and slower, head full of a peculiar madness. I want to laugh and cry at the same time. I want to touch every tree, every rock on the way. I want to know them, to take them into me so they cement out whispers of memory. My head feels full of fuzzy cotton confusion, of *wanting* to remember being here before, but nothing is definite. It could just be the wanting that makes me feel this way, that makes my feet long to walk back and forth over the same places to make me remember them, if not from before, from now.

I shake my head. Aiden told me she knows I'm coming; she'll wonder what has happened to me . . . again. I start walking at a proper pace. What could it have been like for her? For *my mother*. I say the words over and over inside my head, tasting them, but they still don't feel right, don't sound right. I'm *her daughter*—that feels weird, too. I disappeared when I was ten years old. Seven years ago. How do you get through something like that? And then her husband died, a few years after I vanished, when he tried to rescue me. My fault. She might blame me.

And so my feet go faster and slower and faster again for the rest of the walk, as my thoughts tumble inside. When I finally see the house in the distance, my feet stop completely. From Aiden's file I know it used to be Lodore Falls Hotel; Waterfall House for Girls it is called now. The exterior covered in Lake District gray slate fits the foreground of lake below and woods rising behind, the snow-touched fells beyond. It is warm from this distance, like a soft-focus, dreamy castle, even though I know much of it was destroyed in the riots decades ago, then rebuilt with more concrete and less slate. I carry on. The closer I walk, the harsher it gets.

When I finally reach the house, I hesitate at the door. This is it. Will she know me? Will I know her? Eagerness and fear war inside of me, laced with caution. As Aiden's notes pointed out, many girls live here. None of them can realize what we are to each other.

Do I knock? Go in?

As if to answer my question, the door opens, and a girl steps out. She nods and keeps going. I walk through the door before it swings closed.

There are other girls in the entrance area. Two in chairs, chatting. A woman stands near a large desk. She is tall; long blond hair swept back, dark roots peeking through; thin, maybe forty years old. Neatly, *very* neatly dressed. Even her buttons shine. Is it her? Nothing about her is familiar. I walk up to the desk.

"Yes?" she says.

"Uh, hi. I'm Riley Kain. I think I'm staying here."

"You're *late*. I was about to send some of the girls out to look for you in case you got lost in the woods." Is it her, my mother? Her lips are pursed, words calm and clear, but her eyes sweep over me with longing and confusion. She expects me to be blond, to have green eyes. She doesn't know about the IMET?

With my back to the other girls, I take my glasses off, as if to rub my eyes. Green eyes. Hers widen slightly. I put them back on.

"Your ID?" she says, and I take it out. She scans it into a netbook, hand shaking slightly. "You are indeed staying with us, Riley. I'm Stella Connor. You can call me Stella."

I stare back at her. *Stella Connor*: Lucy Connor's mother. But nothing about her or the name is familiar, and bitter disappointment at the lack of memory gnaws inside.

"You've missed lunch, I'm afraid. Tea is here in the conservatory at four, and dinner in the hall at seven. Here is your list of rules." She hands me a substantial number of sheets stapled together, touching my hand as she does so. "We'll talk tonight," she adds, her words such a quiet whisper that I'm not sure I heard or imagined them.

"Madison?" she calls out, and one of the girls looks up. "Can you show Riley to her room, please? The tower."

The girl bounces out of her chair: cute, with dark curly hair, not much taller than me, a mischievous glint to her eyes. She walks over. "Sure thing, Mrs. C."

Stella's eyes narrow. Not happy with the "Mrs. C" thing.

"This way!" Madison says, with a dramatic flourish. I follow her through a door, down halls to stairs. She looks back. "Take her to the tower!" she mimics, one finger pointing dramatically at the staircase, her voice so like Stella's that I have to laugh.

At the top of the stairs, Madison flings the door open. "I can't believe she's put you in the tower. It's been empty for ages. She only let one person stay here awhile last year, and that was just because a bunch of rooms were wrecked in floods and all the other rooms were full, and as soon as one was empty she shifted her out."

"How many girls stay here?" I ask as I walk in and put my bag on the bed.

"Not so many now. Including you, there are, I believe, seventeen of us. Everyone leaves Waterfall-Weirdo if they can get a place anywhere else."

"Why Weirdo?"

"You met the Queen of the Weird downstairs, didn't you notice? Wait 'til you read the list of rules." She takes it from my hand and brandishes it before putting it on the desk by the bed. "Break any of the rules at your peril," she says in her Stella-mimic voice, and I try not to smirk; that *is* my mother she's making fun of. "And then there is her family." She rolls her eyes.

Family? Do I have other family? "Why? Who are they?" I ask, trying not to look too curious.

"Her mother is the JCO for all of England. Not somebody you want to be in the same room with. Thankfully, she hardly ever visits."

JCO? I stare at her in shock. I have a *grandmother*. And my grandmother is not only a Lorder, but a Juvenile Control Officer, and not only that, but for all of England? My mouth falls open.

Madison doesn't seem to notice. "What are you doing in Keswick, anyhow?"

"I'm here for the apprenticeship scheme."

"CAS? That starts tomorrow, doesn't it?"

I nod. There was an outline of the scheme in Aiden's notes, and it was the reason for my hasty trip up here: to make it for the first day. "What do you do?"

"I'm working at Cora's Café. It's my day off today. Can't wait until I'm twenty-one next summer so I can get out of here. I'd just moved into this fab flat with three others when they brought in that latest stupid YP law two years ago, and we had to give it up."

I look at her blankly.

"Don't you even know why you're staying here? JCO Young Persons Law 29(b)." She stands up bolt-straight. "Thou shalt live with either family or in approved structured accommodation with supervision until the age of twenty-one," she intones in a nasally voice, then pretends to strangle herself. "What do they think we'll get up to? It's not like there is much of anything to *do* in Keswick, even if we weren't stuck out here."

Madison opens a door to show me my bathroom. "You may be on your own in the tower, but at least you don't have to share your bathroom. Don't miss rule nine: No more than five minutes per shower. If you go over, she turns the hot water off for the whole house for a day. Somehow, she *always* knows. She does randoms, too: walks the halls in the middle of the night at odd times to make sure you don't breach rules six or eleven."

"Thanks." I smile, look at her. *Please leave.* I need to be alone awhile.

She must see it on my face. "You want me to go, right."

"Ah . . ."

"No worries. See you at tea downstairs at four. *Don't* be late: rule number two."

Alone at last, I circle the room: a double bed, an empty wardrobe, a desk, and a chair. More wardrobes across the room—locked. And a lot of empty space; it's a big room. Did this used to be Lucy's room—my room—is that why Stella keeps it empty? I shrug. No idea. Nothing in it feels familiar.

I pull the curtains open wide. There are windows all around: lake on one side, woods on the other. Gorgeous views, and I close my eyes, try to imagine this room and me in it, younger, looking out the window with my dad, but I can't.

There is an odd noise at the door: scratching? A gray paw appears underneath. I open it.

A gray cat looks up at me, then pushes past me through the open door. It takes a running leap at the bed and sits there daintily, washing one paw, her green eyes on me all the while.

Lucy's gray kitten, her tenth birthday present—one of the very few memories I've had of being her since I was Slated. Is it . . . this cat?

I walk over to the bed, sit on the other end cross-legged. "Is it you?" I whisper. She stalks across the bed, walks all around me in a circle as if checking me out thoroughly. I hold out one hand, and she rubs her chin against it. Soon I've coaxed her onto my lap; I stroke her and she curls up, purring.

The list of rules is next to me where Madison left it, and I pick it up and look at the first page. *Rule one: Be nice to Pounce (the cat).*

"Pounce?" I say, and she stirs, looks at me with slit eyes, then pulls her paws tight around her head as if to say, *Be quiet; can't you see I'm sleeping?* Pounce sounds to me the sort of name a ten-year-old would give a kitten.

Well. Stella might be a little weird, but given what she puts as rule number one, maybe she and I will get along all right, after all.

8

I MAKE IT TO TEA AT EXACTLY ONE MINUTE TO FOUR, stomach rumbling. Madison and the girl I saw her with earlier are there, and two others; there is no sign of Stella, and I'm told the others are at work in various places around Keswick. There is a teapot and a plate of warm scones with jam we all swoop on with delight. They usually just get dry biscuits at tea, Madison tells me. Is this a special treat for me?

After tea, they give me a quick tour of the place. There is a TV room with sofas and fireplaces, a library, and a dining room with one long table already set for dinner.

I wander back to my room to unpack. When we assemble for dinner at seven, Madison pulls me into a seat next to hers. Soon all but two seats are taken. There is a sea of friendly, curious eyes, and names are called out, too many to remember at once. And it all seems . . . nice. Cozy. Not a place to try to get away from.

Stella walks in as a clock chimes seven, and chatter quiets down. She takes the empty chair at the end of the table. She looks at the other empty seat and frowns. "Does anyone know where Ellie is?" There is a murmur of *no,* shaken heads.

"Maybe she's not hungry. Maybe she's not well. Maybe she found something better to do," Madison says, and the room falls silent.

Stella frowns. "Then she should have sent word. Could someone check her room, please?"

Another girl volunteers, and returns moments later. "She's in her room. She fell asleep," she says, and I wonder: Why doesn't Ellie come along now?

The tension on Stella's face relaxes, and gradually everyone else does also. Serving dishes are passed around. I'm relieved I'm too many seats away to have to try to chat with Stella in front of everyone, but now and then can't stop my eyes glancing over, finding hers, then spinning away again. This is so *surreal*: in a room having dinner with my actual real mother for the first time in seven years, yet we sit apart, not speaking. There is a part of me that wants to jump up and say, *Enough already!* And another part happy to keep up the appearance of strangers, to hang back, to observe.

When we're done, everyone starts leaving except two on dishes duty, stacking plates. The others are wandering out in twos and threes; some head to the TV room, some in other directions, and I stand, uncertain. Did Stella mean for us to talk now? But Madison links my arm in hers and draws me along with her; a few others follow us down a hall and up a few stairs to knock on a door. "Come in," a voice calls from inside.

"Did you bring me anything?" a girl asks, and is introduced as the sleepy Ellie. "I'm starving!"

Madison and the others produce rolls and other bits pilfered from dinner.

"I don't understand—why didn't you just come and eat with the rest of us?" I ask. "What was the point in sending someone to check on you, then leave you here?"

Madison rolls her eyes. "You can't have dinner if you're late. Against Weirdo rule number three."

"Don't be so unkind. She's all right," Ellie says, and I'm relieved to hear someone stick up for her. But it doesn't seem to be the popular opinion.

"It's ridiculous making us account for every second of the day. We're not babies," another girl says.

"You know why, though," Ellie answers, and I get the sense that this is a conversation everyone has heard before.

Madison scowls. "Yeah, but how many years ago was that? Shouldn't she be over it by now?"

"Over what?" I ask. An uncomfortable feeling says I already know, but I shouldn't. Do I ask because it would be normal to ask, or do I need to hear it? Hear somebody else say things I know to be true, but can't remember.

"You don't get over things like that," Ellie says to Madison, shaking her head, then turns to me. "Her daughter went missing. No one knows what happened to her. I think Stella is afraid of something happening to one of us; she's just looking out for us all."

Late that night there is a faint knock on my door, and it opens. I sit up, heart pounding.

Hall light frames her: Stella.

She looks different, hair down, a long flannel robe wrapped tight around her; more soft and uncertain. Pounce pushes past her, runs across the room and jumps up onto my bed.

Stella pulls the chair next to the bed and sits in it. She grips my hand so tight, it starts to hurt.

"Lucy? Is it really you?" she whispers. She reaches out her other hand, shaking, to my hair. "What has happened to your beautiful hair?"

"It's changed, permanently: IMET."

"We could dye it, I suppose."

"No. I'm trying to not be recognized."

"Oh. Of course." She sighs. "I can always stop dyeing mine."

"Why? Do we need to match?"

She starts, pulls her hand away. "Not exactly. It's just that I didn't know you when you came in. I didn't know my own daughter. You didn't know me, either, did you?"

I hesitate, shake my head. She looks hurt. "I'm sorry. You know I was Slated, don't you?"

She nods. "She told me."

"Who?"

She looks away. "I don't know. Whoever it was who told me you were finally coming home."

In MIA?

"Tell me your story, Lucy. Tell me everything you can about where you've been these seven years."

I hold still a moment. I came here because I wanted to find out about my missing past, my years here; of course she wants the same in return, to know about the parts of my life she has missed since then. A fair exchange? But much of what has been my life these last years I don't want to say out loud. Some demons are best kept locked up, hidden away.

"Lucy?"

"Could you not call me Lucy? It's just that it is dangerous. No one can know who I really am."

"No one can hear us now."

"But you might slip up when other people are around."

She half smiles. "I'll try, Lu—" She jumps, guiltily. "Riley," she says.

"What should you call me?" Her eyes hunger, and I know what she wants to hear, but I can't bring myself to do it.

"I should call you what all the girls do, for the same reason: Stella."

She frowns, and sighs. "Oh, all right. Tell me about your life, *Riley*."

And I stare back at her. *Should* I tell her everything, no matter whether I want to or not? Is it dangerous to know? "I don't know everything. A lot of my memories are gone."

"What you do know, then."

"I think I was kidnapped when I was ten. I didn't understand why for a long time."

Her lip curls. "The AGT."

My eyes widen. She knows, or guesses? "Yes, it was them. They had some sort of plan, to fracture my personality. So that when I was Slated some memories would survive."

Stella's face wars between sadness and horror. "You must have been so scared."

So little memory of that time remains, but what does isn't good: late at night hearing a doctor's voice saying over and over again, *You have no family; they didn't want you; they gave you to us.* My eyes start to sting, and I blink. "Are you sure you want to know?" I ask. "Everything? It isn't easy to talk about. It might be harder to hear."

Stella hesitates. "Yes. Tell me," she says, and slips an arm across my shoulders, hesitant, and some of the resistance inside melts enough for me to lean into her a moment, and tell her the blackest early memory from *then*.

I hold my left hand up. "They made me—as Lucy—be right-handed. Broke my left fingers so I had no choice." She cradles my hand in hers, staying silent. Nods once to say *go on,* but doesn't press. But I can't bring myself to tell her the thing that happened that finally cemented the personality split: that Dad snatched me back from the AGT, that we nearly got away. But Nico caught us. The gun in Nico's hand. Does she know how Dad—her husband—died?

I straighten up. "Later on, they succeeded: I had a split personality. When I was left-handed, I trained with the AGT as one of them; now and then I was right-handed, and I was Lucy. When the Lorders caught and Slated me, the other part of me hid away and Lucy was dominant, so I was Slated as right-handed, and it was Lucy's memories that were Slated. The later memories I had with the AGT survived. Lucy's early life is gone."

"Why would they do such a thing?"

"As far as I understand, it was all part of a scheme to show the Lorders that Slating could fail: that any Slated criminal could be violent, even though that was supposed to be impossible. That none were safe." I don't spell out what the consequences of Nico's plans would have been. With no way to tell which Slated might turn, what would the Lorders have done to all the Slateds? I shudder inside.

"But if you were Slated, why haven't you got a Levo?"

This is venturing into no-go territory; it would be dangerous for her to know how I was caught between the violent plans of Nico's AGT and Lorder blackmail. How they tracked me to the AGT, and I thought Agent Coulson was going to kill me, but Katran—terrorist, yes, but an old friend who really *cared* about me—raced to my rescue, and Coulson shot Katran point-blank in front of me. How holding Katran as he died made me finally remember my dad's death. Because of Dr. Lysander, the Lorders thought I'd done as they wanted; they let me go, removed my Levo.

"Lucy? Sorry, Riley, I mean. What happened to your Levo?" Stella prompts, and I wonder how long I've been staring into space.

"It was cut off," I say. A small lie. The Lorder method of removal was gentle: a few buttons pushed on a machine, and it painlessly sprang away.

"I didn't think that was possible," she says.

"It is," I say, and this I say with truth. I cut Ben's Levo off with a grinder, didn't I? He survived. Barely, but he did; then the Lorders took him away.

"There is something I don't understand. If you were Slated as right-handed, how can your years here be gone? You were left-handed until you were ten. You *must* remember!" She says the words like if she wants it enough, it will be so.

"I don't understand all the neurology of it. It's like what hand was dominant was plastic; it could be bent and changed. I think doing that was part of how my personality was fractured."

"So young." She shakes her head. "But some memories stayed with you after you were Slated?"

"Not exactly. To begin with, I was just like any other Slated. I had this new family, and—"

"Were they nice?"

"Mostly. Mum and my sister were, though Mum was difficult to work out at first."

She holds still. "You called this other woman *Mum*."

"I was Slated. They told us to do that."

"Sorry. It doesn't matter. And then?"

"I started to get memories back." I hold back *how*. She doesn't need to know that I was attacked, that fear and rage crashed through the boundaries and made Rain emerge: the half of me that was pure

AGT, pure terrorist, under Nico's spell, and ready to do whatever he asked.

"So what do you remember?"

I shake my head. "I'm sorry. The memories I have are from after I left here. With the AGT. Before then is the half that was Slated."

She looks back at me, eyes desperate and pleading. "But do you remember anything about me? Do you remember anything from here, before, at all?"

Something, I don't know what, makes me say *no*. Even though there are some little snippets that *have* come back: this cat, now curled up between us. Playing chess with Dad, and the rook. Is it because, as she said, I was left-handed when I was little? If that is true, then more may come back. Or is it because these are things that Rain knew? The worst memory of all—Dad's death—was suppressed, buried so deep it didn't come back until Katran died.

"Lucy? Riley, I mean. What is it?"

I shake my head. Does she know how he died? Does she know it was my fault? I can't say it out loud. Not tonight.

I look past her, at the bedroom we're in. "Was this my room?" I ask.

She shakes her head no, and I'm relieved. It seemed *so* not my room. I had that right at least. "I put you in here because it's away from the other girls. Easier for me to visit." She hesitates. "It used to be my room. A long time ago."

"Tell me everything I can't remember," I say. "Please. I want to know it all."

She seems to hesitate, then holds out her hand again. A small thing, yet somehow it is so hard for me to reach out and take hers, to hold a stranger's hand, when her eyes are so full of desperate *want*. I do, and she grips mine tight once again. She smiles. "What do you want to know?"

"Everything, from the beginning. Tell me about when I was born. Where was I born? Was . . ." And I hesitate. I've been so reluctant to mention him that it is just penetrating now that Stella hasn't, either. "Was my father there?"

She shakes her head, lips in a thin line. "He wasn't there. He rarely was for the hard bits."

My eyes widen, a retort working its way up, but I bite it back.

"But you, Lucy, were the most beautiful baby that ever drew breath." She smiles. "I'll show you." She gets up and takes out keys from her robe pocket. She goes to one of the locked wardrobes. "I put albums in here for you: photos, all sorts of things you can look through from before. There are eleven albums, one for each year. We'll start making another one now, won't we?"

She extracts an album and brings it over, places it in my hands, and I eagerly turn the pages. Well, okay; I *was* a pretty cute baby. There is shot after shot of my general chubby baby cuteness: in a cot holding out hands and laughing; giggling in the bath; covered in mushy food. Always smiling. Didn't I ever howl? A few have Stella in them, also: hair dark then, smiling in a way that goes into her eyes. And there are empty spaces here and there; someone is missing. Removed? "Why aren't there any photos of my dad?"

She snaps the album shut. "That's enough for tonight. You need to get some sleep. You have an early start tomorrow, don't you?" She slips the album back into the wardrobe, locks it again.

"Can I have a key?"

She hesitates, then shakes her head. "No. You need your rest.

We'll look at them together, all right? Good night, Lucy." She goes out the door.

Well.

The Queen of the Weird: I hear Madison's words echo in my head, then feel bad. That's not fair. She's had a terrible hand dealt to her, hasn't she? Having her only child vanish when she was ten, then back seven years later, Slated, with no memory of her. She obviously had issues with Dad, also. I need to work out what that is about, what I should or shouldn't tell her about him. I sigh. I'm gripped by a need to know all I can of him, all I've forgotten, and more. I wonder if there are photos of him anywhere?

I slip Pounce off my knees, walk across the room to the wardrobe with the albums in it, and assess the lock. A few twists with a hairpin and the lock clicks: open sesame! A skill learned from Nico.

Inside, the wardrobe has clothes hanging on one side—summer dresses, put away for the winter? And the other side is shelves. The first few have albums numbered one to eleven as she said. But if she took Dad out of album number one, chances are the same is true of them all. The shelves below contain things wrapped in tissue paper. Curious, I draw out one bundle, take it to the bed, and open the paper carefully. Inside are neatly folded children's clothes. A girl's. Mine?

I hesitate. I am trespassing on Stella's memories, wrapped up and locked away, for how long? It feels wrong.

But her memories should be my memories. I hold up a small dress, sized for perhaps a nine- or ten-year-old. It is pink and ruffled, really cute; way too cute, in fact.

I hated dresses. Especially pink ones.

I almost stagger, put the dress down on the bed.

She made me wear it.

My head is spinning; I feel ill. I don't want to see any more. I fold them back up in the tissue paper, as careful as I can with shaking hands. This isn't what I was looking for.

Dad. I want photos of Dad.

I put the bundle back where it was. The lower shelves just contain more tissue-wrapped bundles of what feels like clothing. More memories preserved and locked away. I stand back.

There is a top shelf, too high for me to easily reach, and I drag the desk chair across the floor and stand on it. There is a plastic box, pushed back so I didn't see it from below. I pull it off the shelf, put it on the desk, and take off the lid. *Bingo.* Framed photos, ones she has put away, out of sight. There has to be one in here.

But instead there are photos of a woman, one I don't recognize. The ones on top look old, going by the clothes, the hairstyles. Farther down is one of the same woman with a little girl, one hand on her shoulder; another with the girl a few years older. I gasp as I realize the girl is a dark-haired young version of Stella. The woman must be her mother: my grandmother. The Lorder JCO.

I peer closer at her face, but don't see it in her, the Lorder stare. There are more recent ones; she is older, hair swept up and silvery gray, but she looks good for whatever age she must be. Sixty-something at least? She is thin, dressed well in clothes that look expensive but not showy. A kind smile on her face. I hold up a portrait of her and stare at her eyes; for no reason I can identify, I shiver, and hurriedly put it back down.

I continue through the box. At the bottom is one last frame, and I draw it out.

A group shot from a wedding: happy couple in the middle, a couple next to the groom that are probably his parents, and next to the bride, my grandmother.

It is hard to recognize the bride as Stella. Not so much from the unwinding of years or the white dress, but the youthful joy of her smile. And next to her in some version of a suit is Dad. Younger than my dreams, my memories, but there is no mistaking him. I reach out a shaking hand to the frame, to touch him. But he isn't looking at the camera; he is gazing at Stella, with so much love on his face that it is hard to even look at him.

What happened to them?

I pack the photos back away as they were, put the box back on the shelf. Lock the wardrobe and switch off the light. There are more boxes up there, and another locked wardrobe next to the first, but that is enough for one night.

In bed, suddenly aware how cold I have become, I pull the covers up and cuddle Pounce. She stays, warm and purring, and reminds me of Sebastian. I feel a pang of homesickness, for Mum and Amy.

Stella I can't think of as *Mum,* or even as *Mother.* At least, not yet.

The only photo of Dad I've found so far in wardrobe number one is the wedding photo. Did Stella destroy them all, but couldn't bring herself to get rid of that one?

And Stella hides all signs of her mother away in a plastic box in a locked wardrobe. Why?

I suppose her being a Lorder is a good enough reason.

We sneak to the back door.

Daddy grins, holds up one finger to his lips. "Quiet now, Lucy; we're spies."

"On a secret mission?" I whisper, pulling my coat on when he holds it out.

He nods and winks, and we slip under the windows along the back of the house. He looks back at me following. "Hmmm . . . Wait here a second," he says. He retraces our steps and moments later comes back, holding my wellies in one hand.

I roll my eyes.

"Put them on, Lucy. One less thing to get yelled at over." He winks again. I struggle out of my hated pink shoes, already a bit dirty from the great garden escape, and am about to toss them behind the bushes when Daddy grabs them and carefully places them on a windowsill.

"They'll be able to follow our trail," I warn.

He shrugs. "I'm pretty sure she'll know where we've gone, anyhow."

"So why be sneaky?"

"We're spies, remember?"

"But I'm not dressed like a spy." I frown and hold out the ridiculous pink skirt that sticks out under my coat and do a spin in my camo wellies.

He laughs and bows down low. "You are, indeed, the perfect picture of a demented princess spy, Your Majesty. Come on; your official birthday spying chariot awaits." We start to walk toward the lake and the kayaks.

But then a door bangs above. A voice calls out, "Get back in here at once; your grandmother is here."

"Busted," I say.

"Better go back, Lucy."

"Why?"

"She just wants to say happy birthday. Go on."

I sigh and start trudging back to the house, feet like lead. When I reach the window with my waiting shoes, I turn around; Daddy is gone. A distant splash says my spy chariot has launched without me.

At the back door I take off my wellies and slip on the pink satin shoes. They're better for spying in, anyhow. Still in the game, I creep without a whisper of sound; not down the main hall, no. Spies go careful, quiet, down secret ways. I slip through Mummy's study and out the door hidden behind the curtains. Down the tiny hall that goes around the sitting room where I know they'll be.

One more step, then another . . .

Their voices change from a murmur into words I can hear, then wish I hadn't.

9

MEOW? MEOOOOW.

Hmph? I open one eye. It's still dark, and Pounce is scratching at my bedroom door. I get up and open it for her. She disappears down the stairs.

I squint at my watch: 5:20. Thanks for the early wake-up call, cat. I yawn and stretch, shivering as I shrug my robe on and pull it close. There's no way I'll get back to sleep now.

That dream was so *weird,* yet somehow I know in my gut it was real. It happened. Was it that horrible pink dress that brought it back?

It was happy at first, off on an adventure with Dad; then . . . what? I overheard *something* between Stella and her mother. Something upsetting. What was it?

I head down the stairs and up the hall for a drink. As I go, motion sensor lights momentarily blind my eyes, illuminating patches of darkness, then go out just as the next takes over. I start down the wrong hall, uncertain of the way, and double back to find the reception area from yesterday with its tea things.

While I wait for the kettle to boil, I turn the lights off again and wander to the windows that overlook the lake, but it is lost in inky darkness. A spy kayak: Are they still there? I smile to myself, then frown. Dad went off without me, left me to go back and face them alone. *Never there for the hard bits,* isn't that what Stella said? No.

That isn't fair. Trying to rescue me from Nico was a *very* hard bit. Failing was the hardest of them all.

The room is suddenly cast in bright illumination. A girl yawns in the doorway, then jumps when she sees me: Madison.

"You don't strike me as the early morning type," I say.

"Who, me? No, to be honest. But it's a seven o'clock start at the café to take care of all the early breakfast-eaters of Keswick. How about you?" she says, both of us heading for the kettle.

"The CAS thing starts at eight."

"Lucky. Couldn't sleep?" I shake my head. "Nervous?"

I look at her quickly, then realize she means what I am officially here for: CAS. I've been so caught up in Stella and my missing past that I haven't thought about it at all. Another new place, new people, more not knowing what to do or say while trying to remember to answer to *Riley Kain* and not to say anything she wouldn't. Suddenly it is all way too worrying. I sigh.

"Tell you what. Come with me on the six thirty bus, and I'll show you where you've got to go, then I'll make you an amazing breakfast at the café. My treat."

"Really?"

"Sure." She holds up her cup of tea. "Here's to firsts. Jobs, I mean," she says, and winks in a way that suggests she was thinking of something else entirely. She clinks her cup against mine, then winces. "That was loud. Meet me back here in an hour."

An hour and a shower and change later, we're heading for the door. Madison pauses at a table, flips open a folder with pages of columns, writes her name and the time in the Out column, writes *work* under Description. Hands me the pen.

"What's this?"

"Haven't you read your rules yet? That probably breaks one of them." She grins. "This is rule number twelve: Always sign out when you leave, and in when you get back."

I bend to print *Riley—CAS,* and realize that it is the first time I've written my new name.

We step outside into the dark morning.

"I hate this time of year. It's like midnight," Madison says.

"I like the darkness," I admit. I like how it covers and hides, and the chill as well. The ground is frozen, crunches under our feet as we take a path up behind the house through silent trees to the road above.

"No bus stop?" I say.

"No. You just hail them. Comes every thirty minutes or so."

Soon a bus appears in the distance. Madison waves and it pulls in and stops. We scan our IDs as we get on, start down the aisle; Madison aims for a seat near the back.

"Oh my Lord. Is it possible?" a voice says to the side. Male.

Madison pauses, turns. "Is what possible?" she asks.

"Don't sit down yet, I need to be sure," he says, and Madison holds on to his seat as the bus starts up the windy road. He smiles, and something passes between them in the cold air. Is he her boyfriend? Even sitting down he is taller than she is; a rugged, outdoorsy type. Tanned even in January.

He looks between Madison and me, then glances at a few friends sitting in front. "Wow. It really *is* true," one of them says.

"What?" Madison demands.

The one smiling into her eyes answers. "At long last, Shorty. There is somebody shorter than you."

His friends laugh, and she punches him in the arm. Straightens her shoulders as if aiming to be taller, then slips into the seat opposite his. I sit next to her.

"Who's that?" I say, voice low.

"That six-foot brat is Finley." She raises her voice: "He and his friends are total ARSes."

He leans across. "We are indeed. You're just jealous." I look between them, brow knotted in confusion. "We're in ARS: the Apprentice Ranger Service," he explains.

"Generally known as ARSes," Madison adds.

"Only you can get away with that, Shorty," he says, and winks. "Who are you?" he asks, turning his smile on me.

"Riley," I say, managing to get my name right. "I'm here for the apprenticeship scheme."

"Hey, you could be an ARS, too!" Madison says.

He shakes his head, laughing. "I'm sure there must be some sort of minimum height requirement."

With that, the bus stops; we're in Keswick.

"Ladies first," Finley says, and we get off the bus.

With a wave to the boys, Madison slips her arm in mine. She shows me the building where I need to go at eight, then takes me to her work: Cora's Café. We go in the back way; the lights aren't on yet.

"Hello," Madison sings out as she unlocks the back door.

A woman in a chef's hat bustling about a cramped kitchen looks up, and scowls. "Glad you decided to turn up." Madison sticks out her tongue. "And who's this, another waif who needs feeding up?"

"Ah, sorry . . ." I start to say, and back toward the door.

She laughs. "Kidding, kid. I'm Cora; come in." They put me at one of the tables in the front of the café, bickering all the while. Minutes later the lights come on and the doors are unlocked. Early customers flock in, and we're soon busy tackling the most massive and delicious cooked breakfasts ever.

A bit later, too much breakfast churns uneasily in my stomach as I walk up to the government building Madison pointed out earlier. The sign on the door says CUMBRIAN APPRENTICESHIP SCHEME SEMINAR. It looks so *official,* and to me, *official* means *Lorder.* Does Aiden know what he's doing, sending me to this? He usually does. I hesitate, watching others go past me and through the door.

"Hey, it's ES," a voice says behind me, and I turn; it's Finley.

"ES? What's that supposed to mean?"

"Extra-Shorty. Shouldn't you be walking through the door instead of staring at it?"

"Why are you here?"

"I'm one of the good examples. Shocking, I know. Come on." He holds the door open. "Sign in there," he says, and points at a table with a line of people. "See you later." He waves at someone across the room and saunters away.

I wait my turn.

"Name?" says a woman with an overly bright smile and hard eyes.

"Ky—" I cough. A fake cough to cover nearly saying *Kyla. Get a grip.* "Sorry. My name is Riley Kain."

She scans a netbook. "You're not on the list. Next?"

A boy steps up around me.

"No, wait a minute. I should be on it. Can you check again? That is Kain, with a *K*?"

She sighs. Looks again. Smiles. "You're still not on the list." She turns to the boy.

I start to panic. Could Aiden have messed up? No. "I might have been put in last-minute."

She sighs again. "A Late Add—why didn't you say so?" She touches her screen. "There you are. Fill this in so we can put you on the registered list." She hands me a handheld device with my name on the top, blanks to fill in. Starting with date of birth. When was that again?

"Not there," she says. "You're in the way." She points to the side and I scurry away, face pink.

I touch the screen and try to remember the contents of Aiden's file. My new birth date finally comes to me: September 17, 2036. I fill in the rest—address, hair, eyes, height. And then I'm stumped. Emergency contact? Aiden never gave me an address for my fake parents in Chelmsford. Finally, with no other option coming to mind, I put *Stella Connor, Waterfall House,* and click enter.

I approach the table. She ignores me, checking others in. "Excuse me," I say finally.

"About time," she says, takes the device, updates her netbook. "You're all registered now. Here you go." She hands me a folder. "Take a seat, Riley."

I sit down near the back. There are about fifty of us now, a few empty seats here and there still. Everyone else is chatting, seems to know one another. Are they all local? A few glances are cast my way and I try to smile, but they aren't particularly friendly glances; after a while, I give up and ignore the looks. Finley is off to the side, standing with some others. My eyes seek his, and he winks.

A few more shuffle in, and then, abrupt silence.

A man in a rumpled brown suit walks to the front. A half smile on his face, he gazes at the assembled faces, moving across them so every one is acknowledged. His eyes pass over mine with a slight pause.

"Good morning, everyone," he says at last. "I'm pleased to see so many familiar faces have come in for the Cumbrian Apprenticeship Scheme this morning, and a few unfamiliar ones, as well." His eyes touch mine again, and then another's: a boy near the front. "For those who don't know me, I'm Councillor Watson. On behalf of the Central Coalition I'd like to welcome you to this opportunity, the gateway to your futures. The Jobs For All policy of the Coalition is in its twentieth successful year, and the apprenticeship schemes are a vital part of its success. I'm going to hand things over now to your local apprentice-ships coordinator."

There is a polite scattering of applause, and another speaker approaches the front. Out of the corner of my eye, I see Watson exit the hall at the back, and everyone visibly relaxes.

Over an hour the scheme is explained in detail. Representatives and apprentices are here from each section today, and we can speak to them and ask any questions. The sections seeking new apprentices are Administration, Hospitality, National Parks, Transportation, Education, Enforcement, Communication, and Sanitation. Tomorrow we must come in and sign on the dotted line to commit to CAS for five years. Then we pick our favorites, and take aptitude tests.

On Monday we find out which four we get to trial. Then follows weeklong placements with each, and finally a section is chosen for each candidate. He doesn't say who does the final choosing, and I'm guessing, not us.

So, without any guarantee where we'll end up, we must first commit to *five years*? That sounds like forever.

When he's finished, doors are opened to an adjacent room, with areas set aside for each section. Everyone spills out and seems more interested in getting a cup of tea than speaking to the representatives and apprentices. Then I notice waves and hellos exchanged here and there. Do they already know what they want to pick? More, do they think this is just a formality; has everyone already worked out who will go where?

A woman at the nearest table—Education—catches my eye and smiles, and there is something about her that makes me smile back. I walk over to her.

"Hello," she says. "Have you thought about working in schools?"

"No," I answer truthfully.

"Honesty! An excellent trait." She looks at me quizzically. "I never forget a face, and there is something familiar about you, but I'm stumped. You're not local?"

I shake my head, careful to hide alarm; could she see Lucy in me despite the changed hair and eyes, after so many years? "I'm from Chelmsford."

"I didn't think I recognized you, and every child in Keswick goes to my school. But that doesn't matter to me, and it shouldn't to anyone because place of origin is not admissible criteria."

"Really? I was thinking I was heading for Sanitation for sure."

She laughs. "Well, in case you'd like another option, we're looking for three apprentices in Keswick Primary School. You start as a teaching assistant, and if all goes well can move on to teacher training after a year." She starts enthusing about inspiring young minds, and I think of the smiling boy on the train, taken off by Lorders.

"Is everything all right?" she asks.

I start. Am I that transparent? "I'm not sure about Education; I haven't been around little kids much, and—"

"Well, that is the whole point of this scheme. If you pick

Education, you get to spend a week with us in the school, and we'll both soon know if it's for you."

"Thank you," I say, and it isn't just for what she has said, but the warm way she has said it.

She seems to know what I mean, and smiles again. "Go on, talk to everyone else; none of us bite!" She leans in closer and lowers her voice. "Except maybe Enforcement."

I straighten my shoulders and start at one end of the room, visiting each section in turn, but skip Enforcement. The latter aren't Lorders; they are the local force that deals with parking and minor matters, but anything that says *authority* says *keep away* to me, and besides, they'd work with Lorders, wouldn't they?

It soon becomes apparent by foot traffic that there are two main points of competition: Hospitality and National Parks. At the latter there is now a small crowd. An unfriendly crowd, as I find when I try to inch my way into it.

"Hey, it's ES," Finley says, tall enough to see over everyone that I'm there and not making progress.

Finley pulls me to the front and soon I'm face-to-face with his boss, who looks at me and raises an eyebrow. "Considering a career with the National Parks Authority?"

"Of course."

He sighs. "It isn't all mountain trails in holiday sunshine."

I bristle at his tone. "Of course not. It's conservation, public access, education, and safety." I'd been lurking at the edges long enough to already hear the spiel.

"Do you have any relevant skills?"

"I can read maps, and I know how to use a compass. I'm a runner and experienced walker, so I'm fit. I love the outdoors in all weather."

"Really?" His voice is still skeptical, and even though I had no idea what National Parks did until five minutes ago, something about his tone has my back up.

I straighten and meet his eye. "Try me and you'll see." A challenge thrown down.

"Well, well. You never know."

I walk off to hostile glances from many of the other hopefuls; Finley follows.

"You handled him well."

"Did I?"

"But I wouldn't get your hopes up. They'll trial ten and take five this year. But most of the others have been volunteering with National Parks all through school and have staked their claims; even if you make it onto the ten, it's a tough competition."

So much for place of origin being inadmissible criteria.

10

I WANDER INTO KESWICK, THE AFTERNOON FREE. SHOULD I go back to the house? Probably. Most likely everyone will be at work, and Stella and I could talk some more, and isn't that what I'm here for?

But the sun is shining. It's lunchtime, but after the Breakfast of Giants this morning I'm good, and the sun sparkling on the snow-dusted fells above is calling, making my feet restless.

I wander about Keswick to start with, paying no attention to where I am going, and after a while find myself outside Keswick Primary School. That teacher said every child in Keswick goes to this school: It would have been my school. It must be their lunchtime; there are children running and playing all over the grounds. It looks like a happy place, without the undercurrents at the secondary I was at until recently. Do they get visits from Lorders here, too? Do Lorders stand to one side during school assemblies and drag off troublemakers, never to be seen again? No. That'd be ridiculous. It's a *primary* school, not full of potentially dangerous teenagers. I stare a moment at the white buildings, but nothing feels familiar.

All the while the fells are calling me. I want *up*, to climb into the sky and touch the sun. I start to follow a footpath sign that leads out of town, taking whichever way goes up and out. Then I stumble across another sign that points the way to *Castlerigg Stone Circle*. I almost stop breathing when I read the words. Is this the stone circle from my dream, the one with Dad? Counting the stones together: the mountain's children.

I'm walking faster and it isn't fast enough, so I start to run. It's uphill on uneven ground and the cold air catches in my throat, but it feels good to be running. I told that National Parks rep that I was a runner, but how much have I done of it lately? I've barely even jogged; it reminds me so much of Ben that it hurts. But now my mind is full of Castlerigg, of getting there as soon as my feet can take me.

I slow to a walk when I finally see a gate in the distance. It is *the* gate; I'm sure of it. I pull my coat in tight around; despite running and the sun, the temperature seems to have dropped and has a prickle of expectation about it. Snow? Distant clouds are moving closer.

Leaning up against the gate, I can finally see it. A wide field with the stone circle at its center; the mountains, standing guard, are an amphitheater all around. I open the gate and step through, then stand there, staring, something stirring and shifting inside. Not just a dream, I'm sure of it. I *remember*, and the joy of memory makes me laugh out loud. I've been *here*, many times before, in all weather: picnics on sunny summer days, walks in blustery autumn rains and snow-covered magic, searching for bright dots of spring wildflowers. It was our place, mine and Dad's: our special place we came again and again.

I walk to the stones, but don't start counting yet. I have to start in the right place: where some of the stones reach into the circle. We start here so we don't lose track.

Close up some of the stones are huge, but not so much as in my memory when they were giants. Now, some are even shorter than I am. I reach the first one, press my hands against it, then lean into the cold stone: hands extended, face turned so my cheek is against it as well. I close my eyes. Number one.

All I have been and all I have been through these last years seem to fade away, leaving just Lucy. A little girl with her dad. I open my eyes again. Is it this place, these ancient stones? Thousands of years old, do they do something to time, make seven years seem of no consequence? I feel myself stepping back as I was then, and start running between the stones, tagging each one with my hand and counting as I go.

It's getting darker, and colder, and all at once there are fingers of mist wrapping around the stones. The sun vanishes. *Lake District weather: Blink and it changes.* The words are in my mind, unbidden. Who used to say that? Eyes closed again, I lean back against another stone and feel like I'm sinking into it, getting colder but not caring, reaching *back* for something else, without knowing what.

Some sense of disquiet takes hold; this wasn't always a good place. I push the thought away, wanting to stay Lucy, but she is slipping away.

How long have I been here? I'm shaking with the chill, and the light is starting to fade. I should go back, catch the bus with Madison when the café closes at five. I squint at my watch: almost four. I should have enough time to get there by then, but I'm disoriented. Which stone was I up to, and which way is the gate? I don't know. I peer at the mist, but it holds its secrets; I can't see beyond a few meters of frozen field. A shiver runs down my back. What if I had followed my first impulse, and kept climbing up, up, up? I shudder to think of being on the top of a ridge and unable to see the way.

Fine park ranger I'd make.

I step out across the frozen ground in my best pick of the right direction, hoping the mist will lift. Long after I expect to, I hit fence: no gate. No problem: follow the fence around. I start out, keeping the fence close and in sight, but then walk for so long I know I've gone the wrong way. Turn around? No. Keep going; it's the only way to make sure I don't end up going back and forth. I reach a gate, but it looks different from the one I came through. Ah. I'm on the opposite side, the one with the parking lot. Now the gate I want is just as far again around the other way.

Finally I reach it, go through, and follow the footpath down. The lights of town start to penetrate the mist; it is lifting as I reach the first houses, so I run full speed up the streets, back to the center.

As I round the final corner, the bus is pulling away. I wave; he stops. I step on, breathing hard. Flustered, I have a moment of panic when I can't find my ID, but it's in my other pocket. I scan in and start down the aisle. A hand waves: Madison. She scoots across so I can sit next to her in the aisle seat.

"Riley? I thought the apprenticeship seminar ended hours ago! How was it?"

The morning seems like *ages* ago. "Good, I guess. I'm thinking of Parks. Maybe Education."

She looks at me curiously. "What happened to you this afternoon?"

I shrug. "Nothing much. I went for a walk."

"You're going to catch it when we get back."

"Why?"

She shrugs. "Don't worry, it'll be fine. You should have written that in the stupid book when we left; Stella's probably ticked off 'cos she hasn't known where you were every second of the day."

"Really?"

"Don't worry, you didn't know, did you?"

Because I didn't read the rules.

Stella stands by her desk in the reception area, arms crossed, rigid with tension. Her head turns when we come in, and her eyes fix on me. Something changes, relaxes on her face when her eyes reach mine, and I try to say *sorry* without saying anything. She smiles, then looks to my side at Madison, and her smile vanishes.

"Hi, Mrs. C," Madison says. Her arm hooked in mine starts to pull me across the room.

"Not so fast," Stella says. "Riley? I'd like a word. This way."

She turns and walks toward another door behind her.

"Uh-oh," Madison says. "A chat in her private study. Good luck."

I follow Stella through the door, and it swings shut behind me.

"I'm sorry about the book, I didn't realize—" I start to say, but then Stella steps up to me and sweeps me against her in an awkward hug, a tight one, and she is all bones and angles, thin and desperate.

She lets go. "I was so worried. Don't do that to me again!" she snaps, sits at her desk, face cross once again.

"Why do you make everyone account for all of their days like that? If you didn't, you wouldn't worry when someone forgets to write something in the book. You should trust us. Can't we be allowed out in daylight hours? We're all over eighteen. Or are supposed to be," I add, since I'm not, but I'm sure the rest of them are.

She shakes her head. "I'm responsible for every girl in this house, and I take that very seriously."

"Oh. Do you have to do that, as part of this being a supervised house for under-twenty-ones?"

She hesitates.

"You don't, do you. It's just you who makes them do that; makes *us* do that."

She shakes her head. "You're the one who has broken the rules here; don't argue." She softens. "I can't have different rules for you than the other girls."

"Of course not."

She sighs, shakes her head. "I was so scared something happened to you, that they worked out you weren't Riley Kain and took you away from me all over again."

Then I'm contrite. "Really, I'm sorry. I haven't read all the rules yet," I admit. "I didn't know I needed to write down what I was doing for the afternoon."

She opens a desk drawer, hands me another copy of the rules. "Then you shall sit there and read them before dinner, before you can break any more of them accidentally."

And it's not so bad. I sit in an armchair in the corner of her study, a little cold but before long Pounce finds me and curls up warmly on my lap like my own hot water bottle. Stella brings me a cup of tea, and I start at the top. Rule one I've already covered: Be nice to Pounce. I scratch behind her ears and she purrs. The rest of them are mostly easy, logical stuff, like not wearing outdoor boots on the carpets, keeping doors locked at night.

About halfway through, I pause, look up. Is this study the same one as in my dream? There are long curtains that cover the windows and also curve into the room, cover part of the adjacent wall. I slip Pounce off my knees, walk to the curtains, and pull them to one side. There is a door! Just like in my dream. Unable to stop myself, I reach a hand to push the door open, but then hear voices outside the study.

I scoot back to the chair and pick up the rules just before Stella comes back in. She gets something from her desk, leaves again.

I better finish reading these before dinner. *Concentrate.* There is also quite a bit on curfews, random room checks, and keeping track of where we are and what we're doing. "She's a bit of a control freak, isn't she?" I say to Pounce in a low voice.

An uncomfortable feeling inside wonders: Was she always like that, or was it my being taken away from her that made her so?

That night, soon after lights-out—which I know now is eleven P.M.—there is a soft knock on my door, and it opens. Stella peeks in. "Are you awake?" she asks.

"Yes," I say, and she seems to be hesitating. "Come in."

She walks across the room, pulls a chair in next to my bed like she did last night.

"But you do realize it's lights-out now," I say. "And I'm supposed to be sleeping."

"Don't be cheeky. I know you've got an early start again tomorrow, so I won't stay long."

"It's okay. I'm not much of a sleeper." Just now my mind has been full of mountains; ridge walking on high fells.

"You never were. You kept me up half the night until you were four. And then later with nightmares."

"What did I have nightmares about?"

"All sorts of things. Monsters under the bed. Something happening to . . ." And she stops. "Usual kid stuff, I guess."

So was I always like that—with vivid dreams and nightmares? I thought it was just my fragmented memories that haunted my sleep.

"Can we look at more photo albums?" I ask.

"Not tonight. I want to talk to you about something. How'd CAS go today?"

I shrug. "All right."

"You do know if you sign up tomorrow that it's five years, and you may not get one you want."

"They explained it; I know. But—"

"I've got another idea. Why don't you work here instead?"

"What do you mean?"

"Here, at the house. I've usually got two girls working for me, but one turned twenty-one a few months ago and left."

"Doing what?"

"You know: looking after the house. The garden in the summer. Helping with cooking." She looks at my face. "I know it doesn't sound very exciting. But we could spend more time together, get to know each other again. And it would be safer. There'd be less chance of anyone finding out you're not who you say you are."

"I don't know. I'm interested in apprenticing with National Parks."

"That might be hard to get into."

"Did I used to like walking?"

"And running; you were never still for a minute."

"No, I mean in the mountains—the fells. Up in high places."

She hesitates, finally nods. "I think you were born part mountain goat. You loved it."

I read her face. "But you didn't."

She sighs. "No. I haven't got a head for heights. And I worried you'd slip and hurt yourself."

"If you don't like heights, who did I go walking with? Was it my dad?"

She nods, finally admitting he existed. "That was the other reason I didn't like it."

"What do you mean?" She hesitates again, and I jump in. "I kind of get the feeling you and he didn't get along. But he is part of my past, part of where I come from. I need to find out about him, too."

She stares back, finally nods. "Of course. I'm sorry. Yes, your dad took you ridge walking." She pauses and I stay silent, looking at her, saying *give me more* with my eyes, and I can see something relent in hers. She takes my hand. "All right. Your dad—what can I tell you about him? He was always a dreamer, off in some other place in his head. He had a way of taking you along to lands of make-believe, where anything was possible. That was what drew me to him, but it wasn't enough. Not once you came along. Danny wasn't the most reliable person in the world; as quick to anger as he was to joy, and easily distracted. I was always scared he'd forget you were following along and lose you somewhere along the way."

"But he didn't, so you were wrong."

She stiffens. Something shutters in her eyes, and I wish I could take the words back. She lets go of my hand. "That's enough talking for tonight."

She stands, walks to the door. Turns, face softer again. "Please, just think about CAS. Do you really want to sign your life away for five years? You could end up doing anything, not what you think you want. Wouldn't it be better to work here than end up in Sanitation? And you could always leave it for now, and sign up when it opens again in six months, if you still want to."

"All right," I say. "I'll think about it."

"Good night, Lucy. I mean Riley."

• • •

As I'm drifting off to sleep, I do think about it. About being in this house twenty-four hours a day, and only being able to escape if I can come up with a good reason to write down in a column in a book. And having to come back before the reason is up.

And then I think about the mountains: walking in high places, climbing to the sky. With my dad: Danny the dreamer. I have his name now, and I hug it close.

That night's dreams are indistinct, and glorious.

11

THE NEXT LECTURE IS EARLY MORNING ON THE BUS, AND comes from a surprising source: Madison.

"Are you sure you really want to sign up for CAS?"

I look at her in surprise.

"It is *five years,* and they pay next to nothing the whole time. And you could wind up someplace awful. You might even"—her face crinkles in horror—"end up working with Finley."

He turns around from his seat in front of us and winks. "She should be so lucky," he says.

"What do you think? About signing up?" I ask him.

"It was the best thing I ever did," he answers seriously. "I love it."

"But—" Madison interrupts.

"No buts. But if you're counting on Parks, don't. Have a plan B."

Not much later I'm in the seminar room we were in yesterday morning, staring at a contract.

The last time I signed a contract I was a new Slated, just leaving the hospital. That seems such a long time ago. Then, I had no choice; imagine what would have happened to me if I refused to sign? That contract was all about promising to follow rules: of my new family, school, and the community. About doing my best to fit in, not get in trouble. I meant it when I signed, but that didn't last long, did it? If the Lorders found me now, they'd drag me off as a contract breaker.

It is very high on the *thou shalt not* list for Slateds to seek out their old lives. Using IMET to change my appearance, the assumed name, and the fake ID all add to my sins.

But this contract, today, is up to me. I get to decide. I chew on my pen, try to concentrate and read it properly.

Chairs shuffle around me. No one asks any questions; they all just sign without reading and hand them in. Soon eyes will notice my hesitation.

What does it mean? Five years, an apprenticeship. Being trained in a career, whatever it may be: my choice, or theirs.

A life, one of my own. As a Slated I wouldn't have been able to do this until I was twenty-one.

If seven years ago I hadn't been kidnapped by the AGT, hadn't ended up a terrorist, hadn't been Slated, what would my life be now? Would I still be sitting here, at this precise moment in time, trying to make this choice? Maybe *Lucy* would have been happy, excited. Signing the contract, then going out with all her friends this weekend to celebrate. Maybe she'd be sure she'd get her top choice, here in her hometown where everybody knew her.

Would Stella still be there in the back of Lucy's mind, arguing against this, wanting to keep her safe, keep her close, at home?

I sign: *Riley Kain.*

Next is the form to select my top choices. I put National Parks as one; hesitate, then put Education as two. I stare at the others, then, aware I'm one of the last still lingering over paperwork, I scribble the other sections in randomly, with Sanitation and Enforcement right at the bottom. I hand in the forms.

Hours of aptitude tests follow: comprehension, math, strange logic problems, and sequences. When it is finally time to go, we are told to report back Monday morning at eight A.M., when we'll find out which four weeklong trials we will do, and head straight off to start the first one that very day.

Outside, yesterday's sun is a distant memory; the sky is gray, the mountains hidden in cloud. It makes it easier to catch the bus straight back to the house. Time to face up to Stella and tell her I signed on the dotted line.

When I get there the side door we usually use is locked. Lucky I read the rules last night, and so know the door code. I punch the numbers in and step inside. The house is quiet.

I open the book to sign in, and with a start see *Stella Connor* written in the Out column, with *shopping* in the description, and return time estimated as four. She follows the rules, too? Another name, *Steph,* is also down as shopping; is she the girl who works for her? I scan today's page; it looks like nobody is home, and nobody expected back for at least a few hours.

Time to explore.

I'm gripped by a peculiar sense of excitement. At first I creep around, quiet, almost like I'm expecting someone to jump out and demand to know what I'm doing. I start with the public rooms, interconnecting hallways, stairwells: wandering, trying and failing to find something, anything, that feels familiar. At one point Pounce jumps down from a hall table as I round a corner, and I jump and almost scream.

The house is huge. Pounce follows as I wander into the massive shiny kitchen, utility rooms, walk-in cupboards. Nothing is familiar. Though the kitchen looks new; maybe it has changed since I was here? Then I try the door to Stella's study where I was yesterday: locked.

Stella had said the tower room I'm in wasn't my room before. Which was? I try to cast myself back, to stop thinking, to just follow my feet, but nothing works. I've had dreams of my room here before, but if I close my eyes and try to see it, all is uncertain. There is just a sense of proportion, some white-painted wardrobes, a too-frilly bed. Maybe there are photos of it in the albums?

Back in my room, door shut, I get the hairpin out and spring the lock to open the wardrobe. Lugging the albums to my bed, I lay them out in order, number one to eleven.

I open one album, then another. I scan through, looking for photos taken in my bedroom, but soon get distracted when I realize that apart from the first one where I am a baby, each one starts with a birthday. From my first birthday with cake smeared on my face, to a toddler and on up. Birthdays looked like serious business. Each year there was an amazing themed and decorated cake: fairies one year, ponies, pixies.

Mummy made them for me.

A shiver goes up my spine. Mummy? Stella. There are often smiling snaps of her, her arms around me, my arms around her. I was just a few years old when her dark hair changed to pale blond like mine. As I got older and my hair a little darker, so, weirdly, did hers. Almost like she was trying to make us match.

Again there are none of Dad. There are odd blank spaces in the albums as if some photos have been removed, but the spaces are few and far between; he couldn't have been in many of them to start with.

He took most of the photos.

An image of him behind a camera jumps into my mind, then

vanishes. I must ask Stella what happened to the photos she took out of the albums. Did she put them away someplace, or destroy them?

Something makes me push the other albums aside and reach for the last one: number eleven.

First page: Lucy smiling back. Me. Goosebumps travel up my arms and spine: I'm wearing the pink dress. The one in the cupboard, the one in my dream. Pounce jumps up and walks over, peers as I turn the pages. "Look, it's you," I whisper, not sure why I'm whispering. There is photo after photo of Pounce as a tiny kitten: chasing bits of string, sitting on my knee, sleeping in my arms. My tenth birthday present. Then there are photos of me with a big pink iced birthday cake: princess-themed this year. Ten candles, so I had that right.

A few pages later, something changes.

I'm still smiling, but something is wrong. It is on my face; I'm holding something in. I can almost feel this moment, but then it slips away.

What?

I turn another page, and there is a picture of me taken outside on a sunny day, with the peaks of Catbells behind. Pounce is clutched in my arms, and my gap-toothed grin is a real smile this time.

I turn the page: nothing. I scan through more pages to the end, but the rest of the album is blank. Something cold grips me inside.

I shut it. My heart is thudding hard behind my ribs. That last picture of me is the one that was on MIA. The last one Stella had before I disappeared. The one she gave to the website in the faint hope I might be found and come back to her one day.

I don't know how long I sit there, staring at the wall, thinking. I don't know why I've been remote to Stella: Is it the neediness and hunger in her eyes that makes me pull away? What we were to each other back then is all over these pages. To her, our relationship is real and immediate; to me, it is a bare echo, like a song I half heard once but can't really remember.

And now I've signed up for CAS instead of staying here with her.

A distant noise penetrates: a car? I look at my watch. It's almost four; they must be back. I jump up, hurriedly place the albums back in order in the wardrobe, lock it, and go downstairs.

Stella is in the kitchen unpacking boxes of groceries. I stand in the doorway a moment; she smiles to see me when she looks up.

"Can I help?" I ask.

"Of course." We slot things into two massive fridges, and she shows me which cupboards things go in.

"Now for a cup of tea and a chat," she says, and puts the kettle on. "Steph stayed in town, so we should be on our own for a while." She pours tea, and we sit on stools at the island.

"There's something I've got to tell you," I start to say, then hesitate.

"What is it, Riley?"

"I'm sorry, but I signed up for CAS."

I brace myself for her reaction, but she looks back at me calmly, sips her tea. "I thought you would. Though you know I'm not keen on National Parks. Some of what they do can be dangerous. And it'd be a disaster if they put you in Enforcement, with all the enhanced security checks. But we'll just wait and see what apprenticeship they give you; no point in worrying about it yet, is there?"

I stare at her, past surprise into shock. This *so* isn't the reaction I was expecting. "Thanks, Mum," I whisper.

Her face goes all funny. She reaches out an arm, but instead of crushing me into a hug like yesterday, she touches my cheek. She blinks furiously and gets up, goes to the counter behind us, and reaches for a box.

"I got you something." She opens it and holds out a small black rectangle.

"What is it?"

"Look, it's a camera. These new ones are so clever." She touches a small button and it springs open to show the lens and a few controls. It's small, barely a few fingers wide. She shows me how it works. "I thought this way if you must rush off every day, you can take photographs to show me what you're doing. And we can start another album together. All right?"

"Thank you," I say, and then I take photos of Pounce sitting at our feet, of Stella, a few of the kitchen. Then I stand next to her and hold it out at arm's length to take one of us together. She shows me how to look at them, pushing a button and projecting them onto a surface, and a few clicks later there we are, standing next to each other and smiling on the kitchen wall.

"Oh, and I have something else for you." She reaches into her pocket. "I made an extra copy of the key to the wardrobe with the photo albums; you can look at them when you want to. But keep it locked and hide the key. I don't want anyone else getting into it, all right?"

She hands me the key, and I wrap my fingers around it, slip it into my pocket. I feel guilty that I've been in there already without her knowing. I remember I was going to ask her about the missing photos of Dad, but can't bring myself to do it, not today. Not while we're getting along so well.

"Now, enough of that, I've got things to do," Stella says. "It's Ellie's birthday today. Do you want to help me decorate the cake?"

. . .

Ellie's birthday cake isn't as elaborate as my childhood ones: a triple layer chocolate cake with chocolate icing, intricate icing flowers climbing across the top, and twenty candles. It's delicious, and everyone is in good spirits; even Madison makes no sideways comments. She announces the reason for her good mood is that it is her one weekend off this month, and that I'm going with her on a led walk tomorrow up Catbells with Finley.

Even after hearing that, Stella is the most relaxed I've seen her, smiling at the end of the table, looking out at each of the girls. And I see that to her, all of them are her daughters; surrogates for what she lost? Some have been here for years.

It's later that I find out that Ellie is an avid gardener, and she is delighted that the flowers on the cake were copies of ones she'd planted in the garden last summer. And there is a little swirl of jealousy inside.

12

THE NEXT MORNING AS MADISON AND I STEP OUTSIDE TO catch the bus into Keswick, it finally happens: It's snowing.

I dance about on the way to the road, holding my arms up to the sky.

"You're mad," she says.

"I just really love snow. I don't know why."

She shrugs. "Mostly I tolerate it. But it'd be excellent today if it snows really, really hard, and they cancel this stupid walk."

"I thought you wanted to go?" She doesn't answer, and I look back at her. "Oh, I see. Not so keen on walking; more keen on Finley."

She scowls. Then laughs. "Maybe."

"What's up with you two?"

She shrugs. "It's hard to say. He's Finley." As if that says it all.

"And . . . ?"

"He's not known for having girlfriends for longer than five minutes. He's Finley the flirt."

We reach the road and stop to wait for the bus.

"You're wrong," I say. "That may be the way he has been before, but he really likes you. It's in his eyes when he looks at you."

The pink of her cheeks deepens, but she doesn't answer, and holds up an arm to flag down the approaching bus.

When we get into town we go to the Moot Hall. There is a small cluster of people dressed like us, in warm walking gear. Finley is there, along with a man identified as John with a clipboard writing down names of each arrival.

Finley sees us and waves. He gets our names put on John's list, then walks over. "Well, look here: It's Shorty and Extra-Shorty. You both better stick close to me."

"Why's that?" Madison asks.

"If it keeps snowing, you might disappear in a snowdrift. We don't want to lose you up there."

It is snowing great heavy flakes, and there is a little discussion about that and the weather forecast. They decide to wait and consult with the fell checker, due along any moment.

"What's a fell checker?" I ask Finley.

He turns to me, raises an eyebrow. "That is the sort of thing you should know if you want to work for Parks. It's all in the name."

"Let me guess: He checks fells?" Madison says.

"You got it, Einstein. Len goes up Helvellyn every day and checks conditions on Striding Edge. He takes a few photos up top. They post his report so walkers can decide whether to go up," Finley says, gesturing at a display case on the front of the Moot Hall. I walk over to look. Inside is yesterday's report on conditions and weather on Helvellyn. *Icy: Experienced walkers with winter survival gear only. Crampons essential.* And a photo: a thin icy path winding on a ridge, steep drop off both sides.

"Not for the fainthearted," Finley says.

"Not for me!" Madison adds.

"Exactly," Finley says, and she punches him in the arm. But I'm ignoring them both, staring, transfixed by the image in the cabinet. I've been up on that ridge, many times. I'm sure of it! With *Danny the dreamer.*

"Judging by that smile, you're not fainthearted," another voice says, and I turn. It's John; he must have walked over and listened in without my noticing.

"No. Can we go up there today instead?"

John laughs. "No way. Too many beginners here."

"I don't get it," Madison says. "Why do they have some guy go up there to check stuff every day? Why don't they just have a camera installed, and some weather sensors?"

Finley shakes his head at Madison. I jump in before anyone else can answer: "It's conservation. National Parks can't put equipment up there; it's against their mandate." John nods.

Len the fell checker appears. He's older than I expect, long gray hair tied back, a wild gray beard, and a crazy glint in his eyes. He chats with John, and it is decided we're still on for Catbells. As Len strides off, I stare longingly at his back, feet itching to chase after him and ask if I can go up Helvellyn with him instead.

"You coming?" Finley calls out, and I see our group is starting off. John is leading the way, with Finley as back marker, bringing up the rear.

We walk through Keswick to the river, then down the side of it onto a footpath along fields, into woods, and climbing to the turn to Catbells. There is soon more snow on the ground as we start up a steep hill. Madison is gasping, slowing down, and Finley is laughing and pushing her from behind. Then holding her hand. The way they are with each other pulls inside, finds the ache that is always there.

Imagine if Ben were here. Holding my hand as we walk up the hill. Imagine we were alone instead of in this straggling line of walkers.

I speed up and let Finley and Madison drop behind. Giving them some alone time, I tell myself, or is it just that I can't watch them anymore? I push my legs and muscles, and one by one overtake the others who are slowing as the path steepens. Before long I reach John at the front.

"Slow down there," he says cheerfully. "I can't let you disappear ahead, and I can't speed up and let the others drop behind."

"How about if I go ahead, but stay in sight?" I ask, itching to just see open path in front of me.

"Go on then. But don't get too far ahead," he says. "Wait every now and then for us to catch up."

I head out front. The snow has slowed like the weather report said it would, and the sky is lightening; the view opens up ahead.

The open path at my feet calls me forward; every step I feel I'm getting closer to something without knowing what. I force myself to wait now and then for the others to catch up as promised, then take off again. The cloud gradually lifts, and one by one the surrounding peaks reveal themselves. Something inside is letting go, untwisting bit by bit. *This is where I belong.*

I reach some rocks; the wind has swept the snow away from this exposed place, leaving the glimmer of ice behind. A short scramble up is needed. Stella's right: I am part mountain goat. I climb the rocks easily and wait at the top for the others at John's wave. Most get up without much difficulty, but Madison looks alarmed, and it doesn't look like an act designed to get Finley's attention. I scramble back down again and help her up before he notices.

Across the first ridge, another scramble, and then I'm alone on top of the world. The lake stretches out below, Keswick beyond. The other way, higher fells and steeper climbs call out to me, and I promise myself: another day.

Up here you can believe anything; you can be anything. Words whispered inside: Danny the dreamer. I repeat them out loud.

Steps come up behind me; John stands next to me. Did he hear? "True. And these mountains and lakes have been here a long time, longer than people have. They'll be here when we're all gone."

We say nothing else. The world below, and its Lorders and problems, seems remote, of no consequence.

The others catch up, and before long we must leave to make it down in daylight. Back to reality.

That evening at dinner, Stella tells us that an inspector is coming for lunch tomorrow: a JCO. All must attend, no excuses, and be on our best behavior. She doesn't say a name; is this my grandmother, the one Madison mentioned? The one whose photos are hidden away inside a box in a locked wardrobe? Glances are exchanged, nothing else said, but the mood is dampened down, as if she'd just thrown a bucket of cold water over the room.

Madison follows me to my room after dinner in a total black mood. She flops down on my bed.

"I *really* can't believe this."

"What?"

"That that witch has to pick this Sunday, my only one off in an entire month, to come for a stupid lunch. And *all must attend.* Some of us might have lives of our own. Things to do."

"Like what?"

She scowls furiously, but her face wars between that and the edge of a smile.

"Finley?"

She nods. "Yep. He finally asked me out this afternoon; we were going to meet in town, go out for lunch, and whatever. And now—"

"Whatever? What is *whatever*?"

"What does it matter? I've tried to call, but no one is answering. He's going to think I'm coming up with an excuse to get out of it. He'll never believe we're not allowed to miss this stupid lunch. It's this stupid house. None of the others are like this."

"Is it Stella's mother coming for lunch? The Juvenile Control Officer for all of England that you told me about?"

She nods. "She comes every few months or so. Stella never refers to her as her mother, but that's who it is: Astrid Connor, the smiling assassin."

"What do you mean?"

"Oh, you'll find out soon enough." She sighs tragically. "I can't believe this is happening to me."

"I told you so."

"What?"

"That Finley really likes you."

"Maybe." She smiles, then it falls away. "Not that it'll matter after tomorrow."

"Call again tomorrow, tell him you'll meet him later. It'll be fine."

"Sure it will; I bet he'll just go off with some other girl."

"I doubt it!"

"What makes you so wise in the ways of guys, anyhow?"

I don't answer.

"Okay, I've told you mine; now tell me yours. Is there someone? There is, isn't there? Tell me!"

I can feel the shadow cross my face. "There was."

"What happened? Did you stand him up and then he went off and—"

"No." I fling a pillow at her. "No, because he really *cared* so he wouldn't be so daft. Like Finley really cares."

"So why aren't you together, then? If the path of true love is really all forgiving like that, where is he? Why did you leave him behind? Why didn't he follow you to Keswick?"

"He couldn't, that's all," I say, and refuse to say more. Eventually Madison sees I'm really upset, apologizes, and leaves.

I sigh and turn the lights off, get into bed, and pull the blankets around me. If Ben really loved me . . . shouldn't that survive everything? Shouldn't he still feel the same way, deep down inside, even though Lorders have wiped all memory of me from his mind?

It is romantic nonsense to think so. A wave of sadness creeps over me, bit by bit, so deep that it feels as if heavy weights are holding me still, that I'm paralyzed. Later I hear a light tap on my door: Stella? But my eyes stay shut when it opens, my body unmoving, breathing deep, unable to reach out or say anything. Moments later it shuts again and footsteps retreat.

Underlying the grief, an uneasy sense of disquiet remains. Tomorrow, I meet my *grandmother*.

What would she do if she knew I was here? Would she be happy to have her long lost granddaughter back, or is she Lorder through and through?

13

"THERE ARE A FEW NEW FACES HERE TODAY, I SEE." SHE smiles, and her eyes twinkle behind glasses that look a little like mine. "I'm Astrid Connor, and your lovely house mother here is my daughter. Bet she didn't tell you." She looks at Stella and then smiles again. "Daughters!" she says, and shakes her head. Like the last photo I saw of her, her hair is silvery gray, swept up. She wears ordinary clothes; nothing says *Lorder* in how she looks or acts, but there is something about her. The hackles are raised on the back of my neck. Every eye is drawn forward. Some people you don't want to turn your back on.

Stella clears her throat. "There are three new girls since your last visit." She quickly points to each of us and says our names while Steph and another girl co-opted to help are bringing in serving dishes, putting them on the table: We're having a roast. As Stella points to me and says "Riley Kain," Astrid's eyes fall on mine. A brief moment of something crosses her face—curiosity, that soon fades to disinterest? Then she is interrupted by Stella passing her a dish. The curious glance returns.

The usual chatter around the table is gone. Everyone eats silently, even Madison, while Astrid holds court. She talks with Stella about the running of the house; asks about window repairs. Every now and then her eyes fall on one of us and she'll ask a question: about work, or Keswick. All pleasant and chitchatty. No order in it, not working her way around the table or any other logic to it I can see.

Then she turns and her eyes fall on Madison: playing with her food, slumped in her seat, eyes lowered. "Madison, isn't it?" she says.

Madison looks up, nods; her eyes, visible now, are defiant. Something in my stomach twists.

Amusement crosses Astrid's face. "Not hungry today, dear?"

"Not really. Can I be excused?"

Stella's sharp intake of breath is audible in a room too quiet.

"On one condition. Tell me exactly what you are thinking first."

Doubt crosses Madison's face; she shakes it off. *Please, Madison, don't be an idiot,* I plead silently.

"All right, then. It's my one weekend off this month, and I had plans. But *she* insisted we all be here." Madison glares at Stella.

"Oh, I see. I'm sorry you missed your *plans*," Astrid says. "What were they?" A tinge of red crosses Madison's cheeks. "A boy, I'm guessing? My, my. Really, Stella," she says, looking at her daughter now. "They don't all have to be here today, not if they have *plans*. You know I really just come to see how you are. You know what it is like to be a *mother,* to worry about your *daughter.*" There is a malicious twist to her words.

Stella's lips are set in a thin line. "I think I know what is best for my girls."

Madison clears her throat. "I told you what I was thinking, like you asked. Can I go now?"

Astrid looks at her daughter, an eyebrow raised in a question.

"Stay and finish your lunch," Stella says.

Madison scowls. "It's not fair. None of the other houses are run like this. She treats us like prisoners!"

Too far. All the girls look at her in horror; I plead with my eyes: *Stop this; apologize now!*

Astrid smiles. "I think, dear Madison, you would be able to tell the difference between this and a prison, if you ever found yourself in one. You may go now."

Madison looks between her and Stella, like a rabbit caught in the headlights. Stella nods faintly. "Go on," she says.

Madison puts her napkin on the table, pushes her chair out. Walks stiffly to the door and is gone.

Astrid laughs. "What a serious bunch you are! Doesn't anyone have any stories to tell? Perhaps one of the new girls." Her eyes fall on me. "Kylie, was it?"

"Riley," I answer, trying not to react to her saying a name so close to Kyla.

"When did you arrive in Keswick?"

"Earlier this week. I'm here for CAS."

"Where are you from?"

"Chelmsford. But I love the mountains, and I want to work for National Parks." I start to rush out an explanation of what they do before she has even asked. My voice trails away.

She raises an eyebrow. "At last: a chatty one. And how did you—"

"Oh drat. Sorry!" Stella interrupts, springing up as a toppled jug spreads water across the table. Steph dashes for a cloth; Astrid gets up out of her seat before the water can run onto her lap. "Sorry, sorry," Stella says again.

"Stop fussing," Astrid snaps.

She and Stella leave the dining room.

The door swings shut, and as if we all had been holding our breath, we let it out in one collective gasp.

"Is she always like that?" I ask Ellie, seated next to me.

She nods. "She's horrible to Stella, isn't she? Can you believe what she said to her, about knowing what it's like to worry about your daughter, when Stella's daughter is missing? Nasty."

Then everyone starts talking in hushed tones about Madison, what she said, how long Stella will confine her to the house as punishment, but I can't get Astrid's words out of my head. Like Ellie said, it was nasty, but not just the way Ellie meant. There was something *else* twisting behind her words, that niggles and worries inside.

Feigning a headache, I leave the others and wander out, thinking I'll look for Madison. But when I start to cross the reception area, my feet pause. Stella's office; the hidden door. Will they be in the same sitting room they used to go?

I shouldn't. But it'll be locked anyhow, won't it? I look around; no one is here. I cross behind the desk to the office door, reach a hand to the knob; it turns and I push the door open. Too late, I realize my mistake: What if they are in here instead? But when I peek into the room it is empty. Behind me I hear voices and footsteps heading this way. I step through into the office and pull the door shut behind me.

Trapped.

What if they come here now?

My eyes dart about the room, my ears strain for footsteps. All I can hear are some low voices beyond this door—not Stella or Astrid, but some of the girls. They're not moving; they're staying out there, probably in armchairs by the window, and not going anywhere anytime soon.

My feet start the reluctant few steps to the curtains that cover the door, somehow feeling half frozen, each move an effort. I should have gone back to my room, or looked for Madison; anything but this.

Something on the wall catches my eye. A recent photo of Astrid that had been hidden in the box in my room hangs there. I pause, look around, and spot a few of the others.

So. When Astrid comes for a visit, Stella hangs her photos up; when Astrid leaves, they are hidden in a box. I shake my head. What weird family am I part of?

Maybe it is time to find out. I pull the curtain out, step behind it. Push the door open and look through.

And it is just like my dream: a narrow hall. *I used to play hide-and-seek here.* It's dusty, and I put a finger under my nose, try not to sneeze. Not used anymore?

When I step through and let the door shut behind me, I'm plunged into darkness. *A flashlight; there used to be a flashlight hidden here, in the corner.* I feel along the wall and reach down, but find nothing.

I walk, slow and silent, one hand touching the wall. The hall stretches past one room, then turns ninety degrees. There are a few slivers of light from ventilation panels near the floor. And voices.

I crouch down near a panel, and listen.

". . . but don't do it, please don't—I'm begging you." Stella.

"Do what?"

"You know."

Astrid titters. "You should see your face. My, my—so fierce. It's a shame you can't put that energy to better use."

"I see no better purpose to my life. Isn't 'serve and protect the young people of our country' part of *your* official job mandate as JCO?"

"Oh it is, and I take that *very* seriously. The bad apples must go to prevent rot in the barrel, as you well know. These girls, here—they aren't your daughters. You know the consequences of error; that could be a *painful* mistake."

Silence. Even from the other side of the wall, it feels strained. Is Stella caught in her mother's eyes? I shiver.

"I told you I had news for you today about Lucy; you haven't asked me yet," Astrid says at last. "Don't you want to know?"

"Of course I do. Please tell me."

"Stella, prepare yourself for a shock."

"What?"

"You know how I told you weeks ago that Lucy was killed by a terrorist bomb? I've found some . . . irregularities in the Lorder records on this matter."

"What do you mean?"

"It appears her death was faked."

I'm stunned. Stella had been told I died in that bomb? She didn't say; didn't ask about it. And now she isn't saying anything I can hear in response to news that I'm alive—news it seems she shouldn't know. And I'm hoping—praying—she is a good actress.

"I don't understand. Where is she, then?" Stella asks finally.

There is a pause. "I have no idea. She is still listed as officially dead, but unofficially, she is missing. There seems to be some *interest* in finding her, from a number of . . . *interesting* places. I do wonder what that girl has been up to."

"Nothing to worry you, I'm sure!" Stella snaps, too quick, and I'm worried. This is a dangerous game. Somehow, I know—either from traces of memory, or observation today, or both—that Astrid is adept at reading what people say and don't say. Shouldn't Stella be in hysterical tears at the news that I'm alive?

"Really? We shall see," Astrid says. "But no matter. You know I've kept my half of our bargain and found out everything I can about what happened to her. I'll protect her and bring her home safe to you if I can.

Darling girl, despite our differences, you *know* I only want what is best for you. As soon as I find out anything of Lucy's whereabouts, so will you. But don't ask anything more of me. You *will* be disappointed."

Soon their conversation turns to other things; roof maintenance needed, damp in the cellar. I'm stiff and cold from crouching down in this unheated hall. Time to make an escape while they're both still in there and accounted for.

I can't go back the way I came; there are sure to be eyes outside Stella's office door. I stand carefully, ease my muscles, and creep slowly forward, one hand on the wall. Their voices fade as I reach another door.

Carefully I pull the door toward me: nothing! I start to panic. Is it locked? It didn't have a lock before, I'm sure of it. I feel along the door; no padlock, but there is a simple latch. I release it. Step through the door into the utility room that is behind the kitchen, then back along a hall.

Somehow my feet are remembering, more and more, how to get around this house. I look down before I reach a main hall, brush at my clothes to get rid of the dust.

Later, back in my room for the night, my mind is spinning with Astrid: the things she said, the way she said them. The twist of the knife in her words.

And that Stella was told I had died. Was this before I reported myself found, before she knew I was on my way back to her? She never told me, so I can't ask without admitting I was listening in. But *why* didn't she tell me? I don't understand her at all.

Astrid said she's looking for me, that she'll bring me home if she finds me. Yet here I am, and she obviously doesn't know about it; Stella hasn't told her. She doesn't trust her.

But Astrid has noticed something is up with Stella, I'm sure of it. She won't let it go. If Astrid works out what it is, I'm in trouble. Despite her assurances to Stella, I don't trust her, either. If Lorders find out I'm here, they'll come for me.

Danger.

Careful, quiet, each step on tiptoes through Mummy's office, but it is hard to be a spy in this stupid pink dress; it whispers and rustles as I move. I gather the skirt together and bunch it up in my hands to hold it still as I slip behind the curtains.

I push the door, step through, and hold it part open with my foot as I lean down to get the flashlight. Switch it on, then let the door swing shut.

I creep along the wall, around the corner, then crouch down to listen like a spy.

". . . be here soon." Mummy.

"He indulges that child, as do you."

"It's her birthday!"

"Really, Stella. Isn't it about time you tell him the truth? That his precious daughter isn't his; that you don't even know whose she is. Perhaps I should tell him?"

"No! Don't you dare, I'll—"

"Don't threaten me, Stella. You'll regret it."

Their voices continue but I stop listening. Shaking, I stuff my hands in my ears, but I can still hear Grandma's words over and over inside my head: his precious daughter isn't his.

How could that be? He's Daddy.

My daddy!

I start to cry.

14

"IS EVERYTHING OKAY?" MADISON ASKS.

"Shouldn't I be asking you that? Where'd you disappear to yesterday? Why are you going to work so late today? Bets are on that Stella will ground you, between that and what you said at lunch."

She smiles, and it is a *very* happy smile. "I wrote it in the book: *out until late.* I thought I made it quite clear. And Cora will get over it when I tell her why."

The bus pulls up, and we clamber on. Madison sits with Finley, he holds her hand, and some of the boys whistle. I settle into a seat on my own, glad to put some space between us before Madison shakes off her loved-up state enough to ask me again: Is everything okay?

That dream, the things Astrid said—could it be true? Was he really not my father? All my snippets of memory of him—the way he was with me—say otherwise. But what if he never knew?

Then he died for a daughter who wasn't even his.

Later I'm standing in the CAS meeting room, and when my name is called, I collect an envelope. It doesn't seem so important now. But unless Astrid works out what is up with Stella, and who I am, and everything stops, it is for *five years* of my life.

I rip it open.

Dear Miss Kain, blah blah blah. I scan down to the important part: my trials.

Week 1: Education

Week 2: National Parks

Week 3: Hospitality

Week 4: Transportation

Hurrah! I got my top two choices. But I'm puzzled at getting Hospitality. It didn't really appeal to me, so I'd had it far down my order of preference, and it seemed like a popular choice. I turn the pages and find the details for each placement.

The words next to Hospitality jump into stark focus:

Report to Waterfall House for Girls, Stella Connor.

What? How can this be? And I think back to how adamant Stella had been about my not signing up for CAS, especially not for Parks. But then when I went to tell her I'd signed, she was all chilled about it, and I'd thought she'd realized I had to make my own decisions. But I was wrong. She was in town that day. She knows somebody; she must have pulled some strings. What do you want to bet these trials mean nothing, that I'll end up with her for *five years* as some sort of apprentice housemaid?

Eventually it penetrates that the others are leaving, heading off to the first of their trials. Week one for me is Education, and I find the details. Keswick Primary School; I'm supposed to go there now and report to reception. But what difference will it make?

When I arrive I get rushed to an office. Two other potential apprentices are waiting along with the same smiling woman I spoke to last week about apprenticing in Education.

"I'm really sorry I kept you waiting. I got lost," I lie. I knew the way, but my feet wouldn't cooperate.

"No problem, dear, take a seat. I'm Mrs. Medway, Head of School. I also train apprentice teachers and assistants. I'm going to run you through what you'll be doing for the week."

I try to pay attention, for her sake, but it is a losing battle. Some details get through: We'll be shadowing classes two days, spend a day in admin, then two more days in classes, but this time helping with lessons. "Any preference for year groups or subjects?" The others tell her theirs, and eventually she turns to me and smiles. "You're quiet today. Any favorite year groups? Activities?"

"Anything is fine," I start to say, then pause. "Unless they do art? I love art. And running—sports."

"Perfect—our youngest class is doing messy art this morning. I'll put you in there. And there is a sports day on Friday afternoon this week; they can always use extra help. We'll work something out for the other days."

She has us follow her around the school for a tour, telling school history on the way. It was damaged and rebuilt after the riots. Keswick Primary used to be called St. Herbert's Church of England School, but the name changed after church schools were banned thirty years ago. We see children through windowed classroom doors, playing a noisy game of basketball in a gym, heads bent in a library. Then finally we reach an art room, and I peer through the door. They're tiny. Four years old. All sitting cross-legged on the floor and listening to their teacher.

Mrs. Medway knocks at the door, has a word with the teacher. Comes back and squeezes my arm. "Go on in. You'll be fine; don't look so worried." I walk in, and a sea of small faces look up and smile.

Not much later they're all wearing smocks over their school uniforms, and the teacher passes me one to go over my clothes. "It's up to you; you're down for shadowing, so you can sit in a corner and watch. Or jump in if you want to."

I decide to sit and watch for a while. They are finger painting on big sheets of white paper, and the air is full of the smell of paint and excited voices. Despite the resolution to stay put, before long swirls of color on white paper pull me close. I itch to paint.

A small hand pulls at mine. "Miss, look at my painting!" a boy says, and I'm pulled to a table and soon admiring blobs and blotches.

One girl sits quiet in the middle of all the chatter, not joining in. "Hi," I say. She doesn't answer.

The boy looks up. "That's Becky. She's sad."

"Oh, I see. I'm sad sometimes, too," I admit. "But I like painting when I'm sad." Never a truer sentence have I spoken. I kneel on the floor between them and dip my eager fingers into black paint.

"Why are you sad?" Becky asks.

"Mostly because I miss things. Like Sebastian."

"Who's he?" the boy asks.

"Watch," I say. I can't remember finger painting before—I'd rather have a brush in my hand—but a reasonable estimate of a black cat soon appears on the paper.

Becky stares at it very hard. "You miss your cat?" She nods to herself. "Okay. I'll paint something, too." She gathers different paints and soon is concentrating on getting as much mess on herself and the paper as possible. I glance up and the art teacher gives me a thumbs-up. Other kids bring me their pictures to look at, then ask me to show them how to paint a cat. This is fun. Could I be an art teacher?

Not if Stella has anything to do with it.

I stay and help clean up at lunch. The teacher hangs pictures on the walls, puts my cat up next to Becky's painting. Hers could be anything from an alien to a lamppost, but I'm reasonably sure it is supposed to be a man—her dad?

"It's her father," the teacher confirms. "He went missing last month."

I turn my shocked face to hers. "What happened?"

A pause. "It was good work getting Becky to take part. Thank you," she says, not answering my question. If it can't be said out loud, we all know what that means.

Lorders.

When the final bell rings, I'm surprised the day has sped past. Each year group has art a half day each week, and the afternoon was spent charcoal drawing with year five. I gaze at the white-topped peaks as I walk back to the center of Keswick. If I can't get into Parks, maybe this wouldn't be such a bad choice. Then I shake it off. What a joke for me to even think of being a teacher; despite my faked records, I didn't even finish high school. And what about Stella's manipulations?

I should get the bus back to the house now, but there is a kernel of anger inside that says *no*.

Madison: She'll understand. I head for her café. I'll wait there until she's finished; we can get the bus back together.

When I reach the café and pull at the door, it doesn't budge. It's locked? Puzzled, I realize the lights are off inside. A CLOSED sign hangs on the door, yet I'm sure Madison said she was working until five. A sense of unease settles inside. I walk around to the café's back door and knock.

No one answers, but was there a noise inside? I knock again: nothing. I'm about to turn around and leave, but then try the door. The handle turns. It's not locked.

I pull the door partway open, peek in. "Hello?" I call out. "It's Riley. Is Madison here?"

Cora is sitting at the work surface, her back to me. Not turning or answering. Unsure what to do, after a moment I push the door open the rest of the way, walk in, and let it shut behind me. The light is dim, and I blink.

"Hello?" I say again, and walk toward her. Her shoulders are shaking. She's crying? Fear grabs me inside. "What is it? What's wrong?"

She looks up at me, shakes her head. "What could she have done?" she whispers.

Madison? Panic swirls inside. *No, not again.* "What happened? Tell me!" I demand.

"She was helping make cakes for tomorrow, standing there with flour on her nose and telling me about that boy she likes. And they just marched in, grabbed her. Dragged her out past the regulars—all of them just sat there, staring at the lunches she'd brought them earlier. She's gone." Her face drops into her hands.

"Lorders?" I whisper.

She nods.

No. *No.* This can't be happening; it can't. Not here, too. And it feels like quicksand is clawing at my feet, pulling me down into another nightmare.

"What could she have done?" she says again.

I shake my head. Nothing to deserve *this*. I blink, but there are no tears, just an empty place inside as I conjure up the person who must be responsible: Astrid Connor. My *grandmother.* It must be her. Or could it even be Stella? A cold rock twists in my stomach. I'll make her do something. I'll make her fix this.

I stay long enough to make tea, to start tidying up the mess left behind. I get out of Cora that she'd thrown the customers out after the Lorders left. In the front of the café are half-eaten lunches still on plates. I scrape them into bins, put the dishes in the dishwasher, put food away in fridges.

Finally I hesitate by the door. "I should go now. Are you going to be all right?"

She shrugs. "I'll get up in the morning. Thanks for your help."

Her words echo in my ears as I walk to the bus. She wouldn't thank me if she knew who my grandmother was.

A bus is waiting when I get to the stop, and I climb on. Finley: He's there. A sinking feeling twists inside as I realize I have to tell him. I walk toward his seat as the bus pulls away.

"Finley?" He looks up. His face is white, eyes dead. He knows. One of the café regulars or someone on the street must have told him.

I don't say anything. I sit next to him, as if somebody being there could do anything to help.

15

I MARCH INTO RECEPTION. IT'S PAST TEATIME, BUT THERE IS a cluster of girls there, whispering, faces pale. News travels fast.

"Where's Stella?" I ask.

One of them points at her office door, but before I can move toward it, the door opens. Stella comes out, nods at everyone, and starts to cross the room.

"Wait," I say, and she turns.

"Do you know what's happened to Madison?" I ask, and all voices cease.

Stella looks at me, and her eyes are saying *be quiet,* but I'm not receiving.

"You know, don't you? That Lorders came and hauled her away today. Strangely enough, the day after Astrid—your mother—came for lunch."

"That's enough, Riley."

"No, it's not. Not nearly enough; nothing is ever said. What are you going to do about it?" Some part of me is aware that others have come in now, that everyone is silent, with mouths hanging open and eyes big. Eyes that are looking between me and Stella.

"There is nothing I can do."

"But she's your *mother.* Doesn't that *mean* anything?"

She doesn't answer.

I shake my head. I can feel Ellie coming up next to me, taking my arm. Pulling me toward the door to the hall where my room is, and I let myself be led. My feet take the steps, but then I stop at the door and look back at Stella. She's still standing there, frozen in place.

"No. I guess it really doesn't mean anything," I say, and then walk down the hall with Ellie.

Take her to the tower! Madison had said, laughing, the first time she showed me the way to my room.

Ellie tries to get me to talk, but I send her away, close my door. Every friend I ever had: gone. Pounce scratches to be let in, and I even ignore her. I stay where I am past the start of dinner. No one comes to check on me; they know where I am, that I'm not coming, don't they?

No one ever says *anything*. Isn't this the biggest problem of all? If we all stood up—everyone in the whole country, and said, *Stop; this is enough,* every time something happened, wouldn't it have to stop?

I'm starting to sound like Aiden.

There is a tap on my door late that night. It opens. Stella stands there, takes in me sitting up in bed, blankets pulled up, leaning against the wall.

"Still awake, I see. I thought you might be hungry." She holds out a plate of food in one hand.

I shake my head. Arms crossed.

She walks in, puts the plate on the desk. Sits on the chair. "Why are you so angry with me?"

My eyes widen. "Would you like a list?"

"Keep your voice down. No matter what you might think, there is nothing I could have done about Madison. She went too far."

"You never liked her."

"That's not true. She could be difficult at times, but—"

"Then why don't you *do* something? Why don't you call Astrid; she'd have to listen to you."

"She won't."

"So, is that your philosophy? That mothers don't have to listen to their daughters?"

"What do you mean?"

I shake my head. "That's not important right now; Madison is important. Astrid needs to hear from you that what she did is wrong, to get Madison back to us! How could she have her taken away when all she did was answer her question truthfully and say what she really thought?"

"Too much truth can be a bad thing. And careful what you say about your grandmother!"

"What—are you *defending* her?"

"No, not exactly, but—"

"What, then?"

She sighs. "She thinks what she does is right. That she protects everyone else by—"

"Taking out the rotten apple? What a crock. She's a power-mad manipulative nutcase."

"Careful what you say and who you say it to!"

I shake my head. "You *are* sticking up for her."

"She is my mother."

"That's not a good enough reason. People have to earn respect—even mothers."

"Lucy! You owe a lot to her. Don't speak of her like this." And Stella looks uneasy, as if the walls have ears, but even if they do, for once I don't care.

"What? What do I owe her?"

Stella doesn't answer.

"You're as bad as she is."

"What do you mean?"

"Doing what you think is best for me, without any idea what really is."

She looks at me, alarm starting in her eyes.

"Oh yes, I worked it out: You pulled strings, didn't you? You had me put down for *here* for an apprenticeship trial. Will anything I do or say make any difference to where I end up?"

There it is, in her eyes. Confirmation.

"Lucy, listen to me. I just want to keep you safe. You'll get found out if—"

"I'll get found out if you keep calling me *Lucy*, and if you single me out for attention like that. This would never have happened if Dad were here. None of it."

She recoils. "Shut up! You don't know what you're talking about. You don't even remember him!" I don't answer, but she must read it in my eyes, and her face changes to fury. "You do. You remember him, but you don't remember me." Her arms are crossed rigidly, red spots rising in white cheeks.

"Maybe I remember some little things. But if I've got stuff wrong, how can I know if you don't tell me anything? Tell me already!"

"It was him, it was him all along!"

"What was him?"

"Danny was in the AGT. It was his fault! He had you taken. They wanted artistic children no more than age ten to do some experiments on, and there you were, perfectly fitting the bill. He gave you to them."

I stare at her, stunned. That's what Dr. Craig and Nico always said: that I was given to them. Handed to them by my parents, that they knew what was going to be done to me. Could Dad really have done that, knowing what I'd face? I'd always been sure that was one of their lies. But was it because I am artistic, is that why I was targeted? With shock I remember Nico implied as much—that artists' brains have different wiring. Easier to muck with.

But how could Stella know about this stuff? I never told her. Did she get her information from Dad: Is that what proves she is telling the truth?

No. It can't be. "I don't believe you," I say. "How could you even know what the AGT wanted, what they were doing?"

"My mother told me. She's been doing all she can to find you! Investigating the AGT, everything."

Relief fills me, and I sag back with it. It wasn't Dad who told her; if it comes from Astrid, then maybe none of what Stella says is true. But then the inconsistency screams out at me, and I stare back at her. "This doesn't make sense. If Astrid is trying to find me for you, why haven't you told her I'm here?"

Her mouth opens and closes again.

"I see. You don't trust her. So why do you believe her when she says Dad gave me to the AGT? He never would have done that to me!"

"He'd never have done that to his *daughter.*"

No. And I'm shaking my head, and I'm back in the hallway listening to her and Astrid, and Astrid saying, *Isn't it about time you tell him the truth? That his precious daughter isn't his.*

"He wasn't my father," I say, words quiet. I'm still denying it inside, but it doesn't come out as a question.

"No. He found out. And just after that, he gave you to the AGT for their experiments. Revenge—he did the one thing that would hurt me more than anything else."

"He wouldn't do that."

"I'm sorry, Lucy," she says, anger bleeding away from her face. "I'm sorry. I shouldn't have told you."

"I don't believe you!" And I'm curling into a ball on the bed. Stella comes and puts a hand on my shoulder.

"Lucy, I'm sorry."

"Just leave me alone!" I say, and she pulls her hand away. "I mean it. Go away."

She murmurs that she loves me, that nothing can change that. After a while she finally goes. The door clicks shut, and I'm alone.

It can't be true; it can't. He wouldn't do that. My dad wouldn't do that.

But if he found out I wasn't his, he would have been furious; what man wouldn't be? Stella must have been messing around on him, and not just once or twice. What was it Astrid said? That she doesn't know *whose* daughter I am. I could be anyone's. The thought fills me with horror even as I deny it inside. Could Dad have done what she said, found out I wasn't his and just given me away, to get back at Stella?

No. I can't believe it. I won't.

Stella's wrong. She must have made it up. She's just trying to manipulate me all over again, like her mother manipulates her.

The door clicks shut behind us, and we are plunged into darkness. Daddy flicks the flashlight on and holds it under his chin.

"Mwahahaha!" he stage-whispers.

"Be quiet! You're not a ghost. We're spies."

"Oh yeah. Sorry," he whispers back.

We creep along the hall and around the corner, and a faint murmur of voices gets louder.

"I still think we should play ghosts and yell BOO through the grates," Daddy whispers.

I shake my head and bend down to hear, Daddy next to me.

But the words I hear are wrong. They can't be anything else; they don't make sense. There is a clang as the flashlight in Daddy's hand slips to the floor. I look up. "Daddy?"

He has rocked back onto his heels. The flashlight beam points the wrong way, but even in shadow his face isn't how it has ever been when he has looked at me before.

"Daddy?" I say again.

His eyes focus back on mine. "Go to your room now, Lucy. Go!"

And he has stopped being a quiet spy. He runs for the door; soon he is on the other side of the wall with Mummy and Grandma, and their voices are loud enough to not have to listen by the grate.

16

"ARE YOU ALL RIGHT?" MRS. MEDWAY ASKS WHEN I RUSH IN the next morning. I'd managed to avoid saying anything to Stella at breakfast, reeling with what she said the night before. The dream that followed. My father—*he knew*. He was there when I heard those words. Had something inside suppressed the memory that he was with me? I didn't want to know it. I didn't want to see the look in his eyes when he knew the truth.

Is Stella right about what happened?

"You're pale." Mrs. Medway puts a hand on my forehead.

"Really, I'm fine."

She looks at me closer. "Madison from the café was a friend of yours, wasn't she?"

I start guiltily. I'd barely thought of her since Stella's late-night visit. The dream that had woken me to stare at the walls, awake, for hours.

She misreads my reaction. "It's a small town. Word gets around. How about if we give you admin today? There is a stack of filing. But if you want to nap in the corner, that's okay, too."

So I find myself in a locked back office with rows of cabinets organized by year, with student names in alphabetical order and baskets of papers to file. She explains the system, and when I am surprised at paper records, not computer files, she touches a finger to the side of her nose and winks. "Paper files can't be hacked," she says.

She leaves, and I rifle through the stack of papers in the first basket:

absence certificates for flu, appointments. File notes. Test results. I start on the top, find the file for each, and shove them in, glad to have something mindless to do. But after a while I put the basket down.

The cabinets for current students take up the front row; what of those behind? I wander back. They are in year order and go back decades—since the school was renamed and reopened, about thirty years ago.

The years I would have been at this school—the cabinets are here. I glance at the door: closed, locked, quiet. Seven years ago: 2047–2048. I find the cabinet and pull the *A–H* drawer open to hunt for *Lucy Connor,* but come up empty.

Wait a minute. Astrid, my grandmother, is also a Connor; Connor is Stella's name. Would I have had Dad's last name back then, before they fell out? What was his name? I focus on Danny, then Daniel. I lean forward, close my eyes, rest my forehead against the cold metal cabinet, and will it to give up its secrets. I try to let my mind drift, but nothing comes. Frustrated, I start in the *A*'s, scanning through, and realize this will take forever.

I go back to my filing, and the morning finally ends. At lunch I avoid the staff room and wander the school grounds. They are en-closed all the way around, with fences too high for a ten-year-old to climb without a ladder. The only gates have keypads on them: locked, a code needed, and I'm sure the students don't know the code.

It's cold, but there is snow to play with, and the children are out in force: building snowmen, having snowball fights. I see one whizzing toward my head too late to duck. A teacher walks over, yells at the children to stop.

She comes up to me as I brush the snow out of my hair. "All right?" she asks.

"It's fine," I say, and lean against the gate.

"You're one of the new apprentices, aren't you?"

"Trialing to be one," I say.

"Do you like it so far?"

"Pretty much." I look at her closer. "You didn't know for sure why I was here until I said so. Could anyone wander about here in the grounds?"

She shakes her head. "There are cameras," she says, and points them out: by the gate, on the building, a few in trees. "Security will know exactly who you are even if I don't. And the gates are kept locked."

"Was that always the case?"

She shrugs. "Mrs. Medway is security-mad." She looks around; the nearest children are too far to hear, but she lowers her voice anyhow. "Ever since a girl went missing from school. It was about six or seven years ago."

"Oh. I think I may have heard of that; what was her name?" I say, trying to keep my voice light, casual, even as I'm desperate to know: *my* name.

"Louise or something? Yes, that's it. Louise Howard, I think." Then there is commotion at the other end of the school yard: a snowman kicked over to wails of protest. She rushes over to deal with it.

That afternoon I get back to the filing cabinets. *Louise* is maybe close to *Lucy*; could I have been Lucy Howard?

There is no Lucy Howard, or Louise Howard, for that matter. But she got the first name wrong; maybe the second one isn't quite right, either.

I dip farther into the *H*'s and, a few paper cuts later, find it: *Lucy*

Howarth. As soon as I see the name, whisper it out loud, I know it is right. My hands start to shake. I really *am* remembering things, more and more—little things maybe, but more than I ever thought I would be able to. Are they like blocks? Pull a bottom one out, and others must tumble down.

I extract the file. It's bulky. Was I a truant? Somehow I don't think so. Stella wouldn't have put up with it.

On the cover of the file is my registration information: parents Stella and Daniel Howarth—Danny the spy—and contact details. Inside are all the usual things like I'd been filing all morning. Reports by teachers, a few absence slips, but very few; I didn't get sick much. And an artist I was, even back then—winning contests at this school and across the county. If the AGT were looking for young artists, I wouldn't have been hard to find, with or without any help from my family. I hold on to that inside.

There is a separate folder in the back of my file: a missing report. Beginning with a note that I was reported absent from afternoon classes. Written notes follow, then typed ones—how my mother was contacted, then the authorities. Morning attendance was confirmed; I was missing in the afternoon. No one in the school grounds saw me leave; it was a mystery. The file ends abruptly. Lucy was gone. What happened to her? To *me*. They didn't know; the ending is blank.

I put the file back together, shove it into the cabinet where I found it, and go back to filing the endless bits of paper. Not focusing on what is in my hands beyond the letters of the alphabet to file them under, while the minutes tick past.

Where did I go?

Okay, so maybe the gates weren't locked back then, and perhaps there weren't security cameras, either, but it is hard to believe anyone could have snatched me, protesting, from the school, and nobody have seen anything. But what if it was someone I wanted to leave with?

Like Dad.

That night, I try. To explain to Stella why I can't believe Dad gave me to the AGT. I tell her how he infiltrated the AGT guards where I was held, how he snuck me out of my room at night. That we ran across the sand to a boat. Then I tripped, and they caught us. Nico; the gun raised in his hands. Dad on the sand telling me to close my eyes, to never forget who I am. How I couldn't look away. How his eyes held mine as he died.

How watching him die was the brick that finally achieved what Nico and the AGT doctor wanted: I couldn't deal with it, and my personality fractured. It hid what happened away, inside. That the split achieved their objective: When I was Slated, part of my memories survived, waited for the right trigger to come out again so I could fight AGT battles.

Stella cries. Great gulping sobs. She never knew how Dad died, or even that he was dead for sure. She only knew he disappeared and never came back.

She never knew that it was my fault.

But despite the tears, I can tell she still believes it was him who took me away from her in the first place.

I take careful steps like a spy across the school grounds, watching for the teacher on playground duty. I wait for her to be distracted. Some boys push and shove each other; it turns into a fight. Voices are raised and everyone strains to see, then at last the teacher notices and rushes over.

I swallow hard, pull up the gate handle, step through. It shuts with a too-loud clang *behind me. I'm out! I dash up the road, keeping an eye out, expecting any moment somebody will rush out and march me back to school. I can't get caught.*

My hand is still in my pocket clutching the note I'd found under my pillow. Daddy had been gone for days, ever since . . . And I shy away from thinking about that day, my birthday, and what Grandma said. Mummy and Daddy shouting late at night. The empty place he left behind when I woke up again.

But it's okay now, it must be. I pull the note out that I've read and reread ten million times since yesterday.

Dear Lucy, I'm on a very special secret mission, and I need your help! Go to the mountain's children at lunchtime tomorrow, and wait for further instructions. Tell no one.

Love, Daddy

See: signed Love, Daddy. *It was all some horrible mix-up, and he's going to tell me, and then everything will be all right.*

My feet half fly up all the quieter streets where eyes are less likely to spot my escape, then up the footpath and the hill, still going fast. I don't want to miss him. I don't want him to think I didn't come.

I burst through the gate to the field—no sign of him. Maybe he's hiding behind one of the stones? I rush to our beginning place and start around the stones, counting out loud as I go, expecting him to jump out and give me a fright at each one.

I'm at number fourteen when I hear a car the other way. There is parking by the gate at the other end of the field.

After a moment the gate opens, but it's not Daddy. A man, one I don't know, walks across the field toward me, and I ignore him and keep counting the stones, uneasy. Daddy, come out from where you are hiding. Do it now!

But the man doesn't come up to me. He stands in the center of the circle and watches me for a moment, then looks both ways.

"Are you Secret Agent Lucy?"

I stop in my tracks. Only Daddy calls me that. "Who are you?"

"I'm Special Agent Craig. I've got your further instructions from Agent Howarth."

Oh. I stare at him. Daddy is Agent Howarth! But he has never involved other agents in our games. He must be a real agent!

I salute him. "Proceed."

"Agent Howarth orders you to accompany Agent Craig—that's me"— and he winks—"in the spy-mobile. I will take you to Agent Howarth for a full briefing of your mission."

I hesitate as I walk across the field toward the parking area. Agent Craig walks slower, behind me, and I glance back. His careful eyes are watchful, on the stones, on the mountains. On me.

When we get to the car, I pause. "Where's Daddy?"

He opens the door. "Get in, Agent Lucy. You'll find out soon enough where we're going." He smiles, and my feet suddenly feel rooted to the ground, remembering Mrs. Medway at school saying to never go with people we don't know. But I know Daddy, and he is taking me to him. So it's okay, isn't it?

He nods, as if he can hear my thoughts. "It's fine, Lucy; we'll take you straight to your father. He wanted to come himself, but he's being watched. That's why he's been in hiding these last few days."

If he knows Daddy has been in hiding, then it must all be true. I slide into the car; he shuts the door. It clicks locked as he gets in. As we pull away, I look back at the stones through the window, trying to crush a flutter of panic inside that says I will never see them again.

17

THE DRAWINGS ARE LAID ABOUT BEFORE US IN HER OFFICE.
The art teacher smiles. "This is the hard part. Which do you think?"

I try to concentrate after a hard night of not enough sleep and too many painful memories. Sometimes I wish they'd stay buried. I feel jagged and exposed, as if I'm bleeding in front of everyone, and can't believe no one can see the wounds. Did Dad really do it? Set me up with that note? Did he really write it, or did I just think he did because of where it was, what it said?

"Riley?"

There are expectant young artists waiting. I pull myself back to the present.

"It's a tough call, but I'd put these ones ahead of the others," I say, and point out five of the pencil drawings.

The teacher picks her favorites, we compare, and she eventually settles on a top three. We go back out into the noisy classroom, and the year four students settle down. She holds up the ones chosen but is careful to praise all the others. There are happy faces, and disappointed ones. Was I like that? Did I care if I won?

She points out the winners from last year, still up on the side wall, and I realize they start a border that goes around the room. School winners, different grades.

Later, while the students are packing up and leaving to go to lunch, I follow the drawings along the walls.

I stop, frozen, at a landscape: the mountain's children. The gray stones of Castlerigg Stone Circle are drawn delicately, with hidden details to animate: They are dancing. The mountains above have faint faces etched in them, smiling down on their children below. At first glance the movement, the personification, is hidden. A closer look reveals it. And there, written at the bottom corner, a small *Lucy*.

Vaguely I'm aware of movement next to me, but it doesn't really register. I'm some other place, a pencil in my hand, hiding the faces in the shading and texture of the stone.

"It's amazing, isn't it?" a voice says near my ear. I don't answer. "Do you see?" And the art teacher points out the drawing's secrets.

Unable to stop myself, I ask, "What happened to this girl, this Lucy—did she go on to become an artist?"

"I don't know. She left," she says, and abruptly walks away.

Did she leave, or was she stolen? She climbed into that car of her own free will.

At the end of the day, I can't stop myself; I run up the paths that lead to Castlerigg. Now I understand how I felt the other day when I came here, the shadow of fear that colored my connection to this place.

Before anything else, this was our special place: Dad's and mine. I can see the magic in the dancing stones; the faint faces I'd drawn for the mountains are there in the distant lines and shade in the late afternoon sun. I start counting the stones as I did just days ago, but it is spoiled. When I get to fourteen, a cold shiver runs down my spine; I half expect to hear a car, to look up and see Dr. Craig walking toward me. For all his pretending that day, that is who he was: the AGT doctor who deliberately fractured my mind.

And it wasn't just a dream. The blocks inside are pulling out, one at a time; I remember that day. The note was real, but did Dad write it?

My head is fuzzy, but becoming clearer. Is it like Stella wondered days ago? As a child, I was left-handed. No matter that I was forced later to be right-handed, and Slated as such. These other memories were hidden and twisted tight, but are starting to unravel—and me with them.

I thought it was watching Nico kill my father that finally caused my personality to fracture, but maybe that was just the final nail. Maybe it all started with Dad, with that note; with knowing that once he found out I wasn't really his daughter, he didn't want me anymore.

Or was that just what Nico and Dr. Craig wanted me to think?

Whichever is true, one thing I am sure of now: Stella had nothing to do with them. Her exposed secret might have set things off, but she'd never have given me up. She'd never have done anything but cling to me, desperate and tight.

Light is failing, and I run back to town for the bus. It is pulling away when I get to the square, and I wave; the driver pulls in and I clamber on.

Finley is there, in the same seat he's been in before with Madison. Guilt grabs at me when I realize that I was so absorbed with my own stuff, I never noticed I haven't seen him on the bus the last few days. No matter how it feels to me now, what I'm going through is ancient history. Finley's pain is immediate.

I sit across from him in the aisle and try to catch his eye, but his are lowered. I think he doesn't even know I'm there, but then after a moment he glances over. "Hey, Extra-Shorty," he says.

"Hey," I say back. I want to ask how he is, is he all right, but that's stupid, isn't it? Of course he isn't. I try to say it with my eyes, instead. After a few beats, he nods, looks down again.

Does he know who Stella's mother is, that she must be responsible for Madison vanishing? What good would it do if he did? Maybe if Stella could see his pain, she'd do something about Madison. Maybe she'd get Astrid to bring her back.

Or maybe he'd kick up enough of a fuss for it to get back to Astrid, and then he'd disappear, too.

But I can't leave this, and when it comes to me I can't believe it took so long. MIA: We have to put Madison on Missing in Action. As unlikely as it seems, maybe she can be found.

I stare at him, nudge his foot with mine. "Finley? We need to talk." I breathe the words quietly. He looks up with a quick look of hope, one that fades fast when I give a small shake of my head. If *only* I knew where she was.

"Tomorrow—get the seven A.M. bus," he breathes back.

I nod.

That night, I get to work on a drawing of Madison. Why didn't I take a photo of her with my camera when I had the chance?

To get her on MIA I have to get in touch with Aiden. Or do I? He told me how to contact someone who knows him here: Leave a coded note on the community board, then wait until they get in touch.

That was for emergencies. Does this qualify?

Yes.

Getting Madison right turns out to be easy. It's the look of mischief in her eyes that marks her out: Is that what Astrid really objected to?

I'm nearly done when there is a faint knock on my door, and I slip the drawing under the bed. Stella looks in, hesitant, but I nod and she comes across the room.

"I'm sorry about last night," she says.

"Me too. But can we not talk about stuff tonight?" I say. "I just can't deal with it right now."

"Of course," she says, and relief crosses her face. "I've got an idea—let's have some fun."

"How?"

She smiles. Holds up a key. "Like this!" She goes across to the other locked wardrobe, turns the key. Looks back at me. "Come on."

I get up and walk across the room. She opens the doors; inside the wardrobe are shelves, and on them are brightly wrapped packages.

I look at her, not understanding.

"They're for you—your birthday presents."

"Really?"

"Yes. There is one for every year we weren't together; because I never gave up, Lucy. Not once. Every third of November, another joined them." She touches my cheek. "I always knew, somehow, you'd come back to me." She blinks hard. "Here—help me carry them." And she fills my arms with packages small and large, points me toward the bed, then brings the last few herself. We spread them out on the bed.

"Go on," she says.

"I can unwrap them?"

"Of course. They're for you, aren't they? Though some of them might not be much good to you now. Start at the beginning," she says, and hands me one with *11* all over the paper. "Where's your camera? I want birthday photos!"

I smile, shake my head. "How could you explain them if they were found?"

Her smile falters. "Of course. You're right; it's too risky."

"No, it's a good thought. Next year maybe? But my birthday isn't in November."

She goes very still. "What did you say?"

"My birthday is in September now! As Riley, on my fake ID, I turned eighteen on the seventeenth of September."

"Oh. Of course." She smiles, tension falling away. "Have you been using your camera?"

"Not really. Sorry. I'll take it tomorrow."

We start on the presents, and soon I'm covered in wrapping paper and presents for an eleven-, twelve-, thirteen-, fourteen-, fifteen-, and sixteen-year-old me: clothes, many too small now; art supplies. A gorgeous leather portfolio case.

"Last one?" she says, and holds out a parcel, the one for my seventeenth birthday.

I pull the paper off carefully. Inside is a gorgeous pale green sweater of a fine, soft yarn. "It's beautiful," I say.

"Really? Do you really like it?"

For an answer I get up and pull it on over my pj's, hug it close. "It's perfect."

She pulls my glasses off. "Perfect with your green eyes. I made it, knitting late at night."

"Thank you." I put the glasses back on. "But the match to my eyes has to stay secret."

"Of course." She gathers up the wrapping paper, stuffs it in a bag. "I'll burn it," she says, matter-of-factly.

"I'm sorry."

"What for?"

"All this being secret about me is hard for you, isn't it?"

"Anything to have you back." Something crosses her face, she starts to say something, but I interrupt.

"No talking about stuff tonight, remember?"

"Okay. Another night. Now get some sleep."

She helps me hide the presents away in the wardrobe; I keep out the drawing supplies, a few clothes that should fit. She heads for the door, then turns back. "I will say one thing, though. You were right; I shouldn't have interfered with your apprenticeship trials. I'll make sure they don't bias where they put you, all right?"

And with that, she is gone.

Well. I stare at the door she just disappeared through. Did she mean it? Time will tell.

I retrieve my nearly complete drawing of Madison, put the final touches on it, and tuck it into my coat pocket.

Restless, sleep feels far away despite the late hour. I unlock the other wardrobe and pull the albums out. Each one starts with a birthday, and I look at the birthday photos again: presents, cake, smiles. Except the first album, of course. Really, your first birthday should be the day you are born, shouldn't it? You should have a cake with a big 0 on it. Instead the first album starts with photos of me grinning and reaching for toys, crawling across the floor. Very embarrassingly having a bath.

I put them away, and with lights off and eyes closed, I hug the soft green wool close, still wearing it over my pajamas. After the agony of that dream of Dad and his note, and the memories that came from it, at least now I'm feeling warm, feeling wanted. Maybe Stella is enough. One parent who loves me, who would never give me up.

All those presents she searched out every year: They were all stuff I know I'd have loved; still love now. She wrapped them up with care and locked them in a wardrobe, all for a daughter she might never see again. It's so unbearably sad, even though I'm here now.

It's even harder to bear being the one so missed.

18

THE MORNING COMES EARLY. FINLEY IS ON THE SEVEN A.M. bus as planned. I nod to him, but sit down, silent, in the front.

When we get off I walk without comment to the back door of Cora's Café. Finley follows, catches up as I reach the door. I knock; it's locked this time, but soon opens.

Cora sees it is us and a quick look of hope crosses her face. "Get yourselves in," she says, and we step through the door. She checks the back lane before shutting and locking it behind us.

"Is there news?" She looks between us, then as Finley's eyes turn to me, she does also.

I shake my head. "I'm sorry; no news. But there may be something we can do. Have you ever heard of the group MIA: Missing in Action?" They shake their heads no. "This is very secret. There is a website run by MIA where missing people are posted; there is a network of people who try to find them, or what happened to them."

"What happened to Madison is unlikely to be good," Cora says.

Finley winces, shakes his head. "Better to know," he says. "How do we do it?"

"We need a photograph of Madison, a recent one. Failing that, I've drawn her." I pull out the drawing I did last night.

"That's good, but I've got photos," Cora says, pushes her chair back, and goes into an adjoining room.

Finley reaches out a hand, traces Madison's face on the paper with a finger. "I wish . . ." And he stops.

"What?"

He shakes his head. "I wish I told her how I really feel."

"I think she knew," I say, though not sure as I say it that she did. They'd just started out, hadn't they? Did she know what is so obvious now? He loved her. *Loves her,* I correct to myself.

Cora returns with some photos, and we pick one out to use. Seeing the longing in his eyes, she gives another to Finley. "Keep the drawing, too, if you want," I say, and he tucks it in his bag.

"What happens next?" Cora asks.

"I'll take care of it," I say.

Promises to tell no one follow, and as we leave, I wonder why I'm doing this. Not getting Madison on MIA, but letting them in on it. It's a risk, a huge risk, but the only way to give them hope.

This is what Aiden does, what he is about. *Join us,* he'd said. Looks like I have.

I'm still hopelessly early for school, and go for a walk by way of the community notice board Aiden described. It is just where he said it would be, tucked on a side street by a hall. No one is in sight, and I tack the note up: *Seeking chess partner, please contact Anita c/o hall.*

All I can do now is wait.

I take some photos on the way to school, of Keswick as the sun creeps up. The sun seems to go from hidden to clearing a mountain all at once, and first touches of light transform dark shadows to dazzling, clear morning.

Parents are depositing children at the school gates as I walk up, a teacher on the other side watchful as each goes into the grounds. A woman is coming from the other way with two boys and carrying a baby. One of the boys trips, falls, and starts to howl. She shifts the baby in her arms, tries to bend over to help him up.

"Can I help?" I smile, coax the boy up, and he and his brother go through the gate.

"Thank you," the mother says. "Are you new at the school?"

"I'm trialing to be an apprentice teacher."

"You might be this one's teacher one day, then." She smiles and looks at the baby, a soft look on her face. He? She? I can't tell; even wrapped up, it is tiny, wearing the smallest hat I've ever seen over a pink face, and sound asleep.

"You never know," I say. "Maybe."

A teacher walks over and coos over the baby. "How old is she now?"

"Almost four weeks," the mother answers.

I leave them to it, go through the gates. What I know about babies is precisely nothing. But she was *so* tiny. Four weeks old? I frown. In that first album of me, I'm fat-faced and crawling, playing with toys. How old am I when that album starts? Maybe Stella has another album tucked away someplace. She's so photo-mad, it's hard to believe she didn't bother taking any when I was really little. That must be it.

Something niggles inside that day, like a sore tooth that you should leave alone but worry at with your tongue, pushing and prodding until it is loose. I'm out of art and in a year two class today, through all their lessons, and my mind wanders so much that their teacher has to repeat instructions to me more than she does to her students. She must think I'm an idiot.

They have reading after lunch, and there is a birthday girl in their midst, seven today, who gets to pick the next story. The teacher starts reading her choice—an old and tattered book from a bottom shelf, about princesses who rescue animals—and I fade away again, looking at the birthday balloons she has tied to her chair float over her head.

As Riley my birthday has changed to September 17. Funny how Stella is about birthdays; they are such a huge big deal to her. She'd actually seemed rattled when I mentioned my birthday wasn't in November anymore.

That night at dinner, thoughts are spinning through my head. I feel disconnected to what is happening around me. When will I hear from Aiden's contact? It could be anyone, even someone at this table. I grin to think so; Astrid wouldn't like that. Anyhow, I'm sure she keeps a close eye on this place. I glance about at the other girls chattering, Stella at the head of the table. She looks different somehow. She gives me a quizzical look, as if she senses something is on my mind, but I don't even know what is wrong, so how could she? *Mother's intuition,* a voice whispers inside, and I shake it off. What nonsense.

Steph, Stella's helper, has finished carrying serving dishes out and sits with the rest of us. I notice she is as quiet as I am; she eats dinner, looking around at the others much as I do.

I can't shake a deep sense of unease, but can't work out what it is attached to. But somehow, underlying everything else, there is something about that tiny baby today, about the photo albums. The missing early photos. Everything else is in there. Maybe those are ones Stella keeps for herself.

I notice now what niggled earlier about Stella. Her hair is darker; not a huge amount, but the dark roots are gone, blended in, and the overall color is a shade darker. She's been to the hairdresser. I frown to myself; it's like she said when she first saw my blond hair had changed to dark. Bet she goes a shade darker each time until we match.

Why is she so obsessed with matching? Is it just part of her being clingy?

Something does a flip in my stomach. *Wait; think.* There is too much weirdness mixed up together. Stella matched her hair to mine years ago, as if to say we belong together; now she is trying to do it again. Then there is how weird she was about my changed birthday. And that there are no early baby photos.

Dinner is like dust; I put down my fork.

"Are you all right, Riley?" Ellie says, and I can feel other eyes turning toward me, but I don't answer.

Birthdays. Dr. Lysander told me cell testing said I was under sixteen when I was Slated, but if my birthday is in November, I'd have been over sixteen. She said I was a Jane Doe, not identified from DNA. Her eyes had been wrong when she said it; not that she was lying, she just couldn't believe it. That no one knew who I really was. She said . . . *no.* She said I might have been a baby born in an out-of-the-way place?

"Riley?" I hear a voice say again, but it is distant and removed.

What did Astrid say that day? Precisely and exactly. I close my eyes, going back, and I'm spinning, I'm someplace else. A dark corridor, crouching down. Full of a game that is going wrong, trying to hear her exact words . . .

Isn't it about time you tell him the truth? That his precious daughter isn't his; that you don't even know whose she is.

Everything goes black.

19

GRADUALLY NOTHINGNESS IS REPLACED BY COLD FLOOR, voices.

"Lu—Riley." Stella's voice.

I open my eyes and she is holding me, cradling my head.

I stare back at her. "Who am I?"

"She must have hit her head," Stella says, her eyes communicating alarm.

Then Steph is there. She holds my glasses in her hands. "One of the lenses has come out," she says.

I close my eyes. Steph must have seen; she must know my eyes are really green. That the glasses mask who I am.

Who am I? *You don't even know whose she is.*

Stella helps me up. "To bed with you now," she says. And we start across the room.

"Wait," Steph says. "I fixed them. The lens just popped back in." She holds out my glasses and I reach for them, put them back on. Steph looks between Stella and me, a thoughtful look on her face.

Ellie scampers ahead and holds doors open. I want to shake Stella off and walk on my own, but my head is still fuzzy, and it does hurt.

Stella helps me to my bed; Ellie hovers next to us.

"That's fine, Ellie. You can go now," Stella says. Ellie looks uncertainly between us, leaves, shuts the door. It clicks.

Stella looks at me with something like fear in her eyes.

"You're not my mother." I say it like a statement, not a question.

She breaks her gaze, looks away. "What nonsense."

"Listen to me. I was cell tested by Lorders when I was Slated; I was under sixteen, and it was after my so-called sixteenth birthday that November."

"But tests can be wrong—"

"You nearly flipped the other day when I said my birthday wasn't in November. There are no early baby photos of me. And that day, my tenth birthday, when I heard you and Astrid—"

"You remember *that*?" she says, her eyes open wide.

"—Astrid said you don't even know *whose* I am. I thought that just meant Dad wasn't my father, but that's only half of it, isn't it? You're not my mother, either. Admit it!"

Color has drained from her face. She looks back into my eyes with desperation. "I am in every way that counts. I've always loved you, Lucy."

"No! Not in one way that counts. Tell me the truth. Tell me now!"

"You should rest. You might have a concussion."

"I do not. Tell me where I come from! I have the right to know."

Stella is shaking, her face crumbling. "I am your mother. I *am*." She's choking back tears, and something else: the truth. Part of me wants to comfort her, to put a hand on hers, but no. She has to face this. Is it something so buried she can't even say it?

"We can have nothing between us if we don't have the truth," I say, and turn away from her, to the wall.

Time passes. Minutes, more? A hand touches my shoulder, then pulls away.

"All right," she says, voice dull. "I'll tell you. It's a sad tale."

I turn, sit up. "I'm listening."

She doesn't say anything at first, gathering herself, then nods. "Okay. Your dad and I wanted children. Desperately. But every time I got pregnant, I lost the baby. Sometimes a few months in, sometimes longer. I don't know why; doctors didn't know why. Then one last time it happened: I was pregnant again. But this time, I didn't tell anyone, even your dad. He went away for a while; we weren't getting along." She stops, bites her lip.

"And?"

"I was staying with my mother." The way she says the words, there is more to that, but I don't interrupt. "My baby was born early—my darling, beautiful daughter. I had Lucy to adore for days, just a few days. And then, she died." Stella's voice is choked, and I don't know what to say.

She turns to me, takes my hand. "Then Mother, months later, brought you to me. You were perfect. And you were mine. I always loved you, Lucy; that is what makes you my daughter. Don't you see?"

"Wait a minute. Are you saying Astrid just came up with a baby to replace yours that died? Where from?"

"I honestly don't know. I guessed from an orphanage; as JCO, she is in charge of those also. But I didn't ask. I didn't want her to take you away from me."

"And this was months later that you got me? Didn't anybody notice you had a baby, then didn't, then did again? What about Dad?"

"I told you. I was . . . away. At Mother's. Your dad and I didn't see each other for a long time. Then when he finally came back, he saw you and assumed you were ours; we got back together. I didn't tell him the truth about you."

I shake my head at her. "How could you lie to him like that?"

"I had to. Mother threatened to take you away if I ever told. But then, years later, she held it over me, and then one day you and Danny heard us talking about it—"

"News out."

"Yes. He couldn't handle it; he took off. It was a few days later when you went missing. Mother found out the AGT had you, that he'd given you to them. I know you don't want to believe it. Mother tried again and again to get you back, but couldn't find exactly where you were being held."

"You say you always loved me as your daughter. Why would it be any different for Dad? Okay, he had a shock to get over, but I was still *me*. Still the daughter he'd always known." I shake my head.

"Maybe you are right. Maybe he didn't have anything to do with what happened to you." She says the words like they are difficult to say out loud, and the struggle is there on her face. For her to accept he was blameless would be hard after all the blaming she has done over the years. Then to accept how he died. "Does it matter now?"

"It does to me." But then I'm shaking my head, and my eyes are welling up.

"It's too much to take in all at once. I'm sorry you didn't know. I—"

"It's not just that. I think I remember what happened that day. The day I disappeared."

She stays very still, quiet.

"There was this note from Dad under my pillow to meet him at Castlerigg. I went there at lunchtime, but he wasn't there. Somebody else was, from the AGT. He said Dad sent him to get me. But when we got where they took me, Dad wasn't there. I didn't see him for two years, when he tried to rescue me."

Her face goes hard, angry.

"No, wait," I say. "It doesn't mean he wrote the note. Maybe they faked it."

"But how would they get a note under your pillow, or know where to say to meet him, if he didn't tell them?"

I shrug. "I don't know. I don't want to believe it; I can't believe it."

Stella struggles to pull away from her anger. "Listen to me. Whatever happened, he still tried to save you, didn't he?"

"So he died."

"He died *trying* to be a hero." Behind her words is an unsaid echo, one she can't forgive him for. Even if he wasn't involved in my disappearance in the first place. He failed.

We talk a bit longer, but I feign sleepiness, and she leaves. I stare at the wall in the dark.

So I'm back to this, as if I've been Slated all over again. To not knowing who I am. No parents, no place I come from. There is not even a name that is really mine. *Lucy Howarth* or *Lucy Connor*: Either way, it is the name of a dead baby.

I'm numb.

Nothing.

20

"TAKE A SEAT," MRS. MEDWAY SAYS, AND I SIT OPPOSITE HER desk. She closes the door.

"Riley, have you enjoyed your week at our school?"

"Yes, thank you," I say, trying to be in the here and now for her, even though I failed at it most of the day.

She sighs. "I don't quite know what to make of you, my dear. Our art department is screaming for you to be one of our next apprentices; you've made quite an impression there. That is fantastic, but the other days haven't been quite as positive. The thing is, if we take you as an apprentice, you have to spend a year working in every year and class in the school."

"I'm sorry. I haven't been myself these last few days." How could I be, when I don't know who that is?

"I understand you must be upset about your friend Madison. Is there something else?"

I'm startled she mentions Madison again; it isn't the done thing—admitting to feelings about someone taken by Lorders. And her face is full of genuine interest, concern. There is nothing that threatens here. But how honest can I be?

I hesitate. "Confidentially?"

"Of course."

144

"I found out recently that I'm adopted. It's been a shock." I've never said anything more true.

"Oh, I see."

"I was wondering if there are any teaching jobs at orphanages?"

"There used to be." She half frowns, shakes her head. "The nearest is the Cumbrian Care Facility; we used to supply teachers there on rotation. But a few years ago, they hired their own. Shut us out completely. I could ask." She hesitates. "I'm not sure what is going on there. It might not be a good place for you."

"Why?"

"It's isolated, stuck out in a valley with nothing near it but a few farms miles away, and people who work there never come to town." She frowns. "Let's just leave it at that, shall we? Now, what shall we do with you?" She opens a netbook, stares at the screen for a moment, then touches it and looks up again. "Right. I've recommended you for an apprenticeship here. If you decide to select us as your top choice, that should clinch it. But don't decide until you've had the rest of your trials."

I stare back at her, eyes wide with surprise. "Thank you."

"Riley, I'm taking a gamble on you here. I take our responsibility to every child in our care, every child we teach, very, very seriously. There are no off days allowed, however good the reason, when every child counts."

"I understand."

"Now, go. Whatever you decide, I wish you all the best."

"Thank you," I say again, my throat feeling choked. She doesn't even know who or what I am, but she is willing to give me a chance. I hesitate at the door.

She looks up. "Is there anything else?"

I long to tell her that I'm her missing student, Lucy, the one she couldn't account for all those years ago. Does it still haunt her? But I'm not really her, anyhow.

"No, that's it. Thanks again." And I bolt out the door.

I stop by the Moot Hall, where Madison and I met with Finley and went on the walk up Catbells. I'd noticed they had maps up in glass cases on the side of the building, and study them closely.

"There are more maps inside," a voice says. I jump. Finley is standing in the doorway.

"What are you doing here?"

"Apparently, my mind isn't on my job enough to do anything fun, so I'm on duty here." He pauses, glances about. "Any news?"

I shake my head. "I've got word out, but I'm waiting for contact still to get her put on MIA. It should be soon. But don't get your hopes up," I say, gently.

"So, what are you doing—planning a weekend walk?"

"Maybe."

"Can I come?"

"Maybe. Don't ask why, but I want to go past the Cumbrian Care Facility. Do you know where it is?"

"No, but I can find out." He gets me to follow him inside, hunts through indices, and finds the right map. "I haven't been this way before; it isn't on a main walking route. But it'll be good to get out and away from everything and everybody, and up high."

"I know. For me, too. Can we keep where we are going between us?"

He looks at me curiously. "Of course."

We work out the way: We'll have to drive out of Keswick to a point where we can pick up a trail, but Finley says he can borrow a car. He reckons from there it'll take about three hours each way. We arrange to meet in the morning.

As I head back to the house, I wonder: What am I doing? Really. What possible good could it do to go look at an orphanage I may or may not have come from, something like seventeen years ago? Stella only *guessed* I came from an orphanage, and even if I did, there is no guarantee it's that one.

I shrug. I don't know. Something inside wants to go there, to see it.

That night, Stella knocks on my door, peeks in. "May I?" she asks, hesitant. I nod.

"I've brought something to show you."

In her hands is a small album. It doesn't match the others in the wardrobe. She opens it, and inside are page after page of a small baby, much tinier than that four-week-old one I saw yesterday. With loads of dark hair, eyes that don't quite open. Even in the photos she seems very still.

"This is Lucy."

"Why did you give me the same name?"

She shrugs, uncomfortable. "I'm not sure. Maybe I shouldn't have." She sighs. "I'll always regret that she died, but I still loved you—and I still do—for who you are. That doesn't change because of any of this."

"But the name Lucy must always remind you what you lost." I stare back at her, and some inkling of understanding creeps in. She was so afraid of losing me, like she lost the baby in these photos. All the other babies, too. Then, years later, when I disappeared, all her fears came true. I feel like I'm starting to understand her, just a little.

Doesn't mean I always like her.

21

"THERE IS SOMETHING ABOUT BEING UP HERE, THAT NO matter how much life sucks, I feel better." I'm looking through my camera at the lonely fells sweeping around us, valleys below. The climb ahead.

Finley is silent, and I lower the camera. "Sorry," I say, looking at him sideways.

"It's okay. I haven't got the worldwide monopoly on misery; you can have some of it, too. So why is your life sucking?"

I shrug. "Mostly I can't say." I hesitate. "But there is something I can. Between us. Somebody I care for got hauled off by Lorders not long ago, too."

"Somebody?"

"Okay. A guy." *Ben.*

"And you loved him."

"Correction: I love him. Past tense not allowed."

"Deal on that one."

We continue on, mostly silent after that, stopping to check the map a few times when paths branch off, steadily climbing all the way. We reach a ridge high on a desolate path, wind bitingly cold sweeping across it. No snow up here: blown away? The sky is almost clear, but it seems thin, as if even the oxygen has been stolen by the howling wind. We're walking fast to stay warm.

"Nice day you picked," Finley says, but I can tell he doesn't care, any more than I do, about being battered by the weather. But when we dip down again it is still a relief to get out of the wind.

"Nearly there now; the orphanage is in that valley." He points it out; we have a traverse down this hill. "Are you going to tell me why we're going there?"

I look at him sideways. Sigh. "To be honest? I'm not really sure. But it's a long story."

"We've got time."

I shake my head. "How about you tell me a story instead?"

"What about?"

"I don't know. Where do you live?"

"Keswick Boys: land of noise and beautiful toys."

"What?"

"We have a reputation for boat races. And a few other things. It's not far from your place. A quick row across and then a walk, or about an hour's stroll along the lake's edge on foot, up the hill." He shows me on his map.

"I hear it is more chilled out than our house."

He laughs. "Very much so. We come and go at all hours. I couldn't believe what Madison said about your place." His smile fades. "Tell me. Was it because of getting out of that lunch to see me?"

He doesn't say what he means, but I know.

"It's not your fault. Whatever happened to Madison, you didn't do it. Lorders did. And their reasons are their own."

I can tell by the grim set of his face that he's not convinced.

"I know what it's like," I say.

"What?"

"To think what happened to somebody is your fault. It eats you up inside. She wouldn't want that, Finley."

"Neither would your boy. But you can't stop how you feel."

"No."

We've been steadily descending into the valley as we talk, still high enough to see all around, and then, there it is. A cluster of buildings, set in a clearing in some woods below us, along a creek that meanders; a distant fence that wanders around it encloses large grounds. A scenic place, but somehow odd, and cold, and it isn't just winter that makes it so. It looks lonely and devoid of life.

"Look there," Finley says. "Along the fence line." I focus where he points, and dots are moving along the fence, inside the boundary: people? But they are evenly spaced, moving at the same rate. Odd.

I get the camera out again and zoom in. A long line of children is walking along a path on the inside of the fence. I sweep along; where visible, it looks like the path runs all of the perimeter of the grounds.

"What can you see?" Finley asks.

"Children. They're out for a walk, I guess." I frown. "It's weird, though."

"How?"

"They're just walking. Single file. Not talking or laughing or anything."

"Shall we go down for a closer look?" Finley asks, and I hesitate. Something feels wrong, so wrong, but I don't know what, and there is a sense of foreboding inside. One that says we shouldn't be here. At least Finley shouldn't be here.

I pull us back along some trees. Take off my pack. "Can you wait here? I'm going down for a careful look. I don't want us to be seen."

"I don't know. I should come with you."

"Honestly, there is nothing to worry about," I lie. "I'm really good at staying hidden, and it'll be easier without the pack. I'll just creep down, have a quick look, and come straight back up. Just stay out of sight here. All right? I'll be fine. I promise."

"You're just going to have a look and come back."

"Yes."

"All right," he says, and looks at his watch. "I'll give you an hour. If you're not back by then, I'm going down to look for you. Deal?"

"Deal."

I take off my outer coat; it's light blue and might stand out. My wool layer underneath is gray and should blend into shadows.

At first I stick to the path; it is cut into the hill, so with me bent down I shouldn't be visible from below. Then as I get closer to the woods, I cut off the path into the scrub, hugging rocks, then trees, heading for the fence where we saw the children, estimating where I should intersect them with the passage of time. Moving careful, quiet, slow. These skills, so useful now—of moving without noise, using the cover such as it is to best advantage—are things I learned from Nico and the AGT years ago. I stop behind some rocks, the fence a bit less than fifty meters away, and wait.

Before long the first of them round the corner and come into view. As it appeared from above, they are just walking. Smiling. Single file, no talking, nothing. I scan the grounds: no adults in sight.

I should go back now, but creep forward, bringing the layout I saw from above into my mind. If the children stick to this path along the fence line, there will soon be trees, and the way the ground slopes, I should be out of sight of the buildings.

I scurry quickly along the ground, cutting down closer to the fence. It's not high; I can easily see over it. But there are telltale signs—a faint glint of wire along it. Is it electric, or is it an intruder alert? Either way, I'm staying on this side of it. I duck down and wait.

Footsteps are coming this way. I hesitate; this is insane.

I stand up just as the children approach. The first is a boy of about eleven or twelve. Walking, smiling. He sees me; he must see me, but keeps walking. Children follow behind him, a few meters apart, pass me one by one, no reaction. As they go, they are getting younger.

A girl of perhaps seven is approaching now. "Hello," I say.

She smiles. "Hello," she says, but keeps walking.

Some younger ones, about four or five years old, bring up the rear.

"Stop," I say. The last three children look at me, and stop. Saying nothing.

"What are you doing?" I look at the one in front.

"Standing," he answers.

"No, before I said stop. What were you doing?"

He looks puzzled. Smiles. "It's Saturday. We're doing our Saturday morning walk." The three of them smile, make no move to continue. It's like they do what I say when I say it, smiling all the while. Just like the others, all walking at the same pace, smiling. It's almost as if—

No. No, it can't be. It can't.

I start to shake, horror swirling inside.

"Hold out your hands," I say, unable to stop the tremor in my voice. In unison, all three of them hold out their hands. "Pull your sleeves up," I say, and they do.

And there, glinting on their wrists: Levos. I have just enough presence of mind to take some hasty photographs, hands shaking so that I have to balance the camera against the fence to make them clear, forgetting it might be electric until I realize it mustn't be, because I'm still standing here. This can't be; it's completely illegal. Slating is a punishment for *teenage* criminals under sixteen. *Not* little children. What could they possibly have done to deserve *this*?

And as I focus through the camera at them, I see. The last boy: that crooked grin. No. It can't be. The day I came to Keswick on the train. That mother and son. It's the same boy. It is.

I lower the camera, look at him. "Where is your mother?" He smiles back, says nothing, and I repeat the question.

"I don't know what that is," he says, and his smile is the same as on the train, but his look is blank. The giggles and mischief are gone; whatever it was that made him who he was . . . gone.

Clang.

A faint noise, through the trees in the distance. A door? Fear runs through me. Did resting my camera against the fence set off an alert inside? Stupid.

"Put your hands down again," I say. "Walk! Catch up to the others!"

They take off, more running than walking now to try to catch up as instructed. I duck back down behind the fence.

My stomach heaves; I want to be sick. Children, young children, Slated? No. It breaks every law. Four-year-olds like that boy from the train can't be *criminals,* no matter what his mother may have done.

Another distant sound intrudes. Is someone coming to investigate?

Get out of here. I slip back the way I came using as much care as I can to stay down, out of sight. Once there is some distance between me and the fence, I stop behind some rocks. Peer back. The children have reached the house now; taller figures are there. I snap a hasty photograph, looking through the zoom. Half a dozen adults, and I don't need to see their black clothes to know what they are; there is something about the way they move, how they stand, that leaves me in no doubt. Lorders.

A few of them are speaking to the children, and others are scanning the hill, binoculars in hand. I pray Finley has kept out of sight where I left him.

There is no chance I'll get back to the path above without being seen if they're watching properly.

The only thing for it is speed, and misdirection. I race back up, taking a roundabout way to make it look as if I'm heading the other way, not looking back. Then shrink down again and out of sight, creeping along behind undergrowth, rocks, until finally I hit the path. I duck down and race along to where I left Finley behind the trees.

"What's going on?"

I'm breathing hard. "We need to get out of here as fast as we can. Better if we're out of sight and off the path."

He peers through the trees. "There are figures heading toward the gate below." My stomach twists. He holds out my jacket, but I stuff it into my pack instead of putting it on. "Who are they?"

"Run now, talk later."

He gets the fear. "Okay. One sec," he says, and consults his map. "Can you rock climb?"

"Yes."

We take off at full speed back up the path, but then, once we're over the peak and out of sight, go off the path to race across rock and dirt on steep, windy, faint trails made for sheep, not people. But Finley is much like me: He moves like a mountain goat. I can see where we're heading: a steep scramble over a peak. If we make it there and over before anyone reaches the place we left the path, they'll never see where we went.

Unless they've got dogs. I stuff the thought down. Unless they've got them there already, they won't have time to get them until we're gone.

We reach the climb, and straightaway I can see a few places where just because of my height I'll have problems. "I'll need to traverse to get over," I say, and start up the rocks. Some echo inside tells me to always maintain three points of contact when climbing, but I'm going too fast to do that. One foot slips.

Finley, just behind, grabs and steadies me. "No point in being quick if you're dead," he says, and I glance down and see with the traverse there is a steep drop below us now. That was too close.

I slow down, listen to him this time about the best way to go, and at last we clear the top. A quick glance back shows heads just coming up the path in the distance, and we duck down. "I'm pretty sure they didn't see which way we went," I say, not sure if that is true, but we're in trouble if it isn't.

"We're on a part of the trail now I'd wanted to come back on anyhow. But not by climbing over the top without ropes." He laughs.

"You're insane."

"You're crazier than me."

The wind is howling again now that we're on the other side of the fell, and I put my blue coat back on. "Turn your coat inside out?" I suggest. "So we look different."

Finley stares back, then takes his coat off, reverses it, swapping blue for gray. He takes another hat out of his bag and swaps his blue one for a red one. "All disguised?"

"Yep. Now let's get out of here. Fast."

We don't run on the ridge—that would be suicidal—but keep the pace as fast as is reasonably safe. The temperature has dropped, and clouds are pulling in.

Another path joins this one. "That's where we would have joined to here if we'd done it the sane way," Finley says. We continue on, dropping down now and out of the wind. I'm breathing easier, and—

"What was that?" Finley says.

"I didn't hear anything." Then I do. Faint, behind us. "Could they have gone the long way and caught up?"

"No way. It's miles longer, and we were going fast."

"Are you sure?"

"No."

We carry on, faster again; there are some rocks ahead, and we duck down behind them, out of sight and out of the wind. "I'll take a look," I say, and get my camera out. I zoom it back down the path, and *there*. One figure; a walker, and he looks familiar. "It's that guy; he was at the Moot Hall the other day."

"What guy?"

I hand him the camera, and he looks through. "It's Len," he says. "The fell checker."

"Should we take off?"

"Len's all right, and anyhow, there's no point. Soon the way the path opens up, he'll see us no matter what. I vote we stay put and have some lunch." Finley opens his pack, takes out sandwiches and a flask. "Tea?"

"Yes, please! You think of everything."

"I try, but with you it's hard keeping up." He finds cups, pours tea for both of us, and I hug the heat of it in my cold hands.

"So. Are you going to tell me what is really going on?" Finley asks.

"Sometimes it is better not to know," I say, and he stares back, nods after a while.

He opens the sandwiches. "Cheese okay?"

We're well into them when Len rounds the path. "Hello there, young Finley," he says.

Finley nods. "Hello there, old Len."

"Cheeky brat. Good place for a picnic on a cold day; okay if I join you?" Len says, and sits on a rock just above, where he can see the path on both sides.

Finley introduces us, and Len finds biscuits in his pack to share. Part of me doesn't want to move, from the shock of the orphanage, the cold, the protesting muscles from the hasty run and climb. Part of me is screaming in fear at the delay and wants to *run*.

Finley is asking Len about weather conditions and the path ahead, but as Len answers, some part of me is wondering if his eyes are on me too curiously.

Len has stayed sitting on the rock above us despite the wind, now and then looking back down the path. "We'll have company soon," he says, and there is something about how he says it that raises my alarm. He looks back at us. "Shall we get our stories straight?"

Finley and I exchange a glance. The flight impulse is in my feet: I want to race down the path the other way.

"No point in running, you'd be seen," Len says. "Besides, we're just three walkers who had a nice time on yonder ridge today together, didn't we, before stopping for lunch; we've got nothing to hide."

I can hear the approaching footsteps now; they're moving fast. If they've come up from the orphanage, they've moved much quicker than I'd have thought they could. Then two faces appear; they must have split up where the paths diverge.

Len nods. "Hello," he says.

The Lorder smiles; it's unnatural. "Hey there. Good walking today?"

"The wind cuts through you," Len answers. "Just the way I like it."

"Where've you been?" the Lorder asks, and Len gives the cover story while Finley and I eat biscuits with concentration.

The Lorder nods, thoughtful. "I see. Have you seen two other walkers, one a girl? We think they may be lost."

"There were two girls a while ago. They took the last branch, I think, back the way you came."

They move off, talk a moment. Speak into a com, take one last look at us, then go back down the path.

"Well then," Len says. "Let's get the hell out of here before they realize they've been had."

We stuff things away hastily and set off in the other direction. Len sets a hard pace, and every time the path branches we go a different way, winding and twisting around in convolutions we'd never have worked out without him, until we're heading back down again on the other side.

Len gets Finley to lead, slows down in front of me so we drop back. "I think we need to talk," Len says, voice low. And *yes* he has helped us today, but what can I tell him?

"Thanks for your help. But—"

"I understand you're looking for a chess partner. Anita, is it?"

I almost stop dead in my tracks. Len? He is Aiden's MIA contact?

He winks. "You've been a hard girl to track down."

"Were you following us today?"

"That was a bit of luck. Finley borrowed my car; I got out of him that you were going with him. The car keys have a tracker. So, what's up?"

First, a promise. I fish through my pockets for the photo of Madison I've been carrying around ever since I put that note up. "Can you put Madison on MIA?"

He hesitates. "I can. But there's little point," he says, his blunt words softened by the sadness in his eyes.

"Do you know where she's gone?"

"Don't know; guess. There's a women's working prison, out Honister way. At the slate mine. She's probably there, where most taken around here end up."

I breathe a sigh of relief. "Prison: Then she's alive."

"Sometimes that isn't best; no one ever leaves that place. But quick before we run out of time. What were you up to today that had Lorders so interested?"

But before I have to decide what I should or shouldn't say, hellos are called out as another group of walkers catch up to us. They stay with us all the way to where our cars are parked.

"Need a lift, old man?" Finley asks.

"Cheeky brat," Len says. "As a matter of fact, I do. And seeing as it is my car, I'll drive, thank you very much."

Finley reluctantly hands over the keys.

"How'd you get here?" I ask.

"Over hill, over dale." Len grins.

My jaw drops. How many miles was that? He looks ancient and was walking rings around us.

As we pull onto the road, Len glances at me in the mirror. "You're one of Parks' new potential apprentices, aren't you? I take the group on a walk the first day, so I'll see you Monday. We'll talk then."

A slight emphasis on *then*. He doesn't want Finley to know anything.

Finley is whistling as Len pulls onto the road, heads for Keswick. "You're awfully cheerful," I say.

He looks at me sideways. "We just stuck it to them, didn't we? Know you're not going to tell me why they were after you, but I don't care why. Anytime a Lorder doesn't get what they want, I *am* happy."

I know what he means, but I'm not feeling it. Have we really gotten away with anything? All through the drive back to Keswick I keep scanning the road ahead, half expecting a roadblock.

And my camera is burning a hole in my pocket. Aiden *has* to have these photos. The proof is there: Lorders are breaking the law, they are Slating little children. No one could ignore this. Is it the one thing that'll finally make everyone stop, stand together, say *no more* to the Lorders?

There is panic inside that I have the only copies, here, in my camera. If the Lorders ask those boys the right questions, they'll know their Levos were photographed. They'll be desperate to find me. And if they work out who I am . . . I'm dead.

This is way past self-preservation. I have to stay alive. I have to get these photos to Aiden.

We have to get the word out, and make it stop.

22

"**CAN WE TALK?**"

Stella smiles to see me, looks so absurdly happy that I'm seeking her out, that a sinking feeling stirs deep in my chest. "Of course, come in," she says, and I walk into her office and turn the lock behind me. She raises an eyebrow. "This looks serious. Is everything all right?"

"No. Not really."

"What is it?"

And I don't know what to say. The less I tell her, the better for her, really. But despite all the need for caution, I just can't do it to her; I can't disappear with no word. Not again.

Stella gets up from behind her desk, goes to the sofa against the wall. I sit next to her.

"Go on. You can tell me anything."

"You don't want to hear this. I'm sorry, but I have to leave."

She shakes her head. "Leave? You've barely got here. Why?"

"I'm pretty sure my cover is blown; or, if it isn't, it will be soon. They'll come for me if I stay."

"Oh, Lucy. No. I'll come with you. I'll—"

"No. Really, you can't; it's too much of a risk. I'll be safer getting away on my own."

A range of emotions crosses her face, and I brace myself for the storm, but before it gets going, it disappears. She sags back on the sofa.

"When?" she whispers.

"I don't know. Soon. As soon as I can arrange something. It won't be forever, I promise; I'll get in touch. Someday I'll come back and see you, when things are different."

"Oh, Lucy. No. It's not fair."

"Life's like that," I say, sharper than I mean to. But really, when has life been fair to me? Even when I finally thought I was returning to a family that was *mine,* I found out it was all lies.

"This isn't because of me, is it?"

"Of course not."

"Tell me everything. Maybe I can help."

I shake my head. "I'm sorry; it's safer if you don't know."

"You don't trust me," she says, her voice bitter.

"It's not that! But why should I? You've lied to me my whole life," I say, the words spilling out of me before I can call them back.

She recoils. "You've worked it out, haven't you."

"What?"

"That I haven't told you everything."

"What else haven't you told me?" I demand, even as some part of me realizes this isn't supposed to be going like this; I'm supposed to be trying to mend things a little before I go, but I can't stop myself from asking. What more could there possibly be?

"It wasn't my fault!"

"What wasn't your fault?"

"She made me do it, don't you see?"

"Who—your mother? What did she make you do?"

"She was blackmailing me, all these years, into keeping quiet. I was a prisoner back then! She had me under lock and key the whole time I was pregnant, to stop me from talking; she kept Danny away, made him think that was what I wanted. Maybe my baby would have lived if I'd been at home. But then when she brought you . . . she knew she had me. Right where she wanted me. I couldn't say anything, could I? Or you'd be gone. So she finally let me go."

"What are you talking about?"

"No. That's enough. If you want to know any more, you have to tell me your secrets, too."

"I just did. I came here to tell you I was going to have to leave. I shouldn't have told you, it was dangerous to tell you, but I did it." I stand up.

"Wait. Don't leave like this. Please. I'll tell you. But you have to *promise* to never tell anyone."

I pause. I'm seething—again. Something about Stella and I just . . . I don't know. She makes me crazy. *But she'll be so sad when I'm gone.*

I take a deep breath, and sit. "Okay. Tell me."

"I found out some things, put them together. Stuff my mother did years before against the government."

"Against the Lorders?" My head is reeling. No way; she is Lorder through and through.

"No, not exactly. There are factions, you see. In the government. Mother is on the hard-line side; the last prime minister wasn't. He had to go."

"Wait a minute. Are you talking about Armstrong?"

"Yes. He and his wife, Linea." She sighs. "They were so lovely, and—"

"You knew them?"

"Linea and Mother were friends at school years ago. Linea confided in her that her husband was planning to expose some of the nastier side of the Lorders and resign. He never got a chance."

My head is reeling. "No way. Mum's parents?"

She frowns. "Mum? What do you mean?"

"After I was Slated, that was the family I was assigned to. Sandra Armstrong-Davis."

Now it is Stella's turn to look shocked. "You were with Sandy? I didn't know."

"You knew her?"

"Of course. We used to go on vacations together, years ago when we were children. We haven't kept in touch. I couldn't. Not after I knew what really happened to her parents."

"But they were assassinated by AGT."

"Yes. But the AGT were told where they'd be. The information was leaked: It was a setup."

"Your *mother* was behind that? Oh my God. You have to tell. You have to!"

"No. I can't! I never can, not anymore. It's too late, far too late. What would it even mean now? After all this time. No."

"Listen to me. Astrid was blackmailing you using me. If I'm not here, and she doesn't know where I am, she can't blackmail you. Can she?"

"It's not that simple anymore. It's everyone: all the girls here. She'd use them against me."

I try. So hard. To tell her that if people don't say what they know, that if we don't stand up against the Lorders, things will keep getting worse. That it is in our hands to do something. She isn't listening, I can tell.

But how can I complain when all those times with Aiden, I didn't listen, either?

What I don't say is, what if she had spoken out all those years ago?

Told everyone that the prime minister was going to resign and expose the Lorders, that they were assassinated by their own government to keep them quiet. Maybe the Lorder stranglehold we have today would never have developed.

I stand to go.

"Wait. My last request. Can I have your camera?"

"My camera? Why?"

She shakes her head. "I'll give it back. I just want copies of your photos: those of you and us."

I hesitate. "Okay. I'll bring it down." I leave the room wondering if she could see the telltale bulge that said the camera was in my pocket the whole time.

Back in my room, I fiddle with the camera's interactive screen until I work out how to make folders; I password-protect the ones of the orphanage. I long to e-mail them to somebody, anybody, but don't dare without a nongovernment computer. They'd be monitored and stopped for sure, and then they'd have my location.

I bring it back down, thinking I'll wait while she downloads the photos.

"I've got something for you." She holds out her hand, and in it, a key. "Your dad's stuff. Photos, all of it. I wanted to get rid of it, but somehow couldn't bring myself to do it."

"Where?"

"In the old boathouse. Do you remember where it is?"

"I think so. Thanks." I clutch the key in my hand.

"Go on, have a look while I go through the photos on your camera. I'll give it back to you at dinner."

I hesitate, unsure if I should let it out of my sight, but the key in my hand is pulling me another direction. I grab my coat and put my boots back on, groaning a little at sore feet from so many fast miles covered today. I slip out the side door, run down the grounds toward the lake.

Do I remember the boathouse? I try, really hard, but nothing comes to me beyond flashes of a kayak sliding into the water. I wander the paths along the water's edge. There are several outbuildings next to the racks of kayaks, and another farther along, almost hidden by overgrown plants and overhanging trees. As soon as I see it in the moonlight, I know: This is the boathouse.

Dad used to spend a lot of time here.

There isn't a boat in sight; it was a converted workshop, where he'd build bits of things, or just hang out—to get out of the house. Getting away from Stella, I realize now, in a way I didn't back then.

The key fits in the lock, but it doesn't turn. Some trace of memory tells me to push the door in with my knee and try again, and this time it does. The door creaks open.

It smells dusty and damp, and I step forward into cobwebs. I brush them off and sneeze, feeling along the wall for the switch. I find it; it doesn't work, but then my elbow knocks something off a shelf. I stoop to pick it up, and my hand closes around it: a flashlight. I flick it on.

The table, the bench, all still in place; as I see them, the rush of memory almost knocks me from my feet. Instead of tools and stray broken things, they are covered now by plastic boxes. I pull the lid off one, then another: clothes. Dad's clothes, from a lifetime ago; books that were his.

In another under more books is a chess set. His set, the one he taught me to play on: one of my few happy memories. He let me win. I smile, open the box, and touch the pieces inside.

Of course one is missing: one rook. The castle. He used it to reach me in that faraway place, where I was taken, held, and fractured. It's up in my room here, tucked in a corner of my bag. And here are all its mates. Something inside me longs to bring the missing rook down to this place, have them reunited in their little nests inside the box.

Another box is full of photographs, and I dive into them. There are old photos of Stella and Dad, some from their wedding. I hunt for some of us together; there aren't many, but I find a few. There is one of me and him and Pounce as a tiny kitten; all smiles. It must have been taken the morning of my tenth birthday. Before everything went wrong. I tuck it into my pocket, along with one of Stella and Dad laughing together when they were young. There aren't many photos of Dad, if this is all of them, to make the trail of an entire life; he was usually the one with a camera in his hands.

My camera. Some sense of unease returns. How long have I been down here?

"Riley?"

I jump, turn. Ellie stands framed in the door, shivering without a coat on, my camera in her hand. She holds it out. "Stella asked me to give this to you; you forgot it in her office. And to say that it is okay if you miss dinner if you want to."

She turns, dashes back up the path.

I stare at my camera in my hands, confused. I forgot it? She said she'd give me the camera at dinner. Why the change? Did she realize I was going to want to spend loads of time down here, or what?

Maybe there is a message beyond her words. Something isn't right. My skin crawls as if an army of spiders have found me here.

I switch off the flashlight, then slip out into the night. Close the door, slow and quiet; push it with my knee. Lock it. Wonder what to do with the key, then put it on top of the door.

Voices float out on the night air, too faint to discern. There are feet crunching on the gravel above. I slink from one tree to another until figures above are in view, but it's too dark to make out who they are. I get the camera out, put it in night mode, and peer through the zoom. A car is parked to the side of the house; the main lakeside door is open, Stella framed in it. Two others are walking toward her. One is Astrid. The other is a man, his back turned to me. The light is poor, but every move he makes is fluid, sinuous, catlike. I feel as if my muscles and bones are melting, can't hold me upright; I may collapse.

Nico.

Why would he be here, with Astrid? It doesn't make any sense.

He pauses, turns his head, and scans out into the darkness, and I shake, convinced he can sense my presence, that his pale blue eyes can somehow penetrate the night and see where I hide. Without thought my finger pushes the camera button, taking several quick shots of him and Astrid in the same frame.

How can this be? Astrid and Nico—Lorder, and AGT—are sworn enemies. Aren't they?

Movement draws my eyes to the sides of the house. I swing the camera. Figures in black: Lorders. They're watching the side doors. What do you want to bet they are by every door? Fear grips my gut for Ellie. Did she get back inside before they came?

Then I notice one of the Lorders has something strapped across his eyes: night vision goggles.

I sink back down until the dip of the land has them out of sight.

That message from Stella *was* a warning: Has Astrid worked out who I am? My panicked brain can't process Astrid and Nico being together, or what it means. But whatever it is can't be good.

Adrenalin pours through my body. *Run!*

To go right would mean going past an open stretch of the grounds that slopes down to the lake without cover—no way I wouldn't be seen. To go left is the logical escape route: the wooded footpath into town. This is where they will hunt when they realize I'm not in the house.

The lake.

I slip along the water's edge to the racks of kayaks. I almost hold my breath as I lift one off the rack as quietly as I can. The paddles are clipped alongside the kayaks. The desire to get away is so strong that it is hard to pause, but I do, and unclip all the other paddles, and gather them together. Make it harder to chase.

I move along the shore, awkwardly balancing the kayak and paddles. Step slowly into the water so I don't splash, struggling not to gasp with the cold when it goes over my boots. As silent as I can, I get into the kayak, awkward in winter clothes and with all the paddles tucked under one arm. A paddle drops and catches the water; the end jumps up, knocks my glasses off my face. There is a slight splash as they drop into the water. I grab for them, but they're gone in the darkness. What does it matter? They're not going to fool Nico if he catches me.

I set out, and my childhood kayaking soon comes back to me; my strokes are fast and sure, hugging the shoreline so I'm harder to spot.

Once I'm well away from the house, I move away from the lake's edge and slip the paddles out in the open water with a silent apology. I leave them floating behind me as I pour every bit of panicked energy into strokes to get me as far from Astrid and Nico as I can.

23

SHIVERING, I PULL THE KAYAK WELL UP FROM THE WATER, then push it and the paddle under bushes. I focus on picturing the map Finley showed me earlier: Keswick Boys should be nearby.

I don't like going there—it's risky for so many reasons—but what choice do I have? I need to find Len, and the only way I know how is through Finley. Besides, I'm half soaked with January lake water. My feet must still be down there, but are so numb, walking is clumsy. The temperature is dropping and, judging by the thin ice I had to break through on this side of the lake, it's going to get worse. I need to get warm and dry.

There are buildings above me, lights, voices. I hug the path that skirts around the houses, until at last I see a large rambling building set apart above them.

I slip around the side of it. There is a boy in shadows near the back door; a dot of red light says he's having a smoke. Do I wait until he goes and try to sneak in, or brazen it out?

I'm too cold to be subtle.

I step down the path in front of him. "Hello," I say.

He squints into the darkness; I step into the light by a window.

"Hello there, yourself. Where did you magic from?"

I giggle. "Could you tell Finley I'm here?"

"Him again?" He rolls his eyes and stubs out his cigarette on the side of the building. "Wait a sec," he says, and disappears into the house.

A few minutes pass. A window down the end of the building opens with a thud, and a head peeks out: Finley.

"Riley? What are you doing here?"

I quickly cut across to the window. "I'm in some trouble."

"A damsel in distress? One of my favorite things. Come in the back way." He holds out a hand and I realize he means the window. He half pulls me through, into some sort of utility room.

"You're frozen," he says.

I nod, shaking violently and not bothering to try to hide it anymore. "I kayaked across the lake. I'm soaked."

"I'm guessing this has something to do with the Lorders chasing us earlier today."

"Probably," I say, though not entirely sure that they could have worked out who I was and where to find me that quickly. Then I remember Steph at dinner the other night—she saw my green eyes. Is she a spy for Astrid? If so, that'd be weird enough for her to report, even if she didn't have an inkling who I am. I shake my head. "I don't know. It could be that, or it could be something else. Either way, I'm trouble. Are you sure you want to help?"

"Don't be daft. Of course I'm helping you. We'll get you warm to start with. Hang on." He opens the door, looks out. "Coast is clear." He holds out a hand. "Try to look like you're here because of my irresistible charms, not on the run from the law." He winks, takes my hand, and wraps an arm around my waist.

We walk fast up the hall to the end, up a flight of stairs to the next level, down a hall. He opens a door to a bedroom.

Another boy is in there, reading a book on one of two beds.

"Clear out," Finley says.

He looks up, rolls his eyes. "Didn't take you long to get over the last one," he says. Finley stiffens, but manages to keep his arm around me as the other boy leaves.

As soon as the door shuts, we spring apart. "Sorry," we both say in unison.

"He won't say anything?" I ask.

"Of course he will. But only to the lads. Boys' code," he says, and taps the side of his nose.

"Great," I say, then wonder why I care, as long as they don't tell the authorities I'm here. My reputation is far down my list of worries.

He opens a wardrobe, fishes through it. "Get out of that wet stuff and put these on." He turns around, and I shuck my boots, jeans, and socks and pull on his miles-too-big joggers, then some huge wool socks. I'm still shaking. "My bed isn't as disgusting as his. Go on, warm up." I get in it and pull his blankets around me in a cocoon. Finley puts my stuff on the radiator, stuffs paper in my boots.

He pulls a desk chair around. Now come the questions, and he has a right to ask them, but in some sort of crazy delayed fear reaction I'm pulling my arms around my head in a ball. Nico: He must know I'm alive. Why else was he there? He'll find me. Deep shuddering sobs are tearing out of me, and Finley starts patting my shoulder, all awkward but nice, but for some reason it just makes me cry harder.

"Hey there. It'll be all right," he says. But how can it be? "Don't cry. If anyone hears, it'll ruin my reputation."

I draw in a shaky breath and fight for control. A bell rings, and I jump.

"Dinner bell," he explains. "But I can stay."

I sit up and rub a hand across my eyes. "Actually, I'm starving."

"Oh, thank God, me too. Right. I'll get takeout."

"You can do that?"

"Sure. The boys'll run interference while I stack an extra plate. Back in five."

He leaves, and I fight for the composure I'd felt earlier. The certainty that I would get away, and I'd find Aiden, and I'd give him my photos, and he'd know what to do with them. Somehow with all the Lorders in the world potentially after me I wasn't all right exactly, but could carry on. But now that it's Nico, too?

After all he and his AGT have done to me—stolen my childhood, my life, killed my father, programmed me to be a killer—there is a core of cold fury inside. But most of all, overwhelming everything else, is fear. One glance at him in the distance and I was terrified. He must know I didn't die when he set off that explosion; why else would he be here? Astrid knew I survived; she must have told him when she worked out where I was. He'll find me. He always finds me.

I look at the window behind me and the door opposite, jumpy, as if just by thinking of what scares me I can conjure it up.

And Astrid and Nico together: What does it mean? I can't process this. Stella said Astrid was behind the assassinations, that AGT did it but she set it up. It couldn't have been Nico; it was over twenty-five years ago, and he can't be much older than that. But Astrid must have links with the AGT. Is that it, is she still using them for her purposes?

But Nico *hates* the Lorders. How could they be in the same place at the same time? He is AGT through and through.

I shake my head, trying to make sense of it all. After I was taken from Castlerigg to that other place by Dr. Craig, Nico was there. He was involved from the beginning. Astrid was my grandmother—or so

I thought back then—she knew me since I was a baby. She might be the only person who knows where I even come from. Now that I've seen her with Nico, is it too much coincidence to think the AGT targeted me and she wasn't involved? Stella thinks Dad was behind what happened to me, but was it Astrid—her own mother—all along?

Approaching footsteps pull me from my thoughts; my heart races. There is a light tap, and Finley opens the door.

He sees the look on my face. "It's only me. Maybe we should have a secret knock?"

"Sorry, I'm just jumpy. And I'm sorry about losing it before," I say.

"No worries. Here you go," he says, and holds out one of two big bowls in his hands, full of stew with bread on the side, and it smells good. I'd told him I was hungry to get him to go, to give me time to compose myself, but now that I can smell food, I'm famished.

While we eat, Finley looks at me curiously, then pauses in between mouthfuls. "You look different, and I just worked it out: no glasses. But your eyes look different somehow."

"I lost them in the lake."

"Are you going to tell me what's going on?"

I stare back at him. The weak point in my plan, such as it is, is this moment. "Sometimes, it's better not to know stuff."

"Like what you were up to today."

"Exactly."

"It's nice to have a reputation-enhancing houseguest, but no matter how slack they run this place, eventually someone official is bound to notice. You can't stay here forever."

"Just a few hours will be fine. Thanks."

"What can I do to help?"

I can't see any way to get the information I need without the direct approach. "I need to find Len," I say, with a silent apology to Len. He didn't want Finley to know anything, did he?

"Always knew there was more to the old man than meets the eye. That's easy; he lives over the hill. We could go now?"

"I think better to wait until everybody is asleep, then slip out. Tell me where to find him, and I'll—"

"No way. I'm going, too. Don't want you to get lost or bang on the wrong door."

"But—"

"No buts. That's it." He takes the bowls, some things for his roomie, who is bunked down in another's room. Comes back and stays, reading a book in a chair with a grimace at the state of the other bed, tells me he'll watch over me, that everything is okay, to get some sleep and he'll wake me up in a few hours.

Warm at last, I'm convinced I'll never sleep, that it isn't possible. There are my own fears still, and others intruding: What if Nico realizes Ellie saw me last? My stomach turns to think what he might do if he gets his hands on her. Then I'm angry at Stella for using Ellie like that; then I'm scared for Stella. And Finley. It won't take long for someone to remember we spent the day together, to come looking for him, and then if they haven't already connected that with the ones they were chasing from the orphanage today, they will soon. He says he's watching over me, but he has no idea what he could face if they come here.

My fears circle around in my head like black crows, but somehow they become more faint and distant, and drift away.

A small head peeks over his mother's shoulder, giggles.

Get down! *I'm saying inside and with my eyes, but he doesn't get it. He peeks out again.*

This time they see him. Black-garbed Lorders.

They march past me and grab the boy from his mother; she's pleading, he's crying. Everyone on the train stares at their feet, at the floor, at the dead windows. No one moves. No one says anything.

Not this time; it is time to say no. No more. I get out of my seat. "Leave him alone!"

One of the Lorders slowly turns around. His blond-streaked hair is too long and unruly for a Lorder. His pale blue eyes glint with danger. He smiles a seductive smile, and holds out a hand.

Nico? No. It can't be.

24

MY EYES SNAP OPEN. THERE IS A BRIEF MOMENT OF CONFUSION:
Where am I? Finley's room. It is still, silent. What woke me?

I glance across the room, and there is just enough moonlight through gaps in the curtains to see that the chair and other bed are empty. I'm alone.

Then there is a faint sound in the hall: footsteps?

I sit up with a rush of fear. Nowhere to hide. Not enough time to get out the window; nowhere to run.

There is a featherlight tap on the door, and it opens: Finley.

I sag back in relief.

"Oh good, you're awake," he says. "Time to go."

I shake off the panic, and grab my things off the radiator. "Nearly dry."

He turns as I change into them fast.

"Now come on," he says, and takes my hand. "If anyone spots us they'll just think I'm sneaking you out."

Finley peeks out into the hall, draws me out. We walk silently to the stairs, down them, and then out the back door—a real door, not a window this time.

I glance back at the lake; all is silent inky darkness. I frown to myself. Surely once the Lorders realized I wasn't in the house or up the path, they'd work out I took a kayak, that the other paddles were missing? I'd half expected to see searchlights.

We creep along footpaths up and away from the houses and the lake, Finley leading the way. I am sure-footed and silent in the dark; years of woods training with Nico made sure of that. Finley is less so. A particularly loud crack in front makes me cringe. "Keep it down up there," I whisper.

"Don't worry, the tree is fine," Finley says.

"What tree?"

"The one whose branch I just smacked my head into. I'm starting to see that being a Shorty has its advantages."

We reach a road, walk along it for a mile, keeping a careful listen for cars, ducking out of sight whenever one goes by. Then we turn down a long, twisty lane.

"Here we are: chez Len," Finley says. More a shack than a house; the car we borrowed earlier is pulled in alongside. It is silent and dark.

"What time is it?" I whisper.

"Four A.M."

"Hope he's not a heavy sleeper."

Finley tries knocking lightly on the door; no response. He tries the handle: locked. We exchange a glance. "Somehow really banging on the door goes against the whole sneaking around thing," he says.

I pick up a few pebbles and ping them against the window.

Eventually we hear movement inside, locks turning. The door opens, and Len peers out. "This better be good."

Len pulls us into the kitchen, shuts the door. "I don't know about you, but I can't be civil without tea this time of the morning. You can make it while we talk," he says to Finley. Points out the kettle, cups. Draws me into the next room and shuts the door.

"So, Miss Lucy Connor: Your cover is blown."

"You know?"

He inclines his head.

"How?"

"Got a message from your mother."

I stare at him in shock. "She knows you?"

"How'd you think you got put on MIA in the first place?"

I shake my head. "I don't know; I guess I didn't think about it."

"Do you know how they worked out who you are?"

"I don't *know*. But I think Steph—one of the girls—is a spy for Astrid. She saw my glasses come off. That my eyes are green."

"Those were some glasses. Not wearing them anymore?"

"Lost them in the lake. Don't suppose it matters now. I'm sure Astrid was already suspicious that something was up with Stella. Then if Steph told her about my glasses, she must have put things together and worked it out." I lean back and sigh. "I'm sorry about involving Finley. I had to run, and I didn't know how else to find you."

"He's a smart lad. He'll keep his mouth shut. But there's more to tell, isn't there?"

There is a tap on the door. Finley peeks in, holds out two cups of tea. "Can I come in?"

"Not just yet, give us a few moments," Len says.

Finley looks disappointed, but hands us our tea and goes back through the door.

Len has a slurp of way-too-hot tea but looks happier. "That's better. Now tell me: What happened yesterday afternoon to make Lorders be looking for you up that mountain?"

"I found out something, something that puts Lorders in a very bad light. I need to get to Aiden, the sooner, the better. Can you help?"

He stares steadily back at me, sighs. "I'll always help when I can, because I'm a stupid old idiot. Not enough life left to be cautious with.

But getting you out of town will be difficult if they're looking for you. Maybe you should tell me why it's so important."

I hesitate, torn. Aiden trusts him, and that's good enough for me. But is it safer if he doesn't know?

"Look at it this way: If you're the only one who knows something, and something happens to you, nobody knows."

I nod. Gulp. "It's so awful, it's hard to even say." My head aches, and I drop it in my hands.

"Time is tight, Lucy," he says gently.

"I'd rather you didn't use that name—stick with Riley."

"Okay, then; Riley."

I look up, meet his eyes. "We saw them from a distance. A line of children, walking along the fence inside the orphanage grounds. But something wasn't right about them. They weren't like normal children. So I went for a closer look."

"Mad as a box of frogs. And?"

"They're all Slated. Even little ones, maybe four or five years old." The horror I can feel on my face is reflected in his. "They were like . . . robots, almost. No personality, no life."

He grips my hand. "Evidence?"

I pat my pocket. "Photos, in my camera, of Levos on their wrists."

"Bad timing." He curses under his breath. "MIA's website has been hacked."

"What? Could that be how they found where I was?" As a Slated, seeking out my past life is completely illegal. That'd be reason enough for Lorders to hunt me down, without adding in stumbling on their secrets at the orphanage.

"They got into the protected areas of the site. Any information available to administrators of MIA was open to them. If they looked, they'd know you were reported found, but not your location. That type of information isn't stored on the website, not even encrypted. Of course they may have worked out to look for you in Keswick. But all computer communications are suspended while it is investigated, so we can't e-mail the photos as backup. Besides, Aiden'll need you; you're the witness. We've got to get you to him."

"Well. You know how they're looking for Lucy Connor? Things could get worse."

"It can get worse?" Len asks mildly.

"If they put her together with the girl who took photos at their so-called orphanage. And that Finley was with me. And you were seen with us later on. I'm so sorry."

Len calls Finley in; he has tea with us. Len finds some biscuits, puts a hand up when we try to say anything. "Be quiet. I'm thinking."

Finally Len looks at me, then gestures at Finley. "You didn't tell him what you found out?" I shake my head. "Keep it that way." Finley looks about to protest, but Len holds up a hand. "Listen to me. We might be in some trouble. If you don't know, you can't tell. You can try to play innocent. Bit of a stretch for you, I know."

"They don't care about innocence," I say, bitter as I think of the Slated children. Children? Some of them were more like toddlers.

"This is what I think you should do," Len says to Finley. "Go home. Slip back in like nothing is happening. I think chances are low they'll connect you with her."

"Can't he come with me?" I ask.

"No. If Finley is reported missing now, they *will* put the two of you together. They'll be more likely to make the leap that it was you two they were looking for on the hill yesterday."

"No, you can't just send him back! It's too dangerous."

"Listen to me. Something is funny about all of this. If you really found something the Lorder government wants to stay hidden, they'd have jumped on the whole county like a ton of bricks: roadblocks, searches house to house, the works. And there has been nothing."

"What does that mean?"

He scratches his head. "Haven't a clue, but for now I think it works in our favor. My usual thought would be to lie low until things settle down before we try to move you anywhere, but this time I think the faster we get you out of town, the better."

"Right. I'll be off, then, or I won't be able to sneak back in before morning." Finley gets up, comes over to me awkwardly, and stoops down to give me a hug. "Look after yourself," he says. "Don't worry about me; I'll be all right."

Len goes to the door with him. They murmur to each other too low for me to hear, then the door shuts and Len comes back in.

"Do you really think they won't track him down?" I ask.

He hesitates. "No, and he knows it. He's buying you some time. Don't waste it."

25

"ARE YOU SURE ABOUT THIS?"

"Unless you can flap your arms and fly, then yes," Len says. "Trains are out. Even if we could get you another fake ID quickly, they're watching for you now. They're unlikely to be fooled. It's the only way."

The truck, a goods transport, is parked behind an isolated workshop. These are the only sort of vehicles that do long road journeys with the environmental bans on private long-distance car travel. The truck's cab has a false floor Len has taken up, with a small—and I mean *small*—space underneath. It's only ever been used to move around tech for MIA; I am to be the first passenger.

"Let's see if you fit," Len says, and I lower myself in, nesting a blanket around myself. Trying different positions to get my arms and legs in. "I'll try the floor on now," he says. "Knock or yell if it gets too tight."

I give him a thumbs-up, Len slowly lowers the floor in place above me, and I'm plunged into darkness. He lifts it up again. "All right?" he asks.

"I think so, just had to flatten my shoulders. Go on."

He puts it back into place. The noise of the drill as he replaces the screws is unbelievable, and I try to stuff my hands in my ears, but can barely move enough to do it. There is an irrational feeling of panic, like I'm being buried alive in a coffin. The driver is having lunch. He's not in MIA, but bribed regularly to leave his truck unattended. While he knows he is transporting something, he's kept in the dark about what it is. He doesn't know I'm in here. What if something happens to whoever is meant to extract this "delivery" at the other end? No one but Len knows I am trapped in here; he judged it too dangerous to get a message out that might be intercepted. Even though he has drilled out some airholes, already I feel like I can't breathe.

There is a *tap-tap* outside someplace, and I imagine Len giving the side of the truck a double tap for luck to send me on my way.

I half smile, then it falls away. I owe Len and Finley so much. *Please stay safe.* I'd gotten out of Len that he'd told Finley a safe bolt-hole if he gets wind of trouble, but if the Lorders come for him it's more likely that he won't have a chance. It was luck that had me down by the lake when Nico, Astrid, and the Lorders came; if Stella hadn't managed to get Ellie out with that cryptic message, they'd probably still have gotten me. What would they have done with me? Nothing good, I'm sure. Maybe hauled me off to the prison Len thinks Madison is in. Maybe, I'd be dead.

Time passes. A door opens, then slams shut. The truck's engine starts up, and it lurches along bumpy minor roads for what feels like forever. Then it's motorway, smooth and fast. The rocking motion is almost soothing. The small confined space warms with me in it, and lulls me to sleep.

WHRRRRR . . .

I bolt awake, hit my head hard on something above me, then re-member where I am. That noise, reverberating through my skull: The screws are being removed. Are we there, wherever that is, or have we been stopped along the way? I have no sense of time. But now that

I'm awake, every muscle in my body is screaming to move and stretch; one way or the other, I'm getting out of here.

The last screw out, the floor is lifted, and I sit up as it is pulled away.

There is a startled face above me, and the floor is almost dropped on my head.

"Oh my God. It's a girl," he says.

The floor is pulled away and out; another face appears. Both men, in overalls. Clearly not Lorders. I breathe a sigh of relief, swing my legs out. "Ouch. Give me a hand?"

One of them hastens to do so, and I step out of the truck, then almost fall over again, my legs protesting after so long in the same position. I steady myself, one hand on the side of the truck. We're outside in the cold behind some buildings, and it's dark.

"Where am I?"

They exchange a glance.

"Oh, sorry. I'm here for the final act of *The Winter's Tale*." Len had given the words to say, coded words that should get me to authority in MIA quickly.

Things move fast after that. I'm hustled inside a workshop and run to their disgusting bathroom, then beg a cup of tea while hurried conversations happen on the other side of a door. I'm strangely calm. Is it because what happens next is out of my hands? I don't know.

A car appears; I'm bundled into the backseat. A man and woman sit silently in front. I watch out the windows; we go through an industrial area, and then into more and more built-up areas. Not London, and not familiar, but then I see a sign: WELCOME TO OXFORD. So close to home! Or what used to be home. My old school, Lord Williams's, is just miles away in Thame. Our village not far beyond that.

The streets get more crowded with old buildings, busy with pedestrians. We weave down narrow back streets and pull in. I'm given a different coat to wear, a hat, and walked by the driver along rambling cobblestoned streets, past grand old architecture. I long to gawk and stare upward at everything around me, but don't dare draw attention to myself.

We duck through an archway, down a path along a quadrangle surrounded by buildings, then to a door where we are met by a smiling girl a few years older than me. The driver leaves me there. I follow the girl down twisting passages to another door. She taps lightly. "Go in," she says, and leaves.

I pull the door open: a bookshelf-lined study. And there, at a desk? A very startled-looking Aiden.

"Kyla? You're our new witness? Thank God you're all right." He jumps up from his chair, scoops me in his arms for a hug, and I cling on a little tight. Something is melting inside: Aiden is here, he'll know what to do. Am I safe, at least for a while? He finally lets go, but keeps hold of my hand, laces my fingers with his. And I stare at him, shaken by how tight I want to hold on to his hand, how much I missed him. His deep blue eyes. Merry eyes, despite the risks he takes. The way his hair catches the light, fiery glints of red. I smile.

"Ahem." A throat-clearing noise. I turn and see there is another person in the room, a woman in a chair by the fire: older than Aiden, a fierce hungry expression on a face pale with dark-ringed eyes. "I hope we're not using all these resources for girlfriend transport now." She frowns.

"Len wouldn't have sent us anything that way that wasn't vital. Not with an emergency code." Aiden's voice is calm, but a tinge of red creeps up his cheeks.

"So, what is so urgent? Tell us," she says.

I look at Aiden. "I'd rather talk to you alone."

She scowls. "That won't be happening."

"Who are you, then?" I demand.

"It's all right, Kyla. This is Florence—we run MIA together, since . . ." And he stops. "Anyhow, we always work on a double system for hearing witnesses. If more people know, then information is safer."

"Okay, then," I say, and get my camera out, fiddle with it to enter the password for the folder, and to find the screen projection control. "These photos were taken at the Cumbrian Care Facility near Keswick. An isolated fenced orphanage. I saw children walking along the inside of the boundary, moving unnaturally. I went for a closer look, and this is what I found."

There are no blank walls, so I point the camera at the door and hit the button to show the shots: three small boys, wrists extended. Levos clearly visible.

They both gasp. "Oh my God," Aiden says, and they look at each other.

"By how they were acting, all the children at the orphanage were Slated. From these little ones up to age eleven or twelve. About fifty children in total."

"We can't wait any longer," he says. "Not with this and all the other evidence of Lorder atrocities that we have. It's time to get the information we've gathered out to the people. They can't ignore *this*—it will be the beginning of the end of the Lorders."

Florence shakes her head. "We need verification. Photos can be faked."

"No! We have a witness."

They continue, back and forth, and I get the sense of a long-standing argument with different variations, but feel removed from it. I've passed along what I know; it's not my burden anymore. There are other things I want—I *need*—to tell Aiden; personal things. But not here, not now. Not with her in the room.

"Excuse me," I say once there is a lull. "Any chance of something to eat?"

Aiden is contrite. "Of course. But let's get those photos." He holds out a hand for the camera.

"I want to keep the camera; there's my stuff on here, too."

He connects it to a computer and downloads the orphanage shots when I give him the password. Hands the camera back.

"But I thought Len said the MIA computer system is compromised?" I ask.

Aiden sighs. Nods. "It's been an absolute nightmare; our techies are working on it. We've been aware that they monitor the site for years, but this time they've hacked through our defenses and were able to trace backward to MIA website administrators. It's a mystery how they got in, and we're not sure how long they've been spying on us through it or how much information they've extracted. But this computer is offline. So for now the photos are stored here, and still there, of course." He gestures to my camera. "Keep it safe."

I slip it back deep in my pocket. Aiden looks pointedly at Florence. She sighs, gets up. "I can take a hint."

"Could you bring Kyla some dinner?" Aiden smiles his most charming smile, and it is pretty good, but she scowls.

"Don't push your luck." She stomps to the door, looks back. "I'll get something brought, though."

"Can you get the new lad to bring it?"

She looks at him curiously, then nods.

And she's gone.

"She's tetchy," I say, glad she's gone, but even more glad to be alone with Aiden. My hand seeks out his again, and he smiles.

"She has reason. It was her father who started MIA decades ago. His identity was exposed with the computer stuff up. Covers were blown, he's dead, and she's in hiding here. As am I."

"Oh no; how awful."

"But let's not dwell on problems. There's reasons to be cheerful here today."

"They are?"

"You're safe and well. Despite our tech setbacks, we're nearly there, Kyla. We're ready to unleash our truth about the Lorders' world once our systems are up and running. You are the nail in their coffin."

"What a lovely image." But I smile. "Aiden, you were right about everything."

He grins. "I do like to hear that, but about what in particular?"

"Things will only change if everybody knows what goes on, and stands together. I want to do anything I can for MIA. Join you completely."

"Being a witness is good enough."

"No, it isn't. There must be more I can do," I protest. And inside I'm starting to gather all the rest that I have to tell him: everything I didn't before, and what I've learned since the last time we were together. But before I can begin, there is a tap at the door.

"This is your third reason to be cheerful," Aiden says. But he's not looking that way anymore himself; his eyes are sad, and he lets go of my hand.

I look at him, not comprehending.

The door opens.

I blink, look back at Aiden, not believing what I see. Not trusting my eyes.

I look back at the person standing in the doorway, a tray of sandwiches in his hands. At the way his too-long dark hair is tucked behind his ears, his chocolate brown eyes. The way he stands. A smile takes over my face, my whole body.

"Ben?"

26

I STARE, TRANSFIXED, THEN GLANCE BACK AT AIDEN. "BUT how . . . What . . ."

"I'll let Ben explain," Aiden says. He stands and heads for the door. "Get reacquainted; I'll be back later. We need to talk some more." The door shuts behind him.

Ben smiles, a little uncomfortably. He puts the tray on the table. "Kyla, isn't it?" he says.

I nod, trying to stop the wave of disappointment that sweeps through me from showing on my face: He still doesn't remember me, or what we were to each other. When he first opened the door, for a moment I'd thought somehow he was my Ben again, that that was why he was here. But his memories are still gone.

He sits in the chair next to me—inches away, but it feels like a gap of miles when it is all I can do to not reach out and touch him. Instead I just let my eyes drink him in, every bit of him that I was afraid I'd never see again.

Amusement crosses his face. "There is something I need to say to you, but it's hard when you're staring at me like that." A trace of Ben's humor. No matter if his memories are gone, it *is* Ben.

"Sorry, I'll try to stop. What is it?"

"Thank you."

"For what?"

He runs his hands through his hair, the way he always did. "It was you who got me out of that training place. With the Lorders."

"It was?"

"I thought I wanted to be there, I wanted to succeed. To become what they wanted. But all the time there was this little voice in my head, doubting what they said, questioning things. Your voice."

"What I said to you worked? I thought I'd gotten through, for a moment. But then, after, I doubted it. I thought maybe I saw that because I wanted to. But it actually worked?"

"Yes, thanks to you I'm on the run from the Lorders with you and all the rest of the crazies." He grins, teasing.

"Do you know what they did to your memories?"

He shakes his head. "Not really. Aiden's setting up for me to see a doctor, to get scanned and stuff. Don't know what they'll find."

His sleeves are long, and I reach out, pull them up, his skin warm under my fingers. "No Levo."

"No." He grins a wicked grin. Takes my hand and holds it between his. "You don't need an excuse to touch me."

"You don't even remember us together! You're a total flirt," I say, feeling both dizzy with the feel of his skin against mine, and confused. To Ben, is mine the hand of a stranger? This feels weird. He looks and feels the same, but do I know him?

"Maybe I am. But I know we were close once. You must have really cared for me to risk coming to that Lorder place. Seeking me out so close to danger."

I shrug. "I'm just stupid. I do stuff like that."

"Well, I'm glad you did."

"How'd you end up here with Aiden?"

"Long story. It was more that he found me. I ran away; someone from MIA spotted and recognized me. Aiden tracked me down to where I was hiding out. He had a difficult time convincing me he wasn't with the Lorders."

"Of course; you wouldn't have remembered him, either."

"No. I'm afraid I kind of hurt him a little. Until I worked out he was telling the truth."

"Whoops."

"Not sure his pride has gotten over being in a headlock. Actually, not sure he or Flo knows what to make of me. They want to work out what's been done to me, but they always make sure someone is with me. Not quite sure what they think I'm going to do."

"They have to be careful, I suppose." I frown. That isn't the way to help someone get better, though. Maybe he'll start getting some memories back, like I have? "I still can't believe you're here." And I'm grinning that crazy happy grin and staring at him again.

He smiles, self-conscious. "I heard you were hungry; I made them just for you." He nods at the forgotten tray on the table, lets go of my hand.

"Thanks," I say, and grab a sandwich, a poor substitute for Ben's hand. Cheese and pickle, and I don't like pickle, but why would he remember that? When there is so much more important stuff that he can't remember, either.

Ben stays, I eat sandwiches, he makes me laugh a few times, and I try not to stare so much. Can this really be happening? Ben: He's really here. Aiden found him, and he's safe and well.

There is a knock on the door, and Aiden peeks in. "Hello, all right if we come in?"

I nod, mouth full of biscuit. Aiden walks in and with him is Florence, who looks pointedly at Ben. He rolls his eyes, stands up. "Well, I'll be off, then," he says. "See you tomorrow?"

"Hope so," I say. He goes out the door, and I hear him speaking to someone in the hall before it closes. They really did have somebody outside the door the whole time?

"Are you having Ben watched every minute of the day?"

Aiden shrugs, looks at Florence. "Ms. Cautious thinks it is necessary."

She bristles. "We don't really know what makes him tick, do we? I don't think even he does. Until we work out what has been done to him, it is a reasonable precaution."

"You're too careful, with Ben and everything else. We should release the evidence we have, now. Together with Kyla's testimony—"

"Testimony? What is that, exactly?" I interrupt.

"We are taping witnesses—filming them, when we can—for first-hand accounts of Lorder atrocities," Florence says.

"Filming?"

"All you need to do is talk about your story to the camera, just tell it like you told us," Aiden says. "Then when we release the evidence—*if* we ever do, that is," he says with a pointed look at Florence, "it will be part of it."

"We will get there, Aiden," she says. "But to avoid being discredited and ignored, we have to make sure we have firsthand evidence for everything. It isn't good enough if it's all he said/she said. We need to back everything up with evidence; hearsay doesn't cut it."

"But the Lorders must know how close we are to releasing our evidence; otherwise, why play their hand with this cyber-attack? They've been aware of the website for years. Why else now? They must realize the risk. We have to get word out before they stop us."

Florence glances at me. "Enough of that now, Aiden," she says, as obviously as if she'd said, *Not in front of the children.* I bristle, but then remind myself what Aiden told me, about her father, and try not to let it show.

"Do you feel up to doing this now?" Aiden says. "We always try to record evidence at the first opportunity."

"On film?"

"It's best."

I swallow, scared of being committed to a recording, sound and image, but unwilling to let Florence see my fear. "Why not? They're all after me, anyhow; giving them one more reason will hardly matter."

"That's the spirit," Florence says. I have just enough time to wonder if spending most of the day squashed in the floor of a truck does much for my hair when she has set up a camera on a small tripod on the desk. "When you're ready," she says. "Just say who you are, and what you saw." She hits a button and a green light comes on.

"What name do I use?"

She makes an impatient noise, stops the camera. "Have you got a selection?"

"As a matter of fact . . ."

"Use Kyla," Aiden says.

"All right," I say. It's just as true as any of the others, isn't it? She starts recording, and I stare at the camera, say that I am Kyla Davis, that I was walking in Cumbria, that I saw a care facility that houses orphans. What was different about them. I project the photos from my camera; she records them also.

She flicks the camera off. "That should do. I'll check it and let you know tomorrow." She packs up the camera, sweeps out of the room, and leaves us alone.

"Sorry. Flo isn't always as polite as she could be. Thanks for doing that. I know it was hard for you."

"It's fine," I say, shrugging off his words, but it did feel *crazy* to be saying stuff Lorders wouldn't like, and, if that wasn't bad enough, to let somebody record it. "It might move me up on their most wanted list, but does that really matter? I'm already on it."

"That's the way."

"I want to thank you for finding Ben."

He shrugs, uncomfortable. "It was the least I could do. I always felt that it was my fault, what he did."

"It wasn't," I protest. "If it was anyone's, it was mine." *Or Nico's,* I add silently, but Aiden doesn't know about Nico. I sigh. There are so many things I haven't told Aiden. Should I? The main thing that would be grist for MIA is Stella's story: that her mother, a Lorder, was behind the assassinations. But despite the fact that I promised not to tell, it is what Florence called hearsay, isn't it? What value would it be for me to tell something somebody else said if there is no way to back it up?

"You look a million miles away."

"Sorry."

"There is one other thing we need to talk about."

"What is that?"

"Be careful with Ben, Kyla. We don't know what has been done to him. But no matter what that may mean, he isn't the boy you used to know. Without his memories from when you knew him, he's changed."

"He's still Ben."

"Not as he was, but we'll see what we can find out with some scans when we can arrange it. It seems like they've used a Slating-type procedure, but less drastic. His personal memories are gone, but general things like judgment remain, so independent thought and action are possible. Makes them more useful to Lorders as agents, but perhaps also more able to break free from their control, like Ben has."

I don't say anything. I got through to him, didn't I? Somewhere inside is my Ben; I'll reach him, somehow. I have to.

"Enough for one day? We've organized a room for you, but you'll have to share it with a student. I'll show you," Aiden says. I follow him out the door, down a corridor.

"What is this place?"

"All Souls College. It's one of the Oxford colleges."

"I thought the University of Oxford was Lorder-controlled?"

"It is officially, but that is part of the reason we're here, hiding in plain sight; under their own noses, they don't look so hard. And All Souls played a large part in convincing the Oxford Conference of Colleges to not take part in the protests decades ago. The Lorder government granted them special privileges of independence as a result; they didn't seem to get that the motivation wasn't pro-Lorder, but to preserve and protect the university. And we've had connections here for years; Florence's grandfather was a research fellow here, and when they changed the rules to admit students as well as fellows, Florence was one of the first. They take alumni ties very seriously. When we needed help, their governing body voted to provide it."

"The college voted on it?" I'm aghast. "That is a lot of people who know MIA is here."

"Every research fellow and student in the place."

"So much risk to them all." To us if one of them can't keep their mouth shut.

"Yes. We need to get out of here as soon as we can. The only way is to get our evidence released as soon as possible; then we can scatter, go into hiding until things settle down." We reach another door; he knocks once. The girl who let me in when I first arrived opens it. "This is Wendy," he says. "Sleep well."

She shuts the door behind us. It is an irregularly shaped room, with bookshelf-lined stone walls crammed with history books. Two narrow beds. A wardrobe and a long desk with two chairs.

"That one is yours," she says, pointing at the bed by the drafty window. She shows me the bathrooms down the hall, lends me a towel and a change of clothes. Curiosity lurks behind her eyes, but she asks nothing.

Self-preservation had me fight against helping MIA for so long, until I could see it was the only way. What makes all these college students, like Wendy, risk their lives for us, when they don't even know who we are?

Wendy studies while I shower, then pretend to sleep, curled up against the cold. I wonder where Ben's room is, if he sleeps, if he dreams. Despite the danger we're in if the Lorders find us, his closeness is like a drug. Does someone watch his chest rise and fall, even through the night?

What was it Florence said? She doubts even Ben knows what makes him tick. He doesn't know much about who he was, but how can he find out if they keep him under lock and key? I have to remind him.

I'll find a way.

27

NEXT MORNING COMES EARLY WITH A TAP AT THE DOOR. I open my eyes; Wendy is gone, and Florence is peeking through the door.

"You can't sleep all day; there are things to do. Ten minutes and I'll be back."

I rush down the hall for a quick wash and put on a top and jeans borrowed from Wendy. Not a bad fit, but too long—I roll up the bottoms.

Florence returns, comes in, and shuts the door. "Aiden tells me you've expressed a desire to join MIA." One eyebrow raised ever so slightly shows doubt.

"I want to help," I say, a little nervous what help may entail with Florence involved.

"Well, you're going to get your chance. We've got a few witnesses I'm having trouble getting stories out of. He suggested you might be some help. Apparently, my bedside manner sucks."

I struggle not to smirk. "You can be a little confrontational."

"Well, so what? I'm not a nurse or a doctor!" Then she half laughs. "I'll show you where to get some breakfast, arrange your ID. They are issued by the college; keep it on you at all times. Then Aiden will take you and Ben later this morning."

"Ben?"

"Aiden thinks spending time with you might tap his hidden depths."

She rolls her eyes, then focuses on me closely. "There is a condition. You're in charge. If Ben does or says anything that worries you, or would worry us, you have to tell Aiden or me. Okay?"

"Agreed."

"What do you want me to do?" Ben says while I fiddle with my camera, set it to record mode.

"Anything. I just want to make sure I know how to use it. Ready?"

"Go for it."

I hit the start button, look through the camera at Ben. He's leaning back on his end of the sofa, smiling, a little self-conscious, but there is still something about the *way* he is smiling that makes it hard to remember what I'm doing. *Check the sound.*

"Say something."

"Something!"

"Very funny. Tell me who you are, and what you are thinking."

"I'm Ben," he says, and leans forward. "And I'm thinking how gorgeous you are, and that even if I can't remember before, I had great taste in girls."

My stomach flutters, gentle butterfly wings inside.

He smirks. "Try to hold the camera steady."

"Sorry. I was blond back then, you know; I look really different now."

Ben reaches out a hand, touches my hair, and I give up and lower the camera. He moves closer and looks into my eyes; the butterfly from earlier has friends, is taking over, and I can't breathe. I'm gripped by two competing emotions: wanting to pull away from the stranger and move closer to the Ben I knew and loved at the same time.

The door opens, and we bolt apart.

"Ready to go?" It's Aiden.

We get up, walk to the door.

"One suggestion?" Ben says in a low voice.

"What's that?"

"When you're finished, remember to stop the recording," he says, and I hurriedly hit the stop button.

I check the footage in the car on the way. It worked fine; the autofocus kept Ben in sharp focus, and his voice is clear.

Aiden comes with us to the door of a house, introduces us, says he'll be back in a while, and leaves.

So Ben and I find ourselves in the front room of Edie's house with her and her mother. Edie is five, and, according to Florence, saw Lorders shoot her brother in a park. He was nine. Her mother wants her to testify; she says Edie wants to, too, but whenever anyone has tried to record her or even just ask her questions, she has clammed up.

I feel in way over my head; Ben is also awkward and making small talk with Edie's mother while I try to work out what to say, how to even bring up the subject of why we're here. Edie is small and silent, pulled into herself on a chair. It's like there are too many eyes and she is trying to hide.

"How about you show me your room?" I say to Edie.

She looks at her mum. "It's okay, sweetie," she says, and Edie takes my hand, pulls me toward the stairs. I motion at Ben to stay with her mother.

"It's here," she says, and pushes the door open, but as I follow her in she turns and faces me.

"Are you here to ask me stuff?"

"I'm supposed to. But maybe I won't. Because, you know, you don't have to say anything if you don't want to."

"I don't?" she says, eyes wide in surprise.

"No. Absolutely. It's up to you, no matter what anybody else says. Because I'm in charge, and I'm very bossy."

"Murray's like that." She nods very seriously.

"Who is Murray?"

She walks over to her bed, picks up a floppy teddy bear.

"He doesn't look bossy; he looks sleepy."

She giggles. "He's bossy if anyone tries to wake him up. Jack was like that, too."

"Jack was your brother?"

"Yeah." Her smile fades, and she pulls the bear in close against her.

I know why we're here. A little girl with a sad tale: good for public sympathy, like Florence said. But making her go there if she doesn't want to is just plain *wrong*.

"We don't have to talk about Jack."

"Nobody talks about him anymore. They whisper. But Mummy wants me to tell you; she said it might help stop it from happening to somebody else's brother. But I couldn't say anything before."

"Why?"

"Because Mummy was listening. It makes her too sad."

"Oh, I see. How about if just Murray listens?"

She tilts her head to one side. "That might be okay. I can tell Murray anything."

"Are you really, really sure you want to?"

She raises an eyebrow, gives me a look that is way over five. "You're not very good at your job, are you?"

With that, we're soon ready. Murray helps me hold the camera. She looks straight at him. Tells him that her brother kicked a ball that hit a Lorder. When he refused to give it back, Jack chased them. That the Lorder took out a gun. Pulled the trigger.

I'm not sure I held the camera steady enough.

Back at the college that afternoon, we check the footage with Florence.

"I don't know how you managed to get her to open up like that," she says.

I shrug. "Partly I told her she didn't have to unless she wanted to. Partly she couldn't talk about it in front of her mother, but could in front of her teddy bear."

"You've got yourself a job," Florence says.

"What will happen to Edie and her mother when this footage is released? Shouldn't they be in hiding, not left in their home?"

"We offered. Edie's mother wants to stay with her extended family for now. Some do. When we're ready to release the evidence, we'll warn them and take them in then."

"Can you hide everyone? Can everyone be safe?" I persist, unable to get Edie's serious face talking to her teddy bear out of my mind.

"We'll do what we can," Florence says shortly, with a glance at Ben. "See you at dinner?"

Dismissed.

Later, Ben and I wander around one of the internal quads of All Souls College: a gray expanse of dead grass on a cold, gray day. Ancient college buildings rise on all sides, windows like eyes, and I'm suddenly aware of both exposure and confinement. Anyone could be looking down on us, trapped in this place.

"Can we talk?" Ben asks, and I realize how quiet he has been, before with Florence and since.

"How about there?" I say, gesturing to a bench tucked against a wall, and we head there, sit down. "What is it?"

Ben runs his hand through his hair. "How can you believe what that little girl said?"

"What do you mean?"

He shakes his head. "That came out wrong. What I meant is that it is hard to believe anything like that could ever happen; that a Lorder would kill a child just for . . ." And he shrugs.

"Just for being a child?" I snort. "They do that and much worse all the time."

"How do you know, when people tell you stuff, if it's real or not?" His eyes are intent, troubled; joking Ben is gone.

"Why would a child lie?"

"She could have been told to."

"No." I shake my head. "I was looking into her eyes; she was telling the truth. Anyhow, I've seen as bad or worse myself, so I know."

"Even if you see things yourself, how can you *know* what is behind what you see?" Ben's eyes are skeptical.

"Look, I'll show you." And I tell him the story of the Cumbrian orphanage, the Slated children. Get him to look into the camera at a photo of three smiling young boys with unnatural still expressions, silver glinting at their wrists.

"But how do you know those are Levos?"

"It was obvious they were Slated, from the way they were acting. There was no other explanation."

"But couldn't they have been coached to act like that?"

"Four-year-olds aren't great actors. And why would anyone bother?"

"To make Lorders—the government—look bad."

"Well, how about this then?" And I tell him about Phoebe, a girl we both knew from our school, taken and Slated without charge or trial just for making offhand comments about Slateds being spies. About my art teacher, Gianelli, hauled off in front of the whole school when all he did was draw Phoebe and have an impromptu minute of silence for her. About the termination center, where Lorders killed Slated contract breakers by injection and dumped them into the ground. And about Emily, killed by her Levo just because she was in love, having a baby, and not quite twenty-one and out of her sentence. I shy away from telling the rest of the story: that I was there with the AGT, attacking the center.

Ben is quiet, drawn in.

"There is one more story. Do you want to hear it, or have you had enough?"

"Go ahead; tell me."

"There was a friend of yours at school, another Slated: Tori. Her mother got tired of her taking attention and had her returned to the Lorders. She hadn't done anything wrong. She was taken to that termination center I mentioned, and saw with her own eyes other . . ." My words trail away. "What is it? Do you remember Tori?" I'm stung; he doesn't remember *me,* but something crossed his face with the mention of Tori's name. He'd always said she wasn't ever his girlfriend, but she loved him, and she was one of the most beautiful girls I'd ever seen.

"Of course I don't remember her," he says, but his face is guarded, uncertain. "It's just . . . hard to hear all these sad tales. Tell me what happened to Tori."

"She saw other Slateds killed by injection, dumped into the ground.

And then . . ." I trail off. Ben's look of confusion is gone; is there a flash of something *else*? What is it? "Look: These are all things I saw. Some of them you did, too. Don't you believe me?"

"I just . . ." And then, as if a switch is flipped inside, he smiles and takes my hand. "Of course I do."

"One day I'll show you Emily's ring; I hid it in a tree a few miles from home. It's real. Don't you see, Ben; it is all their stories that make what we are doing with MIA so important. They are worth risking everything—to make them heard. To make it stop."

He hesitates, slips his arm across my shoulders, and I lean against him, so aware of *him,* his warmth and closeness, that it is hard to continue to think straight.

Ben points out a tower visible over the roofs of All Souls. "See, up there? That is one of the tallest buildings in Oxford. St. Mary's Church tower. The views are meant to be amazing. I want to go up there with you."

"Okay; I'll ask if we—"

"No. Keep it as our secret; our special place. Leave it until I'm allowed out without a tail."

Later, I mull over our conversation, what Ben said, the things he didn't say flitting behind his eyes. I wonder if this is the kind of stuff Florence meant I should tell them. But that isn't fair. He's had his memory taken away; he's figuring out the world, how it works, what happens in it. He has to ask questions to do that, doesn't he?

But one point of discomfort niggles inside: He reacted to Tori's name, I'm sure he did. Of course I never told him the *rest* of her story. That I was in the AGT as Rain; that Tori escaped from the Lorders and joined, too. And then there was the day that I was followed by Lorders and Tori was captured.

I shudder. I'll never forget the pure hatred on her face, and it wasn't just because she thought I betrayed the AGT; she'd found out from Nico I knew Ben was alive, and I didn't tell her. The venom in the words she screamed before being thrown in the back of a Lorder van rings in my ears even now: *Traitor! Kyla, or Rain, or whoever you are, I'll get you. I'll hunt you down and gut you with my knife.*

There is part of me that is relieved the Lorders caught her, that she'll never get a chance for her revenge. There is another part that is ashamed for thinking so.

28

"FANCY A ROAD TRIP?" AIDEN SAYS, GRINNING, THE NEXT
morning. "No need for crouching in the back of a telephone van this
time; I've borrowed a rather impressive car."

"Sure! Where to?"

"It's a surprise. But it'll be just us and Florence today," he says, and
I bite back my disappointment: no Ben. Now that the sun is up, last
night's worries seem foolish. Ben couldn't remember Tori; it doesn't
make sense. I must have been projecting my jealousy and imagined
his reaction. That is all.

The car is plush and powerful, borrowed from an unnamed fellow
at the college. An hour later we're past Oxford and driving through
country fields, then heading down a long lane to a farm.

"Are we here to see another witness?" I ask as we get out of the car.

"Not today," Florence says. "Come on."

She knocks once on the door, pulls a key out of her pocket, and
opens it. She walks in, Aiden and me behind her, and calls out,
"Hello?"

"Ah, there you are at last." In the doorway to the kitchen stands a
man I'm very surprised to see—what is he doing here? I know the
face, but the rest has changed.

"DJ?"

"Yes, 'tis I." He grins. "And there you are, Kyla; your hair is some of
my best work."

"You've changed. No more purple?"

"That is *so* last week." Today the IMET doctor looks more tiger stripes, both hair and eyes. "Did you forget your glasses?"

"I kind of lost them; sorry."

"There may be something else you forgot."

I look guiltily between DJ and Aiden. "Oh no. I was supposed to tell Aiden you wanted to see him! I'm sorry. Was it a problem?"

"Nice to see how reliable you are," Florence snipes.

"No dramas," DJ says. "It gave me some time to look into things a bit more before we talked about it. To look into *you* a bit more."

"What do you mean?"

"You, my dear, are getting curiouser and curiouser. Like Alice down the rabbit hole, nothing is as it appears."

"I don't understand."

"When we were mucking with your hair genes, we had to do a certain amount of looking at your DNA. I'm connected to Lorder systems as much as is necessary to sort out if people are who they say they are; it is a safety precaution as much as anything else."

"And?"

"At lower system levels, your DNA is marked as unknown. At upper levels it gets more interesting: It is listed as *classified*."

"What does that mean?" I ask.

"Not a clue, but I love a good mystery. And that isn't all. There is coded protection on files relating to it, and not just any code; so high up I haven't been able to bribe anyone to crack them."

All three of them are looking at me, and I cross my arms. "You don't think I know anything about it."

"Of course not. But you know something, don't you?" DJ's eyes are so weird: brown and amber stripes on orange. I can't look away.

"Why does this matter, anyhow?"

DJ shrugs. "To be honest? It may not matter. But—and it is a big one—it has been my experience that when Lorders try very hard to hide something, it is important to find it. Anything they don't want known, I want to know."

Aiden comes to sit next to me, slips my hand in his. "Kyla? Do you know anything that might help?"

"I might."

"It's okay to say anything in front of DJ. He's one of us."

I sigh. "Look. The main thing I know is that I don't have a clue who I am. Happy?"

"Hang on," Aiden says. "I'm not understanding this. Didn't you just meet your mother in Keswick? Actually, wouldn't her DNA be classi-fied, then, too—whatever that means?"

"Aiden, I was going to tell you about this, but I haven't had a chance to talk to you properly. She's not my mother."

"What? She reported you missing on MIA. All the records show her as your mother."

I shake my head. "Her baby died; I was given to her as a replace-ment. She doesn't know where I came from."

"Given by whom?" DJ asks.

I swallow. "Her mother. Astrid Connor. She's the JCO for all of England. Stella—that's my adopted mother," I say for the benefit of Florence and DJ, "thinks Astrid might have gotten me from the or-phanage there, but doesn't know for sure."

"So that's why you were nosing about the orphanage," Florence says.

I nod.

"And so the curiosity continues," DJ says. "If that is true, why would an orphaned baby have classified DNA? And you would have been tested at school, at your medical center: Why didn't it get registered then?"

"You tell me." I shrug.

"What *else* haven't you told us?" Florence demands.

"Sorry I wasn't bragging about not knowing who my parents are; is that okay? For all I know, I could have been abandoned, unwanted. I couldn't see how it was important to anybody but me."

Aiden raises a hand. "She's right, Flo. This is personal stuff. Kyla didn't have to tell us; it's her choice."

Not that I was given much choice today. "What do you think it means?" I ask DJ, who has been very quiet, little wheels of thought spinning behind his eyes. Or is that just the tiger stripes?

"I don't know. But something tells me we had better find out."

I drop my head in my hands. Stella hadn't sworn me to secrecy about where I came from, but sometimes you don't have to have said the words "I promise" to know that you've broken one. But what about the rest of her secrets? I *definitely* promised Stella I wouldn't tell anyone about Astrid being behind the assassinations; without evidence, what use would the information be to MIA, anyhow?

"Kyla?" Aiden's hand is on my shoulder. "Are you all right?"

"There's more she's not telling us," Florence snaps. "What is it?"

Aiden asks the others to leave us alone.

"What is it, Kyla?" he asks, once they are gone and the door is shut.

"I don't know what to do."

"I can't help you if you don't tell me more than that."

"It's Stella. There is something else she told me—it's not about who I am or anything like that, but it's important. And I promised not to tell."

"That's a tough call. All I can really say is that you should do what you feel is right, in here." He pats his stomach. "Go with your gut." He hesitates. "Is not knowing going to hurt anyone?"

I shake my head. "It's ancient history. Besides, there's no way to back it up; it's hearsay."

"What do you think you should do?"

"I think I need to think about it some more. How did you get to be so understanding?"

"It's all part of being a superhero," he teases, and I remember I called him that, ages ago. When he found Ben hidden away at that Lorder place; Aiden the superhero, helping people find those they care about. Trying to set the world to rights.

I'd thought he was a no-hoper on the last one. But more and more I am *hoping,* clinging to strands of future possibility, that things might be fixed by MIA *without* using guns and bombs. That he and the others can really do it.

That *we* can do it.

"Thank you," I say. "For everything."

His eyes hold mine, warm, and for a moment it is hard to breathe. Then he shakes his head, looks away, and calls the others back in.

"Well?" Florence demands.

"That's enough for today," Aiden says. Florence protests; Aiden replies, "We don't work like that; we're not Lorders. She can tell us when she's ready, *if* she's ready. I'm satisfied it's not critical to us now."

And I'm scouring my brain, looking for something, anything, that might help, and then I have it. "Wait a minute. There is somebody who might know something about my DNA."

"Who's that?" DJ asks.

"I always thought there was something she wasn't telling me, something she was hiding, but I don't know. Maybe I imagined it."

"Who?"

"My doctor at the hospital. Dr. Lysander."

Aiden's eyes sharpen. "She was your doctor?"

"Yes. She said it was on my records that I was a Jane Doe; that even though everyone is supposed to be DNA-tested at birth, they didn't know where I came from. She said that was all she knew about it, but there was something hiding behind her words. She never lied, exactly, but she hid things by twisting words around."

"*The* Dr. Lysander—the very doctor who invented Slating—was your doctor?" DJ says. "Interesting. I bet that wasn't a coincidence. But why would she tell you anything about your records?"

"We were sort of close. She told me loads of things she shouldn't have. Broke rules to help me."

"We need to talk to her."

"She's always surrounded by guards, and the hospital is a fortress."

"If we can get you to her, will you do it? See if you can find out what she knows?"

"Of course."

Aiden protests. She is a Lorder doctor; however close I thought we were, it would be too dangerous.

I shake my head. "She wouldn't turn me in. Never."

In the car on the way back to Oxford, I sit in the back, staring unseeing out the window. Pondering other coincidences.

What did seeing Astrid and Nico together really mean? How did

I end up with the family of the assassinated prime minister after I was Slated? My two families—Mum and Amy, Stella and Astrid—somehow their histories and what may yet come to be are entwined and twisted together, with me caught between. Yet neither family is truly mine.

Everything is crowding in on me; there is only one solution.

I need to run.

29

"BET YOU CAN'T KEEP UP," BEN SAYS.

"Oh yeah?"

Ben takes off up the path, and I'm on his heels. It's too narrow to run side by side, but at last we are doing something that until recently I thought could never happen again: We are running together. It's cold, dark enough that running full tilt on an unfamiliar path is a little dangerous, but he has set the pace. There is no way I'll let him pull ahead.

It used to be we'd run to get our levels up; endorphins from running would have them high, even in the 8s. We could talk about anything without risking a Levo zap from dropping levels sending us off to a blackout.

So much has changed since then. Neither of us has a Levo anymore; we don't need to run to stay level, but today, I needed it. Yet I was surprised that Aiden said all right, that he let us leave the college grounds together. Maybe, he understands. Maybe he understands too much.

There is a sudden *thud* in front; a cry. Ben flies through the air, lands heavily, and I almost trip over him.

"Ouch," he says.

"Are you all right?"

"I think so." He twists his foot from side to side. "Yeah, it's fine. Just caught it and fell over, not sprained."

I give him a hand up, and he brushes himself off. "Let's walk a little," he says.

"Sure you're not hurt?"

"I'm fine. Was it a tough day that made you want a run?" Ben asks. He takes my hand in his as we walk up the path.

"You could say that."

"Want to talk about it?"

I stay silent a moment. "Do you mind if we don't?"

He stops walking, pulls me around toward him, his eyes dark pools in the moonlight. "Talking is one option. There is another." One hand slips around my waist, the other under my chin. And it is as if I'm in two places, here, and another: the first time he kissed me. It was at night after running, and so like this that my mind is here and there at the same time, drifting, falling between past and present, between the Ben I knew, and the Ben I don't. And then I'm shaking and crying.

He pulls away. "What's wrong?"

"I don't know. Who are you? Who am I? What does this mean?"

"That's way too much thought." He smiles. "Stop thinking." And he kisses me again, and again, until the past is gone, the tears are gone, and we are here. Now. There is nothing else.

We sneak back in late. Ben holds my hand tight; I protest when we get to a corridor and he pulls me the wrong way. "My room is the other way."

"No, you're coming back with me. We still have some talking to do."

Another corridor and a turn, some stairs. Ben still holds my hand. It's late and I'm tired, but every bit of me is *alive.* Talking?

"Now for the 'be quiet' bit," he whispers. He opens a door, peers in.

Someone is fast asleep on a bed in the dark; we creep past him to another door. Ben opens it. "Wait in here," he whispers. "I'll tell my jailer I've returned so he doesn't check if he wakes up."

I step through the door; he shuts it behind me, and I'm plunged into darkness.

There are low voices through the door; then it opens and Ben steps through. "Give him five minutes and he'll be out like a light," Ben whispers, pulls me close. Kisses my cheek, my neck, and I can hear my heart going *thud-thud* so loud I worry the student through the door will hear.

But then Ben lets go, turns, and puts on a small desk light. Darkness retreats, reveals a small student room. Desk, wardrobe.

Single bed.

"Ben, I should go."

"You're not escaping that easily." He smiles, pushes me down to sit on the bed, sits next to me. "We need to talk."

"Talk?"

He grins a wicked grin. "Talking is one option," he says, and takes my hand. "Tell me. Why were you so upset before?"

"It's a long story."

"I've got nothing but time."

And once I begin, it all comes flooding out—all I've wanted to tell him for so long. Inside me, things are letting go with the words, loosening and coming free. Ben wraps a blanket around us against the cold, just holds me while I talk, and cry, and talk some more. I even tell him that I don't know where I come from, about being kidnapped by the AGT and what they did. Why I was Slated, and what happened after he was gone. I tell him about Stella, but not about her mother and the assassinations; that isn't my story to tell.

Finally Ben says, "Enough. I have a question. With all of that, why is it that what really upset you earlier was my kissing you?"

I shake my head. "No, that wasn't it. That was lovely." I blush. "It's this: How can we be anything together when we don't know who we are?"

He shakes his head. "I haven't any idea where I come from, either, or anything of what happened before I was Slated, so you're ahead of me on that. At least you know who raised you. But it doesn't matter."

"It doesn't?"

"No. Kyla, all we are is what we are, here and now."

And he kisses me again, and that *is* all that matters. Now. But a little voice inside knows that in the morning, the sun will come up. Tomorrow will come one way or the other.

30

I'M WARM, IN A DARK, SLEEPY HAPPY PLACE. THERE WAS something: a sound? A click. I stir, then remember where I am.

I sit up fast. Light is coming through under the curtains just enough to see. Ben is turned away, putting something in the wardrobe.

"Ben?"

He whips around. Smiles. "You look cute all sleepy."

"It's morning? I didn't mean to fall asleep! I need to get out of here before anyone notices."

He shrugs. "Stay. Who cares?" He slips a hand around my chin, kisses me, but I pull away.

"I care." I slip to the door, open it quietly. The student outside is sound asleep.

"He's a crap guard," Ben whispers. "He could sleep through *any-thing.*" He kisses my cheek. "See you here tonight?"

His eyes hold mine, and somehow the words come out without any thought or volition. "All right."

I get down the halls without seeing anyone, and to my door. Open it.

Wendy is at her desk. She turns, smirks. "Good run with Ben last night?"

"We were just talking, and I fell asleep!"

She laughs. "Sure, I believe you." She winks. "Don't worry. Your secret is safe with me."

I protest a few more times, cheeks burning, then head for the shower. Will she keep it to herself? Why does it even matter? Somehow I don't want it known I was out all night, for things to be assumed.

Something nags inside. Mostly it's that I don't want Aiden to find out, and I'm not sure why. He had Ben brought here; he must know how I feel about him. Yet somehow I know Aiden wouldn't like it if he knew I'd been in Ben's room all night; he's protective, and he'd worry. And he is the last person I want to hurt, after all he's done for me. That is the only reason I don't want him to know. Isn't it?

The day passes. Florence takes me out to record some more witnesses; adults this time, so not as hard as the last, but their stories still tear inside. Ben isn't with us, as they've finally found a doctor to take him to who will do scans without asking questions. And after each witness I'm telling myself *just get through the day.* Then I can be with Ben.

When Florence and I get back to the college, as we walk across the quad I stare up at the St. Mary's tower, where Ben wanted to go. "Can you go up there—up the tower?"

"Sure. If anyone from the church is there, just smile and flash your student ID. It's thirteenth century; check out the gargoyles. Great views."

We get to the office, and I fidget impatiently while Florence copies today's recordings from my camera to a computer.

"What's with you?" she asks.

"Nothing."

She looks skeptical, but before she can say anything else, the door opens: Aiden.

"Kyla? Are you done? I need a quick word."

Florence hands me my camera. "All finished. Away you go."

Aiden holds the door open; I step through, heart sinking. Has he heard something about last night? No. His eyes are sparking. "Quick, grab whatever you need until tomorrow; we're off on an adventure."

"Where are we going?"

"To see Dr. Lysander."

"But how—"

"No time for questions; you can ask on the way. Don't tell anyone! Meet me out back in five minutes. Go!"

I race to my room to grab a few things. Wendy isn't there, so I can't ask her to tell Ben I had to go out. I can't leave a note with Aiden's "tell no one" ringing in my ears; there is no time to run to his room, if he's even in it.

As I rush to meet Aiden, I wonder: Is Ben going to think I stood him up?

"How are we going to get to Dr. Lysander? She's always guarded."

"Bit of luck on that one. DJ found out she's speaking at a medical conference tomorrow; we've got connections in the conference center, so can get in to where she's staying. We hear she refuses guards in her own quarters, so they stay outside the door. We've checked the room for bugs and cameras; it's clean."

"So what is going to happen?"

"We get you in there tonight; she's arriving early in the morning. She's got a few hours' scheduled rest time before the conference starts."

"Which is when I make an appearance."

"Exactly. Kyla, there isn't much we can do if she sets off the alarm."

"She won't. But I still don't understand why we're going to all this effort to find out about *me*. Even if she knows where I came from, which I doubt, how could it possibly matter?"

"Not a clue. DJ's really pushing on this, and we're going along with it."

"Who is he?"

Aiden glances at me sideways. "Even I don't know his real name."

"That's not what I mean. How does he fit into MIA? I figured he just helped with changing identities like he did with me. But there is more to it, isn't there?"

Aiden laughs. "It's on a need—"

"—to-know basis." I roll my eyes and try another tack. "Is he from Ireland?"

"That you can get from the accent, so I'm guessing it is okay to say yes." Aiden hesitates. "There is international support behind MIA, not just from United Ireland. They know some of what goes on here from people who we've snuck out of the UK, and there is international pressure to get all the hidden stories out, to make them public and do it soon. They want to stop the human rights violations. This is why the Lorder attack on our computer systems was timed so badly; it's held things up."

I stare out the window. Why would people in other countries far from us care about our human rights, when almost everyone here seems to turn away and pretend not to see? "I don't think that is what is most important. It should be about taking the wool off everyone's eyes *here*. Making them face up to what is happening in their own country, under their noses, so we can fix it on our own."

"Both are important. But the simple truth is, we can't do it alone, not when the Lorders have all the power. Sometimes you need help."

Aiden turns into a small village, then parks next to a van behind a hall. "This is where we part company until tomorrow," he says. "Are you sure you want to do this?"

"Yes. DJ's reasons for being interested in my origins might be different than mine, but I still want to *know*."

"Be careful," he says, and looks about to say more when the van driver's door opens and a man steps out.

"Evening," he says, nods, and opens the door to the back of the van. Reaches in, hands me a bag. "Clothes. Change into them." And with a wave good-bye to Aiden, I climb into the back.

The van soon lumbers up the road, and I get myself into a uniform in the dim light. Looks like a maid's? There are a few in different sizes, and one seems to fit well enough to not draw attention. There are no windows in the back; we drive perhaps thirty minutes. Then I hear a faint beep and we drop down and around a circular ramp. The van stops, and I'm starting to feel nervous. What is this place? I don't know what I'm doing. If anyone asks me anything, or—

The door opens.

"There you are, lass. Now don't worry about a thing, it's all worked out. I'm taking you up tonight as no one is around until tomorrow. Best leave your coat and other things there in the van; they'll be fine there until the morning."

I take my coat off, extract the camera from a deep pocket. Maybe I should have left it back at the college, but something tells me I'll need it to get anywhere with Dr. Lysander. There's a pocket in the uniform, and I slip it in.

I follow him through the underground lot to an elevator. He calls the elevator with a key, and it is there in seconds. Up we go. "No one should get on, but if anyone does, nod but say nothing. I'll handle it," he says.

I hold my breath, but the elevator doesn't stop until the selected floor. The doors open, he peers through, then gestures for me to follow.

We go down a plush hall, where all the doors have wire taped across them.

"What is that?"

"Security-sealed electronic tape; the rooms were checked, cleared, and sealed a short time ago."

Then he opens a door at the end that leads to a narrow hall with little doors all along. He counts them and stops at one. "This is the service hatch into your friend's room; they are normally used for breakfasts and so on. Listen very carefully. You can't open these with the electronics on without setting off an alarm." He glances at his watch. "The electronics will go off shortly for one minute, the maximum possible without setting the alarms off. It should be just long enough to open it and for you to climb through into her room. I checked that you were a little lass; I couldn't do it. Once through, make yourself comfortable; there are spare blankets and pillows in the wardrobe. Stay out of sight of the door. Your friend is due tomorrow between seven and seven thirty A.M., and you don't want anyone to see you when she comes in and they bring her luggage. Speak to her, then come back out the same way at exactly eight A.M. The electronics will be switched off at exactly eight A.M. for one minute, and that is it. Here is a watch for you—it is coordinated with the hotel system so the time is exact. Understand?"

"Yes," I say, slipping the watch onto my wrist. It is digital, with hours, minutes, seconds shown by a faint green pulsing light.

He is watching his own watch, hurriedly explaining how the

service hatches work. Telling me not to touch the windows or doors in the room, as they're all alarmed.

"It's time," he says, and yanks doors at the back of the hatch open; it's like a mini elevator. I climb through into a small box, struggle to open the door on the other side when there isn't enough room to extend my arms properly, and manage to pry it open.

"Hurry," he says.

I crawl through; the doors swing shut.

"Good luck, child." His voice is faint on the other side.

My heart is beating way too fast; that wasn't easy to do in a minute. I'm sitting on the plushly carpeted floor in Dr. Lysander's soon-to-be room, wishing I'd asked more questions—like can I turn on the light? Is there anything to eat?

I feel my way around the darkened room. Large bed. Desk. Chair. Wardrobe. I open that and feel along the bottom. Under the promised pillows and blankets, my fingers curve around something cold and round, with a switch: a flashlight. I flick it on.

"Thank you, mystery man," I whisper to myself. I explore the room again with the flashlight carefully angled down, and decide the only place I feel safe is actually inside the thankfully huge wardrobe. What if I fall asleep and don't wake up until she arrives?

I arrange the pillows on the wardrobe floor, settle onto it with the blanket. I try with the door shut, but it feels too enclosed, so I push it ajar. I'm sure I'll wake before she gets here; I'm not convinced I'll sleep at all.

For a while I stare at the wall, imagining what I can say to Dr. Lysander to get her to tell me everything she knows about me, rehearsing the words. Finally I close my eyes. What is Ben doing now? I bite my lip; I hope he doesn't think I'm avoiding him, or don't want to be there. Would anyone tell him where I am if he asks?

I slip into uneasy dreams, of wardrobes: Stella's wardrobes, full of photos and tissue-wrapped memories; college student wardrobes with narrow spaces, too small to hide in. *Click . . . switch.*

31

THE LOW THUD OF A DOOR; FOOTSTEPS.

I open my eyes with a start, glad to see I'd pulled the wardrobe shut in the night.

"Yes, just put it there. Thank you." Dr. Lysander's voice? Another voice, male, asking if she needs anything. "No, thank you; just some peace and quiet." But you can't always get what you want.

A door shuts, and there are footsteps in the room.

I struggle to shake sleep from my mind; it had been late when I finally drifted off. I squint at the digital numbers on the watch. 7:40? Oh no. She's late. We haven't much time.

But I stay silent, unmoving. What if I'm wrong and when she sees me she raises the alarm? She wouldn't do that, not after everything we've been through. Would she?

I listen very intently to make sure she's alone. There is a faint zipping noise—a suitcase?

It's now or never.

I nudge the door open and peer through the slit, just in time to see she is approaching; the door is pulled open.

"Dr. Lysander?" She jumps about a foot in the air. "It's me, it's Kyla."

"What?" She is half poised to run the other way, to her door, but looks, really looks at me this time. I hold my hands out to show I'm unarmed.

Her eyes are wide, face pale, but otherwise she looks the same as always: thick glasses, long dark hair tied back, with maybe a few more gray streaks than it had before. Eyes that can see through me. She takes one of my hands to pull me up from the wardrobe. I stand next to her.

"Kyla?" She smiles. "It really is you? Your hair. But it's you!" And she does something she has never done before: pulls me close for a quick hug. Then, like she realizes what she's done, releases me just as quickly.

"They told me you were dead."

"I'm sorry about that. I'm fine."

"Why would they do that?" She shakes her head. "How are you here, hiding in my room? What is going on?"

"I haven't got very much time. I need to ask you a few things, but first I'll tell you where I've been." I realized last night, if I don't tell her what I found out, why I want to know, she'll never reveal what she didn't before. I have to give her a reason, and do what we always did: trade information.

"I went to who I thought was my mother. From before I was Slated. You know how I told you the AGT took me at a young age? I was kidnapped from my mother when I was ten. I went and found her, to get to know her again. But not long after getting there, I found out she wasn't actually my mother."

"Explain."

"She was given me as a baby after her own died, and raised me from then to age ten. She doesn't know where I came from. Her mother is a JCO and gave me to her, so it may have been from an orphanage. Before I could find out any more, my cover got blown, and I had to leave in a hurry." This is the part of the story I'd struggled to formulate. I can't tell her details of where I am now or who with; I can take risks with myself, but not with those who've helped me. "Since then, I've been with friends. One of them found out that at higher security levels, I'm not a Jane Doe: My DNA is classified. Who am I? Tell me if you know anything; I have to know."

She looks back at me carefully, considering. "Why do you need to know?"

"Wouldn't you want to know who you were if you found out you were adopted?"

She shrugs. "Maybe less than you. My family was never close, and often difficult. Why seek out another?" She touches my hair. "IMET, isn't it." A statement, not a question. "Is this where the DNA came into it? I'm worried about you, Kyla. How much trouble are you in? Can you come back from it? Does learning more help, or hinder? What do your new *friends* really want with you? Are they any better for you than your AGT friends turned out to be?"

I'm so frustrated, I want to scream. As usual, she's homed in on the one thing I won't talk about: my friends. I breathe deeply. "You must know by now how wrong the system you are part of is. But in case you don't, I'm going to show you." I need to shock her, to *make* her help me. It was the only way I could think to do so.

I pull the camera out of my pocket. "You know how I said I may have come from an orphanage? I went to look at the local one. Don't know why." I shrug. "It's not like I was going to recognize a place I left when I was a baby. It was isolated, fenced in. I snuck in close, and this is what I found." I open the camera folder, project the image of the small Slated boys.

Her intake of breath is sharp. "These children, so young? No. Slating is not for them. Who would do this? Where is this place? Tell me," she demands, her face coldly furious.

"Lorders have done this, and they are doing it. There were about fifty children I saw." I glance at my watch: 7:51. "The other thing I found out is that this JCO, the mother of the woman who raised me, had something to do with the AGT and having me taken. Please. I've told you all I know about it. I have to leave at exactly eight or I won't be able to get out. Tell me what you know."

Dr. Lysander is silent a moment, thinking, and I don't press. She finally nods. "I told you before. You were on the hospital records as Jane Doe. There was no mention of being classified; no other information as to your origins at all."

"But there is something else?"

"Yes. A few curious things. Remember when you saw your records on the hospital system? Where the hospital board had recommended termination; it said I overruled." She shrugged. "I don't have the power to overrule the hospital board, and, in any case, never tried to do so. It happened at a higher level; somebody made sure you were kept alive. Also there was more interference and care at times; the longer stay in the hospital and the Watchers you had at night are examples. They were above the entitlement of assistance. Someone was meddling, and it had my curiosity."

"Is that why you took special interest in me, why I was your patient?"

She inclines her head. "That part of the motivation followed. There was an initial reason, as I've told you before."

"That I remind you of someone you used to know, someone who died in the riots."

"Yes" is all she says, but something else crosses her face in that moment, for seconds only, then is gone.

"When you changed my brain chip number on the computer to make it untraceable, was that at request from someone above?"

Her lips quirk. "No. That was entirely my own moment of insanity.

The Lorders are more interested in you than they should be. I made it harder for them."

"One other thing. My memories—there were things from my childhood coming back when I was at the place I was raised. I was left-handed to age ten, then forced to change, Slated as right-handed. Could my memories be coming back because my handedness was changed?" This was Stella's theory, and asking about this isn't on the list of reasons why DJ got me in here, but last night I knew I had to ask. I may not get this chance again.

She's thinking again. Finally nods. "It's possible that the only inaccessible memories from your Slating were those associated with being right-handed. Others may be suppressed, but accessible in the right circumstances. But this is conjecture. To my knowledge what happened to you hasn't been attempted before, so who can say?"

I'm about to ask her more when her eyes drop to my wrist. "Kyla, your watch says 7:59."

I bolt up and run for the small doors at the service hatch at the back of her room just as my watch changes to eight o'clock. "I'm sorry we can't talk longer," I say, and wrench the doors open, then curse: The car isn't there, and what is between me and the doors on the other side is a chasm that drops far down into darkness. Then the opposite doors open; hands are there to help, and I launch myself across to them. One ankle bangs painfully against the door in Dr. Lysander's room as strong arms drag me across.

"Where was the orphanage you visited?" Dr. Lysander says urgently as I'm pulled through on the other side.

"Cumbria," I say back quietly as the doors close. Unsure if I should or shouldn't say, but there is the trade, as always. She answered another question; so must I.

As I pull myself to my feet, the mini elevator whirs into action; a car in motion is heading this way. That was close. My ankle hurts, and I bend down to check it; a small cut.

"Are you all right?"

"Just a nick; I'm fine."

I follow the van driver back down the hall, listening as he explains what to say if anyone says anything, then we get on the elevator. There are other staff on it, but they smile and nod, and no words are spoken. They get off at another level. We go back to the van in the underground lot.

"Sorry, but you'll have to stay in here, very quietly, until my lunch break. There is some food for you on the seat."

He opens the door, I get in, and it shuts behind me. I change back into my own clothes, then find a sandwich and cookies wrapped up and eat hungrily while I think through all that was said.

Hours later the van driver returns as promised and takes me to a rendezvous with Aiden. On the return to Oxford I tell him what Dr. Lysander said, hoping he or DJ will make more sense of it than I did.

Why would some faceless higher-up capable of overruling the hospital board and everything else they've done be bothered about me? I can't answer the question, but deep in my gut I'm sure of one thing: It can't be good.

Dr. Lysander didn't know what they are doing at that orphanage, that is very clear. I go cold inside, afraid what she will do with the knowledge. Will she end up in even worse trouble than she did the last time, all because of me?

32

"BEN CAME LOOKING FOR YOU LAST NIGHT," WENDY SAYS. "SO I'm guessing you weren't with him all night long this time."

"I wasn't *with* anybody."

"Don't look so fierce, I believe you. Just listen to me a moment."

"What?"

"I know I don't know you very well, and I know enough about why you are here to know I shouldn't ask questions. But be careful."

"What do you mean?"

She hands me an envelope. "Just be careful."

She leaves, and I rip it open.

Ben's handwriting: It looks just as it always did.

Dear Kyla,

My scans were good, so I've been sprung from constant supervision, hurrah! Came by to celebrate last night—where were you?

There is only one way to make it up to me. Meet me at the top of St. Mary's Church tower—the views are supposed to be amazing.

Don't keep me waiting again.

Love, Ben

But there is no time specified on it. Maybe he has already been waiting there for hours!

I scramble for clean clothes, which are in short supply. I borrow a top of Wendy's, leaving an apologetic note behind. Tuck my camera in a coat pocket and slip out of our room, down the hall.

I step out a side door of All Souls and soon find the entrance to the church. Wave my student ID at a warden and get him to point out the way to the tower.

And I start the climb. Stairs in the church, then in the tower, take me ever higher until I reach a narrow spiral staircase. The farther I go up the ancient, worn stone steps, the narrower and steeper the way, and despite wanting to be there *now* I have to slow down, take care.

Finally I reach the top and step out onto the tower platform, into the cold wind. No sign of Ben. The platform is irregular and narrow, enclosed by a stone railing with more stone curving overhead, almost as if the platform has been gouged into the tower. Hugging my arms around myself, I follow the platform all around the tower, ducking into linking tunnels on the way, until I reach a dead end.

No Ben.

Either he was here already, got bored of waiting, and left, or he hasn't come yet. Why didn't I ask Wendy when he gave her that note? If he has been and gone I should go look for him. But then what if he comes back and I'm not here? I decide to wait, and do the circuit again, this time with more of an eye to the views across Oxford, and the gargoyles leaning out with wide gaping mouths as if to swallow buildings below. Finally I huddle against cold stone, shivering and staring at All Souls College. Patches of both quads are visible from here, including the bench where Ben and I sat and spoke.

I'm so happy about Ben's scans being okay, but then start to think about it. What does that mean, exactly? How could scans reassure Florence and Aiden enough to give Ben more clearance? They might show how much of his memory has been mucked with, but won't show what he is thinking. I don't understand. I frown to myself, then my misgivings disappear with the dim echo of approaching feet on the stone steps below.

He's here!

The steps get closer, and my smile, wider. Ben said this was our secret, a special place for us. A new special place, for new memories to replace the old.

But the face that appears in the doorway isn't the one I'm expecting.

"Aiden?"

"Where's Ben?"

"I don't know. What are you doing here?"

"More to the point: What are *you* doing here? You know better, Kyla, than to sneak out without telling anyone where you are going."

"What do you mean, sneaking? I wasn't sneaking! I just . . ." I stop. Once I got the note I was in such a hurry to meet Ben that I didn't think about it. I look closer at Aiden and see what I missed. "Something's wrong. What is it?"

"Ben's guard has been found in a wardrobe. Dead. We're hunting for Ben, but he hasn't been found."

"What? Dead? Has something happened to Ben?"

"Apart from killing his guard, not that I know of. Were you meeting him here?"

"He couldn't have done that, it can't be him. I don't believe you."

He shakes his head. "Tell me everything you know, and do it now."

My knees are shaking; I lean on the stone railing. Ben's guard, dead? That student, the one who could sleep through anything?

"Kyla?"

"Ben left me a note. He told me his scans were okay, that he didn't have to be watched anymore."

"Lies, Kyla. The scan results aren't even back yet."

I hesitate, then pull the note out of my pocket, hand it to Aiden. I swallow. "I don't understand. Why would he lie?"

Aiden reads the note. "I don't know, but nothing I can think of is good."

"Did you follow me here?"

"No. It was a hunch; Florence said you'd asked about coming up here. We need to raise the alarm—"

Bang.

Gunshots? Below, over at All Souls: There are people running across the quad. Dim shouting on the breeze.

No. *No.* This can't be happening.

I whip my camera out to see better with the zoom. "There are figures in black at the exits of All Souls. Lorders."

"Do what you do best, Kyla; be a witness." His words are bitter.

I'm recording. Lorders push all the students and research fellows, and those they were hiding, out from the buildings into one end of the quad. Against a wall. They open fire. There is chaos, screaming; some try to run but don't get far—Lorders guard every exit. But in the midst of it all some stand erect, arms linked; Florence is at their center. Facing the Lorders with calm contempt as they are shot. There are bodies, more bodies. Red stains the ancient stone, the dead grass of winter. Somehow through it all my hands stay steady, recording; a numb witness, as dead inside as those in the quad.

Then there is silence.

Two figures in black guard one of the entrances to the quad near the bench Ben and I were sitting on just days ago. One turns and faces the tower, looks straight at me, as if he knows I stand here, watching. The other slips her arm around his waist. She's laughing.

Ben. And Tori.

33

MY ARMS FINALLY DROP; THE CAMERA IS A WEIGHT. THIS can't be happening. Aiden is silent, his face a mirror of mine: shock. And agony.

Florence.

Wendy.

A whole college of nameless fellows and students who voted to help us: dead.

I stare at the camera in my hands, full of witnesses. Recordings of pain. Ben? No. I can't—he couldn't have . . .

But Ben was standing there, part of this massacre. I can't deny what my own eyes have seen, even as everything inside screams they must be wrong.

I'm a witness like all the others hiding in this camera. The only recording left of them now.

Edie is one of the witnesses—Ben went there with me. He knows where she lives.

Run!

The thought is barely in my mind when my feet are running down the spiral steps.

Aiden clatters behind, calls out to be careful, to wait, but he drops behind. Out in the air and sunshine—how can the sun shine on today?—I run, and Aiden can't keep up, he is gone behind me. No one is in sight at any of the nearby colleges that are part of Oxford University; everyone must be hiding under their beds.

I run the fastest I have ever run. My feet feel like they're not touching the earth; I'm flying, skimming the surface of a world I don't want to be in anymore. But for one child. If I can save one child, somehow I can . . . No. I can't think of an after, or a before. Just *now,* only now. Or I'll stop, won't be able to take another step.

I'm still flying when miles later I reach Edie's street. Then her front door.

Her open front door?

I step through it, gasping for air.

"Hello," I call out, voice ragged. "Edie?"

The lights are on. There are half-eaten plates of food on the table. *No, no, no . . .*

I run from one room to another, all through the house. It is empty. The house is empty.

Except for Murray. He's on the floor in the kitchen. I pick him up, stare at his smiling teddy bear face, dazed. Disbelieving.

No. This is a nightmare. This whole day. Nothing is real. It can't be real. I'll wake up in a minute.

I take a swing at the wall as hard as I can. My knuckles crunch into plaster, cracks form from the spot. Pain. Blood.

But I don't wake up.

I'm not asleep.

I clutch Murray tight in my arms, fall to the floor, curl up in a tight ball. The tears finally come. Wave after wave of agony claw through and shred everything I am inside until there is nothing left.

* * *

Later, I don't know how much later, there are footsteps. My eyes are still clenched shut tight like the rest of me, rigid.

"I thought I might find you here."

Some part of my brain registers: Aiden's voice. Aiden is here. Why? It's all my fault. Why would he come?

There is movement close by; something warm touches my hair, strokes it.

"We've got to get you away from here." There is another murmured voice. Then arms slip around me, lift me up.

I can't move, can't speak. But if I could, what is there to say?

I'm carried; there are car door sounds. Placed lying down on a seat. Something warm tucked around me.

Low voices, the car engine starts, and we pull away.

Everything goes black.

I lie still, as a statue on a grave. Unfeeling and cold. Eyes shut.

For a long time all around me is quiet, the absolute silence of the dead. Why aren't I one of them? I long to be. The bullets missed even as I tried to jump in front of them, to stop them from hurting anyone else. I failed.

Then there are footsteps. Faint at first, then closer.

"She must be here someplace," a voice says. Ben. I stay still as death, facedown on cold earth. There is movement, another voice.

Then someone grabs my hair, yanks. Turns me over.

I open my eyes.

Tori smiles and holds out a knife.

240

34

"SHE'S SUFFERING FROM SHOCK PERHAPS. AS ARE WE ALL TO some extent. All the evidence stored at the college is gone?"

"Yes."

Words penetrate, and the meaning drifts around, looking for explanation, while other details start to come through. Not in a car anymore. On a sofa? Evidence; what evidence?

It all floods back, pain like being kicked in the stomach. I groan and open my eyes.

Aiden is across the room; he comes over. "Hey. You're awake?"

"I guess," I whisper.

I sit up. The lights are down, but I know this place: Mac's house. Skye is pressed against the sofa next to me, looking up, tail wagging softly, but as if she knows things aren't right, doesn't jump up like she usually does.

My hand hurts and I hold it out, check it like it belongs to somebody else. Nothing broken; just bruises, a few split knuckles.

"What happened to it?" Mac asks.

"I kind of punched a wall."

He hands me a glass of water, tablets. "Painkillers. The ones you left here after your IMET."

I take two, not the recommended one, and shake the container; a few rattle inside. "There's not enough."

"Enough for what?"

"There's too much pain. No, not my hand. Is it all real, did it really happen? At the college. And it was Ben?"

They exchange a glance. Aiden pushes Skye out of the way, sits next to me.

"It looks that way."

"I don't understand. Why did Ben leave that note, get me out of there?"

"Maybe he didn't want you hurt."

"Funny way to show it. Does Ben know this place?" I panic, looking at Mac. No more. No more friends dying.

"He did before his memories were erased, not since," Aiden says. "It should be okay for a while."

"*Should be* isn't good enough. We need to get out of here before they find us."

"We will. Soon," Aiden says. "It's all over."

"What do you mean?"

He shakes his head, drops it into his hands. "MIA, what we were trying to do. It's over. Florence and all the others—friends, every one of them—murdered. Our evidence destroyed, computer system compromised. We're beat." His voice, so tired, so full of pain.

"It's all been for nothing?" My voice is small. *It's my fault.*

"You and I must be high on the Lorders' most wanted list. You're getting out."

"What do you mean?"

"Going to United Ireland. It's being organized."

"No! You're telling me to run away. I'm done with running."

"We'll try to rebuild. One day." He shakes his head. "I have to stay, to do what I can, but I can't think straight if you're not safe. You have to do this for me. Go."

"Why? After everything that has happened. Ben betrayed me; I can't run away from the mess I created." The words are dull, unreal. "He betrayed all of us. He wouldn't have been there if it wasn't for me."

Aiden shakes his head. "I brought him there. Stupid! I was letting feelings cloud my judgment. It's my fault."

"No, you're both wrong," Mac says. "You were giving him a chance; that is what MIA is about, isn't it? Trying to save lost souls from the Lorders' clutches."

Aiden shakes his head. "So many dead. Was it worth it?"

"Wait a minute. I don't understand what you said before. What do you mean, letting feelings cloud your judgment?"

"Isn't that obvious yet?"

Out of the corner of my eye, I see Mac backing out of the room, shutting the door.

Aiden sighs, leans back against the sofa, eyes half closed. He opens them again, turns to face me. He looks young, bewildered almost, not himself. Aiden is always strong, certain of what he does and why he does it. This isn't him. It feels like the only bit of solid ground under my feet is falling away.

I reach for his hand, take it in mine.

"You can't give up on MIA. You're superhero Aiden."

"No. Just Aiden. Just a man, no superpowers. And I messed up. Royally and completely, and we're finished. That's it."

"How did this happen?" I swallow. "How could Lorders do what they did? And how could they change Ben, make him betray us. Make him a killer."

Aiden touches my cheek. "I'm sorry. No Lorder was holding a gun to Ben's head. The things he did, *he* did. He made choices and took actions. It was in him to do what he did, no matter why he did it."

"No, I can't believe that. Ben wasn't like that; it was what they did to him." But even as I say the words, doubt creeps in. The AGT did everything they could to make me a terrorist, to make me a killer. But at the end of it all, I couldn't do it. Even when I was sure I should, that it was the only way, something inside stopped me from taking that step. If Ben was the same, wouldn't something in him have stopped him?

Aiden sighs. "It's all my fault. And I've been such an idiot. If only I'd been honest with myself."

"No! You couldn't have known Ben would—"

"That's not what I mean. I thought getting Ben back would make you happy. And that you being happy would make me happy. But I was wrong. Seeing the two of you together made me miserable."

I stare back at Aiden. His words now, other things he has done and said, are all starting to fall into place, but I can't take it in.

"Then every doubt I had about Ben I discounted. I thought it was because of how I felt about you that I questioned him, his motives. I argued with Florence when I should have listened. She was right about Ben all along."

I shake my head. "Lorders did this; he's not the Ben I knew. They changed him."

"But did you ever really know him?" Aiden asks. "How can you love somebody without knowing all of them, everything they've stood for, what they've done and not done?"

I'm silent a moment. His words are sinking in, settling. "What you are saying, really, is that no one who was Slated—who has no known past—can ever love or be loved. I was Slated."

"Then why do I love you?"

35

I WAKE IN THE EARLY MORNING; THE HOUSE IS SILENT. Aiden's words are painkiller-fuzzy, but I remember enough. I passed out on him from the tablets almost as he said it.

I shake my head. He wasn't himself. Everything that happened cut him wide open. He didn't mean it.

Then I'm not sure which thing he said alarms me more: that he's given up on MIA? That he is sending me away? That he loves me. It is all tinged in unreality like everything that happened yesterday. The pain at Ben's betrayal, and what followed from it, threatens to overwhelm everything I am. But even more: Without Aiden's certainty to anchor to, I feel lost.

I get up, as if I can walk away from it, Skye at my feet. Wander into the kitchen. Catch my breath at the sight of the metal owl sculpture Ben's mum made, up on top of the fridge. I can't stop myself; I reach for it, pull it down. Run my fingers across the interlocking wings, the sharp beak and claws. Trap the square of paper and pull it: Ben's handwriting. His "Love, Ben" identical to the note he left to get me away from All Souls, safe up the church tower.

I don't understand. Why'd he leave that note to get me away? If he is this cold Lorder-created killer Aiden says he is, that I saw with my own eyes yesterday, why not have me shot along with everyone else? Would that have hurt any more than how I feel now?

Maybe somewhere inside him, despite everything he did, he cares.

Just enough to save me. And I don't know if clinging on to that makes me feel better, or worse. But if he cared, why send me to the one place in Oxford where I would have to watch it all?

And Tori. I shudder. Why was she there? A Lorder now, like Ben. Last time I saw her she was being hauled away by Lorders, screaming threats. Was she subjected to the same treatment as Ben? But there was something in her eyes, something vindictive in the way she laughed, as if she remembers me and knew I was watching. Or did I imagine it? Even zoomed in through the camera, could I really have read her like that from so far away?

I'm overwhelmed by too many questions. Were there clues to what Ben was going to do? Could I have stopped it from happening if I'd noted them, told Florence and Aiden?

I wander back to the front room, pick up my camera from the table where I must have left it last night. I stare at it in my hands, wanting to and not knowing if I can handle it at the same time. I breathe in deep, turn it on, and find the file of footage I took of Ben the day I tested my camera.

Ben's smiling face projects onto the wall. I run it back and forth, looking for clues, for hints of what was to come, but see nothing. He's just Ben as I remember him from before, isn't he? He was more jokey than he used to be if anything, less like a Slated. Bolder. I pause it, stare at his eyes on the wall, and the pain is starting to reach for me, to pull me under.

I switch it off. Concentrate on breathing in and out, casting my eyes about the room, looking for something, anything, to distract myself, and that is when I see something I'd forgotten: Murray the bear, stuffed up on a bookshelf. I pull him down.

"Can it really all be over?" I whisper to him. All we'd dared to hope:

that stories like Edie's could get out, could make a difference. Where is Edie now? Maybe she'll end up Slated in an orphanage. Or worse.

She's still in my camera. I pick it up again, look at the list of files: Edie is there. Along with another three witnesses I recorded. The Slated children at the orphanage. And the massacre at the college. Could it be enough? I stare at Murray. His fuzzy face seems to be saying something—or is that just the painkillers?—that we can still do this. Do it fast, before anything else goes wrong.

I go to shut off the camera, then frown. In the file list is one I don't recognize, don't remember having noticed before. Labeled *SC,* it is before the shots I took of Astrid and Nico.

Open file; click play. Stella appears? Of course; *SC* is *Stella Connor.*

I sit and listen to her message. When it is over, goose bumps trail up my arms.

"It was there, all this time?" I say to Murray, stunned.

Then I run to the back of the house, Skye on my heels, and bang on bedroom doors. "Wake up, get up!" Skye barks, and Mac and Aiden rush out, half asleep. Alarmed.

"What is going on?" Aiden says.

"We need to talk, and we need to do it now."

"What about?"

"Listen to me. I'm not going to Ireland."

Aiden starts to protest; I hold up a hand. "There's more. Just shut up and listen. But first I have a question. What is up with MIA's computer systems? Can we get information out?"

"We were pretty much ready to go for it, but not through the usual computer channels," Mac answers. "After our systems were breached, we'd worked out a better alternative through Ireland. DJ's contacts think they can hack the Lorder communication satellite, broadcast from there across the whole country and internationally when we're ready."

"Broadcast what?" Aiden's voice is skeptical. "Most of what we had is gone—either stolen from the hacked systems or destroyed at the college."

I hold up my camera. "I've still got witnesses' testimonies: Edie and three others. There are the photos of the Slated children at the orphanage, the footage of All Souls yesterday, and—"

"It's not enough," Aiden interrupts. "Our view—Florence's dad, then Florence—was always that we needed meticulously documented evidence and witnesses. We haven't got that anymore. We can't back it up."

"If we don't tell their stories, they died for nothing."

The room is silent.

"We at least have to try," Mac finally says.

Aiden looks between us. Does something *change* in his eyes? Then he shakes his head. "I never completely agreed with the careful long game, but is there really enough to—"

"There's more. Watch this," I say, and point the camera at the wall.

Stella's face fills it, a nervous smile. "Uh, hi. This is Stella Connor. My daughter, Lucy—and, Lucy, I will call you that, you will always be the daughter I love to me"—and she smiles—"a short time ago got a confession out of me I thought I'd never tell. She tried to convince me that I had to tell this story, that it had to get out. But I refused." She sighs. "I'm old, and I'm a coward. I've always been one; I'm just starting to see how much. Anyhow. I best get on with it.

"I'm realizing Lucy is going to have to leave my life again, no matter what I do. And on this camera I borrowed from her, I found the reason why. And yes, Lucy, you did password-protect the photos so I wouldn't see them, but I did set up the camera, so I have the admin override, and I snooped. And there were these very young children, Slated." She shudders, sits up straighter. "Everything keeps getting worse, so now I have to be brave and tell my story.

"My mother is Astrid Connor: Juvenile Control Officer for all of England, and steadily rising in Lorder ranks. Years ago I overheard her speaking to a subordinate about the assassinations of Prime Minister Armstrong and his wife, Linea, *before* it happened. I was a child, I didn't really understand what I'd heard, and when I asked her she said they knew about it before the media did, and I didn't question it. But years later I worked it out and confronted her. She admitted— bragged, really—that a hard-line Lorder faction she was in deliberately leaked information to the AGT for these assassinations to take place. Our family was friends with the prime minister's family; Linea had confided in my mother that Armstrong was going to resign and expose violent excesses of the enforcement arm of the Lorders that he'd unearthed. It would have toppled the Lorder government.

"Mother had me locked up to keep me from saying anything. I was pregnant, and my baby died. Months later, she gave me Lucy: the most beautiful baby. I don't know where she got her from. Once she could see that I loved Lucy completely, Mother let us out. Said if I ever said anything, she'd take Lucy away.

"I love you so much, Lucy. I'm sorry I didn't tell you everything from the start." Her hand reaches for the camera. The recording stops.

I'm struggling to keep my composure. Stella must have made this when I was in the boathouse. Got Ellie to bring it to me with that cryptic message when she somehow found out Astrid was on her way; brave, at last. I hope, so much, that she is all right.

I blink hard. "Well? Is it enough?"

Aiden and Mac are looking at each other in stunned silence. Then Mac grins. "We've got the bastards, don't we!" He holds up a hand in the air to Aiden. After a second's hesitation, he raises his and high-fives.

Aiden's got his determined look back again. "Yes! We can do this." He grabs me in a hug, then lets go abruptly. "You still have to leave first."

"No. I'm the only living witness you've got to back anything up. I'm not going anywhere." I stare back at Aiden's blue eyes, not wavering, but neither is he.

"How about we interrupt this staring contest with breakfast?" Mac says, and fills the kettle, plugs it in. "Then perhaps you'd like to record me telling what happened to Robert after the bus bombing."

Aiden holds up a hand, thinking. "There is one other thing. One other witness that'd really help." His eyes are on mine, apologetic.

"Who?"

"We need Armstrong's daughter, Sandra Davis. Your mum here."

"No. No way." I stare at him, horrified. "Mum and Amy being safe is one of the things that makes me able to go on. Don't take that away from me."

"Listen to me: People will believe her. They don't know who Stella is. But if she sees what Stella says and backs it up, and backs up Mac's story, well. We're home."

Mac slips an arm around my shoulders. "He's right, you know. It's time to stop being safe, to risk everything." I shrug his arm off, go back to the sofa. Murray stares up at me, with a *he's right* look on his face. I shake my head. Next thing, Skye will lecture me. On cue she jumps up next to me, puts her head on my lap, and looks up.

"Okay. We can ask her, but no pressure." She won't do it, will she? I'm beyond her protection, but she won't do it if it means putting Amy at risk. "How are we going to get word to her?"

The front door bangs open. "Hello," a cheery voice says. One I know. I turn, and there is Amy's boyfriend: Jazz.

36

"I'M SERIOUSLY NOT HAPPY," JAZZ SAYS, BUT HIS GRIN ARGUES against that. His arms seem to have me trapped in a permanent hug since the split second that, changed hair or no, he realized it was me. "Why didn't you tell me she was alive?" he demands of his cousin Mac.

I squirm. "Let me go already!"

"You're really okay?"

"All in one piece," I say, not able to think of how I am as okay, exactly, after everything that's happened.

He loosens his arms, but keeps me in front of him with a hand on each shoulder. "Amy has been so . . . Can I tell her?"

"Need-to-know," Aiden interjects.

Jazz glares at him. "Yeah, well, whatever: Amy needs to know."

"Why not?" I say. "It'll be out soon enough. What'll it hurt if he tells her now? She won't say anything." Not after the last time. Amy had in all innocence told about drawings I was doing for the AGT, and a snatch and grab in a black van and Lorder questioning and blackmail followed.

"And your mum?" Jazz asks.

"She already knows."

"No way. She never let on."

"Need-to-know," we say in unison, and I find myself laughing along with Jazz, some part of me surprised that I still know how.

"It's good to see you," I say. "Now let me go." He lets go with one arm, but keeps the other around my shoulders, and it feels good. Amy's boyfriend has always felt like a big brother to me.

"We need to set up a meeting," Aiden says to Jazz. "Between Kyla and her mum. And *don't* say anything to Amy, not just yet."

"Fine. Sure, give me a message. Which reminds me." He takes a small box out of his pocket. "Mail call."

"What's that?" I ask, mystified.

Mac takes it, holds it up. "The latest from DJ, I'm guessing."

I stare at Jazz. "You mean you're involved with all this, too?" A big brother with secrets of his own.

He grins. "Always was their messenger boy; just extra busy lately with computer communications being out. You didn't need to know, I guess." I smack his arm. To think all that goes on under the surface of people's lives, right in front of my eyes, and I had no idea. None.

Mac opens the small box. "Brilliant; at last." He holds his hand open: a com. As if on cue, it buzzes. "I'm pretty sure it's for you," Mac says to Aiden. Aiden straightens his shoulders. Answers it, disappears down the hall, and shuts a door.

Mac and I exchange a glance.

"Does DJ know what happened yet?" I ask quietly.

"I'd be surprised if he doesn't. But he probably wants to hear a firsthand account."

"What's happened?" Jazz asks.

"Need-to-know or not—believe me, you don't want to know," I say.

Mac works out a plan with Jazz about when and where we can try to meet with Mum while I drift about the kitchen, making toast. Wondering if DJ will go along with our plan. What if he thinks we haven't got enough to go public? What if he says no? We can't get it broadcast without his help.

I leave the kitchen, make for the back room. Knock once and go in.

Aiden's still on the com with DJ. He meets my eyes, gestures for me to be quiet. "What is the time frame for that? . . . I'm not sure we can . . . I see."

"Let me talk to him," I say.

Aiden mimes pulling his hair out. "Fine. Talk to her, then." He holds the com out to me.

"Hello?"

"Hi, Kyla. Aiden's been telling me that—"

"DJ, just listen to me a moment. We need to do this broadcast as soon as we can. No more waiting for more things to go wrong. We've got to move before—"

"Slow down. I agree with you."

"You do?"

"Yes. And, Kyla hon, I hear you've had a rough time. I'm sorry." He pauses, but this time I stay silent. What is there to say? "Aiden wants me to ship you out of the country."

I narrow my eyes at Aiden. "I'm not going."

"That's my girl. I think we need you involved in our little movie production. Aiden's given me the rundown on Stella's recording, the other things on your camera, the possibility of Sandra Davis's involvement. You need to make it happen."

Now I glare at Aiden. "We haven't even asked her yet. She may refuse."

"One way or the other, we need to get this wrapped up for transmission tomorrow, or we'll have to wait months for another opportunity. A bit techy, but all to do with choosing the right moment to interfere with their satellite without detection; we can mask our intrusion as solar activity if it coincides with a geomagnetic storm. And wild weather with thunderstorms later is predicted as well: Their satellite and terrestrial communications should be interrupted to-morrow evening if both solar and weather predictions are correct."

"Tomorrow? So soon?" I say, looking at Aiden. He raises his shoulders in a shrug.

"Can you do it?"

Waiting might give us more to broadcast. But look what happens with waiting: All Souls. That's what. "Yes. We'll do it."

"That's the spirit."

"DJ? I have a question."

"Yes?"

"Did you hear about what Dr. Lysander said, about someone high up interfering with my hospital records?"

"Yes."

"Did you find out anything else about me? My DNA?"

There is a pause, barely perceptible. "Still working on it."

37

I'M JITTERY, NERVOUS. CAN'T SIT STILL. AIDEN LOOKS AT ME.
"What's wrong?"

"Nothing. Everything." I look at the time. "She's late."

He glances at the clock. "Only about twenty seconds. It'll be all right."

"It's just I don't want anything to happen to her. Everyone who gets too close to me seems to pay the price. I don't want her involved."

He takes my hand. "Because you care. You want her out of harm's way." He doesn't say anything else, but I know what he's thinking.

"I couldn't go."

"I know." He sighs. "It's part of what makes you who you are. But I had to try."

The door opens.

"Mum!" I jump up and run to her. Her arms wrap around me quickly, a tight hug.

She looks over my shoulder at Aiden. "Who's this?"

He stands up. "Pleased to meet you, ma'am. I'm Aiden."

She turns to me. Shakes her head. "Why are you back? It's too dangerous."

"I tried to tell her, but she wouldn't leave," Aiden says. They exchange a look.

"Stubborn, isn't she?" Mum says. "Now, why am I here?"

"We need your help."

Mum sits down, and Aiden explains what we—MIA—are planning to do.

"So this really will broadcast across the whole country? And in other countries?"

Her eyes turn in, thinking, then meet mine with a spark of excitement. "That could work. Though I'm not sure what you think I can do."

"I'm really sorry to show you this," I say.

"What?"

I get the camera out. "Do you know who Astrid and Stella Connor are?"

She frowns. "Astrid Connor went to school with my mother; they were friends. Stella is her daughter. We used to be in touch when we were kids; not lately, though. She stopped answering my calls, years ago." She shrugs. "What do they have to do with anything?"

"They're my family. From before I was Slated. I was adopted by Stella; she raised me from when I was a baby until I was ten. It was her I went off to see."

"What?" Mum's eyes are round with surprise. She shakes her head. "Small world. But I can't see what this has to do with me."

Aiden and I exchange a glance. I'd wanted to warn her what was to come, but he thought it was best for her to see and hear it for herself.

"Okay. Here's a recording Stella made. She hid it on my camera, and I only just found it recently. I'm sorry."

I project it on the wall, hit play. Her face goes pale as she watches and listens, and she grips my hand tight.

After it ends, Mum looks away a moment. Then she meets my eyes. "If only I knew what my parents were planning to do. All these years, I could never understand why my father set up the Lorder government, with all it has led to. I always thought he didn't know what was really going on, but he did, and he was planning to put a stop to it. Thank you for telling me."

"You see," Aiden says, "this is why we need you. To introduce Stella's recording in our broadcast; it'll give it credence. Make people listen. Also we've got a witness who saw your son, Robert, alive after the bus bombing. You could talk about him being missing, also."

Mum nods. "I knew from another source that Robert survived the bombing, but disappeared afterward. I always assumed he was Slated. If my parents could have said and done what they wanted, would our world be a different place? Would I still have my son. I want to do it for them, to say what they were stopped from saying. Yet this isn't just about me; things could go wrong. I have Amy's safety to consider. I need time to think about this."

"I'm sorry. That is one thing we haven't got a lot of," Aiden says.

"When would we need to do this?"

"Tomorrow afternoon at the latest. There are technical reasons why the broadcast must happen tomorrow night. Jazz can bring you, if you decide to help us."

They talk some more about details, but I just hold her hand tight. Imagine the shock; all this time being told one version of why your parents died, and then finding out it was all lies.

"I should go." She hugs me tight. "Take care of her," she orders Aiden, and then is gone.

"What do you think she'll do?" Aiden asks.

This is so reminiscent of another time, another decision. When she had to decide whether or not to tell the whole country on that live recording what she thought really happened to her son. Then, she didn't do it; she wouldn't do anything to put Amy or me in danger. Will this time be any different?

"I don't know." Part of me hopes she will be there tomorrow; part of me hopes she stays away.

That evening, Aiden is working in the computer room, and Mac has gone off with Jazz to set up for tomorrow and to copy the footage and photos from my camera and start putting it all together. DJ wants me to do an introduction, to explain how things I witnessed fit together, and I'm trying to think what I can say so I won't stare at the camera like an idiot.

What can I say about All Souls that explains what happened in a way that makes any sense? What can I say about Ben?

What can I say—what am I *willing* to say—about my life. My crazy, confused, Lorder-tainted life, and all those it has damaged or destroyed.

I'm stalking back and forth in the front room; Skye gets under my feet. I almost trip over her and curse.

Aiden's door opens; he comes in. "Is everything all right?"

"Just stage fright," I say, but look at my feet. I can't look him in the eye.

"It'll be all right."

"Just like everything else has been all right so far?" And I'm shaking. I don't know why; is it a delayed reaction, fear, pain, all three?

I look up and take a step toward him; Aiden takes one toward me. Meeting in the middle. His arms slip around me, just gentle, not holding but comforting, like you would a sister, or a child. I nestle my head against his shoulder. I fit against him different than Ben; Ben is taller. His hand smooths my hair; he's trying to make me feel better, but it's not enough, nothing can ever be enough to take the emptiness away. And I pull him closer and closer. His heart is beating faster and so is mine. I reach up and pull his head down, kiss him. I don't know what I'm doing, I don't care. All I am is cold, dead, empty; Aiden is feeling, warmth, and life.

And at first he kisses back. Then gradually, gently, he pushes me away. Shakes his head. "Not like this."

And I start to cry. Why? Another loss, another cold space. He pulls me to the sofa, wraps a blanket around me.

"Don't go," I say.

"I'm not going anywhere. Ever. As long as you don't want me to." But he stands up. "Back in a sec." He goes down the hall and comes back with a guitar in his hands.

"I don't play very often, but it always makes me feel better. Close your eyes, Kyla. Tomorrow will be a long day. But we'll get through it. And I'll be there."

And he plays; he's good. Some songs I know, some I don't. And somehow my eyes close. I slip to a dark, dreamless sleep.

38

THE PROMISED WILD WEATHER HAS ARRIVED. THE COLD WIND whips bits of branches off trees and swirls dead leaves as I run.

I'd said I just needed a run, bolting out, not able to meet Aiden in the eye after last night. Half expecting an argument, or an escort. But they let me go.

My feet fly up the canal path, pushing hard to make everything go away, but it's not working. I dig deep for *more*: more effort, more speed. And the miles fly by, and it gets closer. This run wasn't only about escape and release. Will I be able to find it?

Not at first. I know I'm close to where it should be, that there was a particular bend of the path, a climbable tree not far from it. I slow to a jog and retrace my steps until finally I think I see the right one.

The wind is crazy as I climb up the branches, like it's going to pull me off and throw me to the ground. I squint to avoid getting grit blown in my eyes. How far up was it? I think I've come too far and look back. Anything could have happened to it. A bird or a squirrel with an eye for shiny things could have taken it, the branch it was on could have been victim to the wind. It might be the wrong tree. Now that I'm not running, I'm freezing; I feel around with numb hands, having trouble keeping my footing when I can barely feel my feet. I'm about to give up when my fingers brush something cold, something metal.

I twist to reach it better, and pull it off the branch it is hooked around: Emily's ring. Clutch it tight in my hand a moment, then start down.

Back on the ground, I peer at the inscription: *Emily & David 4ever.* I took it off her hand after they both died, victims of Lorders and Slating like so many others. I need this; I need a reason I can hold on to, to get me through what has to be done today. I start to put it in my pocket, but then slip it on my finger instead, and start the long run back.

After a shower I come out to the kitchen, where Mac is making sandwiches. "Is everything okay?" he asks. Then retracts. "All right, stupid question. Anything not okay that I can do anything about?"

"No. Thanks." I smile at him.

"At last: a smile. Of sorts. Sit down and eat up, it's about time to go. Aiden? Lunch," he calls.

Aiden comes in, squeezes my shoulder with one hand, sits down opposite. He looks into my eyes, nods once, and his steady gaze says things are okay. A knot of anxiety inside me eases; just a little, but it's enough.

"Welcome to our movie studio," Mac says, and opens the door to a run-down farm outbuilding. Up a path a few miles from his house, from the outside it looks abandoned, but as I step inside, I gasp. It's like an Aladdin's cave for computer geeks; there are bits of tech everywhere.

"You clearly didn't just set this up for today," I say.

"No. It's been one of MIA's hidden tech centers for ages; there's all sorts of different stuff to play with out here. Movies are new. But we've got the transmitting equipment here to link up with DJ's relay to the satellite. And Jazz and I cleared a place to do recordings last night."

Aiden and I follow him around a crammed-high row of shelving; behind it, there's a clear area with a stool, a tarp hung to block equipment behind it. And a camera on a stand in front with lights.

"That looks a bit more high-tech than my little camera," I say, touching my pocket where it is once again, returned this morning after they copied the relevant content last night. ·

"Nah, it's easy. I'll show you, then we can record my part."

Mac starts to explain the controls to both of us when there is a loud knock.

"Hello?" Jazz's voice. And another: Mum?

I bolt around the shelves, and it's not just Mum; Amy is here, too.

Amy runs over to me and grabs me in a hug. "You crazy girl. Don't you ever do that to me again!"

"You've cut your hair," I say, shocked. Her gorgeous thick hair is gone, cut to a short pixie.

"Hey, if I knew where you were to check for fashion advice and that I didn't need a séance, I'd have done so. Besides, you're looking a bit different, too."

"You're both here?" I say to Mum, who has held back, but walks up to us now for a group hug.

Mum smiles. "Both my girls together! I realized this was a family decision. I had to let Amy in on what was happening, and then we had a vote."

"And?" Aiden asks.

"Amy says go for it. I'm still not sure, but there are three of us. Kyla?"

And all eyes are on me.

No. Don't make me do this. Don't make me decide.

I swallow. "If this goes wrong, it could be a death sentence for everyone involved."

"Including you," Mum points out.

I shrug. I don't want to say, out loud, that I don't care anymore about my own life. "It's different for me. They're already after me, anyhow."

"You told me once before that sometimes the most important thing is doing what is right."

"The problem is working out what is right, isn't it?" Amy says.

And I stare back at Mum and Amy, standing close together. Amy was Slated, assigned to Mum like I was, but that doesn't change what they are to each other now. What we are. But we're not the only ones. "This isn't just about us. It's about every mother and daughter, every father and son. Now and in the future."

Mum looks back at me, slowly nods. "Okay, then. Let's get this show on the road."

Mac goes first while I operate the camera. He tells about the day his school trip went so wrong; when stray AGT bombs took out most of a busload of fifteen- and sixteen-year-olds. How he had a minor injury. How his friend Robby—Robert Armstrong—was hauled off the bus, away from his dead girlfriend. Screaming, but unhurt. Then later was on the list of the dead.

Then it is Mum's turn to tell us about her son, Robert. How she'd heard rumors for years that he'd survived and been Slated, but could find no trace of him.

She pauses, looks me in the eye behind the camera. "But that's not the only tragedy in my life. You know who I am: Sandra Armstrong-Davis. My father, Prime Minister William Adam M. Armstrong, and my mother, Linea Armstrong, were murdered by AGT bombs when I was fifteen. But that is not the end of the story. My parents were preparing to expose Lorder atrocities; my dad, to resign as Lorder prime minister and dissolve the government. My mother confided in a school friend, Astrid Connor, who deliberately leaked the information of their whereabouts to the AGT to have them assassinated and silenced. You will hear about this from Stella Connor—a childhood friend, and the daughter of the Lorder who did this."

She pauses. "How was that?"

Mac, behind the camera again, gives a thumbs-up. "Brilliant. Thanks."

I take a deep breath. "Is it my turn now?"

Aiden comes over. "I could do the bit on All Souls. I was there, too."

I shake my head. "I'm the one who took the footage, and I was looking through the camera zoom and saw what happened as it happened in more detail than you could. I have to do it."

"Are you sure?"

"Yes. And there's more I can testify about. Mum, can you and Amy stay? I want there to be no more secrets. This is all going to be out there; I want you to hear it from me."

I settle on the stool under the lights. Amy straightens my hair. "It's not a fashion shoot," I say. She sticks out her tongue and gets out of shot.

"When you're ready," Mac says.

I stare down the camera, pretend I'm going to talk to myself. That no one else is here; that Edie's teddy bear is staring at me behind the lens, and no one else can hear a word.

"Hi. I'd like to introduce myself, but I can't: I don't know who I am. Before I was born, a woman you'll hear from soon was a prisoner. Her name is Stella Connor. She'd found out her mother—a Lorder JCO,

Astrid Connor—had engineered the assassinations of Prime Minister Armstrong and his wife. Stella was locked up by her mother to keep her quiet; she was pregnant at the time, and her baby died.

"Then Astrid gave Stella another baby: me. She threatened to take me away if Stella ever said anything, and then let us go. Stella and her husband, Danny Howarth, who thought I was his, loved and raised me as their daughter.

"When I was ten years old, I was kidnapped by the AGT. I was subjected to conditioning to fracture my personality, trained by AGT terrorist Nico, and then he deliberately set me up to be captured and Slated by Lorders when I was fifteen.

"After I was Slated and assigned to my new family, my fractured personality and memories started to come back; even though I was Slated, my Levo stopped controlling my actions when my memories returned. The AGT plan worked. I rejoined the AGT, but Lorders threatened me to try to make me betray the AGT.

"On Armstrong Memorial Day, I was present at the speeches given by my assigned mother, Sandra Armstrong-Davis, who you'll be hearing from also." I pause, unable to say what comes next, twisting Emily's ring on my finger and fighting for control. "I'm sorry. I had a gun strapped to my arm. Mum—Sandra—was next to me, and if she didn't say what the AGT wanted her to say, I was supposed to kill her." I blink hard, will myself to not look at Mum and Amy, to keep going.

"I couldn't do it. I didn't stay for the second ceremony in the grounds; I ran back to try to save Dr. Lysander, who was being held by the AGT because I'd betrayed her. Later I found out that a com Nico gave me and concealed under my Levo was a remote-controlled bomb; he'd meant to set it off during the second ceremony, when I should have been next to my family and Prime Minister Gregory."

I breathe in and out a few seconds, fight for control. Then continue. I tell them everything I did with the AGT and what happened with Nico; the bomb that the Lorders said killed me. Going to stay with Stella and finding out she wasn't my mother, visiting the orphanage, seeing the Slated children and realizing I was going to have to run, to take this information to MIA. Seeing Astrid and Nico together. Going to Oxford, finding Ben. That Ben had been subjected to unknown procedures by the Lorders; that he betrayed us. My voice wavers as I describe the massacre at All Souls College that I filmed.

Then I stare at the camera. "I still don't know who I am. Or what Astrid Connor, Lorder and JCO, was doing with Nico, the AGT terrorist who trained me and countless others to attack Lorders. But it's hard to imagine she wasn't involved in everything that has happened to me from the beginning, and the plot to assassinate my family and Prime Minister Gregory.

"But one thing I do know: The truth needs to come out. All of it. If everyone knows what really happens, what Lorders really do, what happens to the missing, then they—you—will put a stop to it.

"*Everyone* needs to know."

I'm finished talking. Still and silent now, I can't look up, can't meet anyone in the eye. I'm aware Mac has stopped filming, but no one says anything.

I hear footsteps: Mum's. She walks up to me.

"I'm sorry," I say.

She slips her arms around me. Dimly I'm aware the others are walking away, out of sight.

"Why are you sorry?"

"I almost killed you, you and Amy. And loads of other people as well."

"You didn't know you had the bomb."

"I knew I had the gun. I thought I was going to use it. I thought I had no choice."

"But you didn't."

"No. I couldn't. But everything else I've done. And what happened at All Souls, because of Ben. It's my fault."

"Caring for someone is never a bad thing, even if it doesn't work out."

"It hurts," I whisper.

"I know. I'll tell you one thing for free."

"What's that?"

"If I could get Astrid and Nico in my sights right now, they'd both be dead."

I half smile at the thought of Mum as avenging gunslinger, not a picture that readily comes to mind. "I'm not good at killing people. I'm better at getting them killed."

Aiden steps back around, and clears his throat. "We're going to get this movie into production now. Go if you want."

"I should get Amy out of here. We're going to go stay in a quiet place with some friends for a few days, see what happens if—when, I mean—that hits the airwaves. Come with us? Please?"

"No. Sorry. I've got to see this through."

"Okay."

Amy comes around; her eyes are red. She and Mum give me hugs, and go.

Mac and Aiden get busy on computers with the different bits of recordings, still photos, our pieces from today. After a moment pulling myself together, I walk over, watch over their shoulders.

Aiden catches my eye. "Thank you," he says.

"For what?"

"For having the courage to do what you just did."

I shrug. "I've been a coward for a long time. You shouldn't thank me for that." I look away, not able to meet him in the eye.

It was Stella and Mum who finally made me face up to telling the truth. They both did, so how could I not? Staring at everything I've been and done, I struggle to keep myself contained when inside everything feels like shattering glass. There are no walls, no illusions left to hide behind. Mum knows. Aiden knows. Soon the whole world will know.

Finally Mac declares it done. "Do you want to watch a run-through? No problem if not."

"I'll watch," I say. Mac projects it on the wall. At the beginning, titles run across the screen: *Need to Know—an MIA production.*

I try to watch the whole fifteen minutes of it dispassionately, objectively. Like I don't know anyone in it, and I'm Joe Public sitting on my sofa about to get the evening TV surprise of a lifetime. But when the footage I shot from the church tower comes up, I can't watch. I look away. A warm arm slips around my shoulders: Aiden. I want to look up at him, but I'm afraid what I'll see in his eyes.

BANG.

A massive crash makes us all jump, then laugh when we realize— it's thunder. The storm is here.

Aiden grins widely. As if on cue, his com rings: DJ? He answers. "Hello? Yes. It's ready." He pauses, listening. "Got it, 'bye." He clicks end, then turns to us. "We're to transmit at six, when the storm should be at its peak. It'll be on then instead of the evening news. It *will* be the evening news!" he says. He and Mac give high fives, excited, and part of me is, too. All we've worked toward is finally really happening.

But part of me is with all those who suffered, who died. Florence, Wendy, all the other students. Those small children who were Slated.

"What is it?" Aiden asks.

"How can we celebrate? We can't do anything for those who died, for their families."

Aiden puts his arms around me, and I lean into him.

"We can remember them," he says. "And, through what we've done today, make it stop. Make their loss have meaning."

Without discussion, the three of us stay silent; a minute, two. Then another massive crash of thunder hits, and again I jump. I don't mind storms; normally I like them, the wilder the better. Not today. I'm as jumpy as . . .

Skye.

I pull away from Aiden. "Skye will be scared alone with the storm. I'm going back to the house."

"Do you want me to walk back with you?" Aiden asks.

"No. Stay and have your moment. I'll be fine."

"Wait a sec," Mac says, does something with the computer and my camera, then hands it over. "I put a backup copy of *Need to Know* on it. Just in case we're struck by lightning."

I scowl at him. "Don't tempt fate," I say, and head out the door—fresh air, storm or not—and escape.

It's about two miles back and just getting dark, but now and then the sky lights up with crazy, jagged lightning. Each time the thunder crashes, seemingly right over my head, I almost jump out of my skin, annoyed at myself for being so jittery. I'm about halfway there when it starts: huge, heavy, freezing cold raindrops. So I get cold and wet; so what.

As I run, I wonder at how I feel; I should be celebrating with both of them. Instead, I feel empty.

What is next? What is my future? How will Aiden feel now that he knows all the things I have done?

Mum said caring for somebody is never a bad thing, even if it doesn't work out.

Do I care?

39

I'M NEARLY AT THE LIGHTS OF THE HOUSE WHEN THEY GO out, and all is darkness.

A power failure, because of the storm? I hope that doesn't affect the transmission. Knowing Mac there will be a backup generator.

It's inky black now, and despite the freezing rain, I slow to a walk to find the path at my feet. Tonight the dark is unnerving, not comforting as it usually is, and without thinking about it I switch to moving silently, every step taken with care.

Another blinding flash, and everything is lit up—a split second only. *There!* By the house, near the back door. Two figures in black?

Fear whips through me as all is plunged into darkness again. Lorders!

Did they see me?

Panic finds my feet, and I run blind, no longer silent, headlong back the way I came. Cries sound behind: spotted or heard, either way, they're on to me. When the path branches, I go the other way, away from Mac and Aiden. I can't lead them there; anything but that. I should be able to lose them. I can run faster than almost anybody I've come across.

But I'm not pulling away. I can hear pursuit keeping pace behind. Now it sounds like just one runner, a long, loping gait. A familiar gait, and when there's another blinding flash I can't stop myself from glancing back.

Ben.

My feet falter, then I push on; I'm gathering speed again, but it's no good. Bit by bit he gains. I can hear him getting closer, and knowing it is Ben has confused my feet.

Then all at once he's flying through the air and I'm knocked to the ground. Winded, under him, I struggle to breathe. He holds my hands with one of his and gropes at my pockets. No! I twist, but he's got it. My camera.

He pulls me to my feet, presses something cold and hard against my back. "Walk!"

"No. Just shoot me already, if that's what you want to do. I don't care anymore."

He twists my arm behind my back and pushes; I stumble forward. What is the time? I have to delay them. I have to stop them from finding Mac and Aiden, from stopping the transmission at six.

I trip and sprawl forward. With an exclamation of annoyance, Ben scoops me up and carries me, my arm still twisted. A gun pressed into my stomach so hard it hurts.

"How could you do it?"

He doesn't answer.

"Everyone, all those students, just shot against the wall. Dead."

"They were traitors. They deserved what they got. As will you."

"You're the traitor; you betrayed me. You used to love me, you acted like you still did. How could you do it?" My voice is too soft, plaintive, and I hate myself for it.

"Ah, sorry about that. Seducing you *was* difficult. But I had to get you to fall asleep somehow."

"Why?"

"Scanned you while you slept. How do you think we found you?

Somehow your records were wrong, and we needed the scan to track you by your brain chip."

No. Dr. Lysander had changed the number; Lorders worked out they couldn't track me, so they got Ben to take care of it.

Now I'm full of rage, and struggle, but despite a few AGT tricks I know, the Lorders must have taught him how to hold someone. Or maybe the pain inside is making me too weak to fight back.

When it hits me, I almost sag. He let me go, so he could track me here. I'd thought some part of him couldn't bring himself to hurt me, but I was wrong. "You're evil."

"Sticks and stones."

"And that little girl; how could you?"

"What girl?"

"Edie! You knew her address. I ran there, and they were gone."

His shoulders move slightly: a shrug? "No idea. I didn't tell them her address." His voice is uncomfortable; he should have told the Lorders he works for everything, even that, and he knows it. Is there some part of the Ben I knew inside him still? Can he be reached?

We're at the door to Mac's house now; the lights are back on, and the door is held open. Ben pushes through and drops me on the kitchen floor. At Tori's feet.

A golden streak rushes past: Skye. She jumps up on Ben in excitement, licking his face. He tries to push her off, but she's not having it.

"That's Skye. Your dog," I say.

"My dog?"

Skye barks as if to say yes.

"Your mum and dad gave her to you when she was a puppy. Look, Ben—your mum was an artist; she made that owl sculpture. Made it for me."

His eyes start to follow my gesture to the owl on the fridge, but then Tori pulls me up by the hair and starts dragging me across the floor into the front room. I scream, and Skye flips around, growling, starts to leap at Tori, but Ben grabs her collar. "Down," he says sharply, and she's confused.

"Let Kyla go," he says to Tori, and she pauses, surprise in her face. "Until I get rid of the dog."

Tori lets go of my hair, and my head thuds painfully on the floor. She smiles, but her eyes are full of twisted hate. I was right, wasn't I? She remembers me. Did the Lorders think she was of more use with revenge to drive her?

Ben pushes Skye into the hall, shuts the door. She starts whining mournfully on the other side to get back to him.

"Aren't they here yet?" Ben says to Tori.

"No. Not yet," Tori says, and something hides behind the glee in her eyes, some lie. She wants to deal with me all by herself.

"Are you waiting for reinforcements?" I say. "She hasn't called anyone in. They're not coming."

Ben frowns, looks at Tori.

"Don't listen to her," she says, and slaps me so hard on the side of the face that tears come to my eyes. I blink furiously.

"You remember me, don't you, Tori. You want to hurt me, don't you?"

"I don't just *want* to, I'm going to." She pulls a knife out of her pocket. "You know I'm good with knives."

"You killed a Lorder with a knife once. I can't believe you could go from that, to this. Don't you remember that day we attacked the termination center, and Emily, the Slated who died?" I slip the ring off my finger, throw it at Ben. He catches it. "That's Emily's ring, the pregnant girl I told you about at the college. Everything I told you that day is true, Ben, and Tori knows it. She was there."

Tori looks at Ben as he reads the inscription on the ring. "She's lying. She could have gotten that ring anywhere."

"You hate the Lorders, don't you, Tori? For what they did to you: Slating you, then taking you to a termination center. The Lorder who pretended to rescue you—do you remember him, what he did to you? Is working for them worth it, just to get back at me? Or is it to be with Ben: That's it, isn't it. You always wanted what you couldn't have. You're just a jealous little girl."

Tori starts to advance on me with her knife; I shrink into the wall. Too much?

"Tori, wait," Ben says. "Leave her be a minute."

"What?" She scowls, turns to him.

"You do remember her, from before." A statement, not a question. "Explain."

She looks between us—wary. Trapped.

Is it working? My eyes find the clock on the mantel: 6:02. The transmission has started! Delay and distract. I've no doubt she'll kill me or, if she doesn't, eventually they'll make the call and more Lorders will come and they will. I'm detached from it. I don't care. What is there to live for? If the transmission is made, I'll welcome death.

"I don't know what they've told you, Ben. But Tori is here for revenge: nothing else. Because Lorders followed me to her, arrested her, hauled her away."

"And you never told me!" she says, and hits me hard again across the face, this time with the flat side of the knife in her hand, and the cutting edge bites in and cuts my cheek. Tears spring to my eyes.

"Oh, is that why you're so miffed? Because I never told you Ben was alive?"

"Tori, is this true?" he asks.

"Ben, I—"

"Why haven't you told me this before?"

"Ben, think for yourself," I say. "It's lies, all of it. The Lorders and Tori have been filling you up with lies, to make you do what they want. All those people dead, all because of you."

"No," Ben says. "You're the traitor! It's because of you and Aiden they died. You twisted the truth and turned them against the government. We had no choice."

There is thumping behind—Skye is throwing herself at the hall door.

"Not even Tori believes that; she just doesn't care."

He looks at her.

"Shut up," she shouts. She lunges with her knife; I'm on the floor, up against the wall, weaponless. Limp and lifeless already; where has my fight gone? This is it. This is really it.

A foot swings out; the knife flies through the air. Ben. He's kicked the knife out of her hand.

"What have you made me do?" he screams, and I don't know if he means stopping Tori from killing me, or Tori's lies and what they led to. Or if he even knows.

Tori screams in fury. She reaches behind her back to a holster. A gun is in her hand. She raises it at Ben.

A crash: The thin hall door has given way.

A flash of fur—Skye—jumps between them.

The gun goes off and Skye yelps, falls, red in her golden fur. Tori stares, disbelieving.

My fight is back. I'm on my feet, and I take the biggest swing I've ever taken to punch Tori full-on in the face. She drops the gun, falls to the ground. Unconscious. And then the gun is in my hand and pointed at Ben.

Who am I kidding? I put it down.

Ben is holding Skye, pushing at the red spreading in her fur. It's her shoulder. I grab a curtain tie off the wall, tie it tight around and around to try to stop the bleeding, and she's whimpering, but still licking Ben's face. He's shaking.

"Ben? Do you remember Skye? Remember!" And then he's crying, convulsing, and I'm holding both of them.

That's when the front door is kicked down. A man steps through.

Nico?

40

I TWIST, DIVE FOR TORI'S GUN, BUT THEN THERE IS *PAIN*—A sudden explosion of agony in my head so severe, I drop and curl into a ball.

"This is why we track the trackers," a woman's voice says. "They really can't be trusted to get anything right. Young people today have no sense of focus or purpose."

Footsteps approach. They stop; a hand strokes my hair. The pain is so intense, it's all I can do to open my eyes and look up at the ones staring into mine: pale blue irises. Nico. His eyes used to mesmerize me, hold power. Not any longer.

"Poor child. You see, over there?" He gestures to the front door, and my eyes follow. It's Astrid, and in her hands is a device. "Once a Slated, always a Slated. Just key in the brain chip number, hit a button, and bingo: pain. Or even death."

Tori is stirring on the floor. "Allow me a small demonstration," Astrid says, and taps at the machine. Tori screams, convulses, then lies still.

As if to emphasize the point, Astrid taps again; a new spike of pain explodes in my head. My vision goes fuzzy. All the Lorder talk of second chances for Slateds: all lies. We're still in a prison. They can strike us down whenever they want to.

"Enough for now," Nico says. "She'll pass out." He lifts me up onto the sofa. Ben is held between two Lorders, and Tori and Skye are unmoving on the floor.

The pain subsides a little, enough that I can turn my head, fix Nico once again with my eyes. I swallow, try to speak with a mouth that is thick and dry. "Why are you here? You hate Lorders."

"Ah, my dear, love and hate have nothing to do with winning. I was always with Astrid. The side of strength." He leans over me, close, and I try to pull away but can't convince muscles to respond. He kisses my cheek.

I fight to think through the pain. Is Nico in some sort of self-serving alliance with Astrid, or was he actually a Lorder all the time? But Nico ran from Coulson's Lorders when they tracked me and attacked the AGT; Coulson *was* hunting Nico. Or was that just an act? If Nico really *is* a Lorder, that may explain why all the attacks Nico and Katran planned just fizzled out: sabotage.

The clock over the mantel says 6:08. The transmission is well under way! I have to keep them talking, keep them from stopping it.

With great concentration, I manage to turn my head to Astrid. "It was you who set up their taking me when I was ten. Wasn't it."

She smiles, and it is a grandmotherly, gentle smile. Shivers run up my back. "Of course it was, my dear. You had a glorious purpose on Armstrong Memorial Day. Shame you didn't fulfill it."

A glorious purpose? That of suicide bomber. *Concentrate; delay her.* "It was no accident I was assigned to that family, that I was there that day."

"Of course not. It just took a little meddling to arrange it."

"How could you do that to Stella? Take me away from her?"

Her face goes hard. "My daughter dared to hold information over me, threatened to tell; she had to learn. And then having you back with her in Keswick, without telling me?" She shakes her head in disgust.

"So you really did have the prime minister and his wife killed, all those years ago."

She smiles. "First rule of politics: Eliminate the opposition."

"How did you know I was at Stella's?"

She shrugs. "It was obvious Stella was hiding *something*. A little information, and the conclusion was apparent."

"From Steph. My green eyes."

She raises an eyebrow. Amused. "Indeed. And it didn't take long to work out it was also you and that Finley at the orphanage that day."

No. She knows about Finley? She must see the horror on my face. Her smile widens.

I'm going cold inside. If she knows Finley was there, that he helped me, he's dead. And all these things she is saying to me; I'm not leaving here alive, either. None of us are. Not with all the things we know.

But there is still one thing I want to know more than anything.

"But why me? Who am I? *Why*?"

Astrid laughs. "That is quite enough family reunion time, dear. Now, tell me. Where is your camera?"

"My camera?" I frown. "I don't know."

"This is the price of failure to cooperate." Her fingers move to the device she holds, and I brace myself for a slam of pain that doesn't come. But there is a cry to the side, and I turn.

Ben is curled up in a ball on the ground.

"Now answer my question."

I think fast. Does it matter? It's just a backup copy. It is 6:12; the transmission should be nearly over.

She raises her hand to the box again.

"Wait. Ben took it from me; he must still have it."

She nods at one of the Lorders, who goes through Ben's pockets, then holds up my camera.

The back door opens; there are footsteps in the kitchen?

"Ah, your other friends are arriving, at last," Nico says. The door from the kitchen opens. More Lorders, dragging two prisoners along with them. They throw them on the floor.

Mac, and Aiden. Both of them bloody and beaten, Aiden's arm hanging at an angle that is wrong.

"No!" I sag back.

"Yes, I'm afraid we stopped them; no movie premiere for you tonight. And we'll round up all the insurgents who appear on your little production as well. We've got some of them in custody already. But don't worry, they won't be in custody for long."

They'll be dead.

So will I.

The Lorder with my camera takes it over to Astrid. She puts down the device she was holding, her box of pain, to look at the camera.

It doesn't matter anymore, does it?

I fill myself with every bit of resolve I can find inside, every reserve of strength, every fragment of AGT training. One last flood of adrenaline before it all ends.

Tori's knife, the one Ben kicked out of her hand. It lies just out of sight, under the edge of a chair near Astrid.

I dive for it and for her.

41

I HOLD THE KNIFE AGAINST ASTRID'S NECK, POSITION HER body between them and me. "Drop your weapons," I say to the Lorders. They look at her.

"Do it," she hisses, and they hesitate, start to bend down, to put guns on the floor.

"Don't bother," Nico says, walking slowly toward Astrid and me, his gun still in his hand and pointed at us.

"Don't take another step!" I say.

He stops. He smiles, amused. "Really? Don't forget I know you, Kyla or Rain or Lucy or Riley or whoever the hell you want to be today. You can't kill anybody. Can you?"

The moment is stretching, each second a slow eternity. After everything, is it this moment, this one defining, ending moment of my life? If I kill her, I'll die. If I don't, I'll die. She deserves it, she deserves it more than anyone I can imagine in this world, except maybe Nico. Push the knife into her neck. Cut her throat. Watch blood spill down her body; revenge for so many.

But I can't do it. I can't be like them.

And he knows it.

The knife loosens in my hand. I swallow.

Nico smiles and steps closer; he takes the knife.

Astrid pushes away from me, her face twisted with fury; she

reaches for her box of pain. "You never could do what I wanted you to, could you? No more."

"Let me take care of her outside," Nico says to her. "It's about time."

She smiles, puts the box down again. "As you will. But make it quick. We've got to get out of here."

Nico slips an arm across my shoulders, gently pulls my hair back. Kisses my cheek. "We have unfinished business, you and I."

There is a scuffle behind Nico; Aiden cries out as a Lorder twists his injured arm behind him.

Nico opens the front door, pushes me out into the night. I trip on the step, sprawl onto the muddy ground in the cold rain:

Run.

I glance back; he stands there. Watching and waiting.

It's what he wants me to do. He wants me to run, doesn't he? So he can shoot me in the back.

I stand up. Face him down, like Florence did at All Souls.

He shrugs, raises his gun.

"Good-bye, Rain. It's been fun."

And I stand there, stare back at him. He's waiting for me to cry, to plead. I won't do it.

It's a funny thing. Earlier I thought I was ready to die, but I'm not. Despite everything, I want to stay, to breathe this air, to *feel* even if all there is to feel is pain. I'm fighting tears that threaten, fear that trembles through my body as he slowly points his gun straight at my heart. He smiles, and then—

BANG!

And I flinch, anticipating impact, pain, being pushed to the ground, but instead am full of confusion.

Nico has fallen? It is Nico clutching at his chest, *red red red* spreading. Nico dying.

Footsteps approach.

It's Coulson. Gun in hand, looking at Nico at his feet. But Coulson is a Lorder; Nico is with the Lorders now. Isn't he? Other Lorders run in behind him.

"I'm not dead," I say.

"Correct," Coulson says. He opens the door, looks back. "Come on," he says. Dazed, I step around Nico's now-still body, walk back into the house behind Coulson.

Astrid's eyes go round with shock. Her Lorders aren't looking happy, either, not that it is easy to tell with Lorders. But Coulson is a Lorder. Aren't they on the same side?

Coulson gestures at the other Lorders in the room. "Get out," he says. They look at Astrid. Indecision plays on her face.

More Lorders step in behind us.

"Do as he says," Astrid says, and they are ushered out.

Coulson checks the room, holds an arm out the door. A gesture.

In walk two people I was never more surprised to see: Dr. Lysander? And with her is Prime Minister Gregory.

Dr. Lysander rushes to the injured. Checks Ben, Aiden, and Mac. Skye. And Tori, too: But this time Dr. Lysander shakes her head. She closes Tori's eyes. Tori . . . dead? Another shock that I can't take in, can't believe. "Paramedics are needed for the others," Dr. Lysander says. "And a vet." Gregory nods, and a Lorder speaks into his collar. They're not going to be killed, but helped?

"So glad you came along, Prime Minister; lovely to see you as always," Astrid says to Gregory. "But things were well under control."

Gregory raises an eyebrow. "Really? What, exactly, is it that is under control? What operation were you conducting here without my knowledge? Did you know anything about it?" he says to Coulson.

"Not a thing through any *official* channels. Luckily, my unofficial sources are rather good."

"Well. If my head of security knows nothing *officially,* and I know nothing, how should I take this?"

Astrid is pale. "I learned of this plot to discredit the glorious Central Coalition with lies. They were attempting to hijack our television transmission and broadcast across the country tonight. I've been protecting you, on a need-to-know basis."

So Lorders use that phrase, too.

Gregory shrugs. "I may not need to know, but if Coulson doesn't know, how can that decision be made?"

She starts to speak again, but he holds up a hand.

"Be silent. I'm reserving judgment until I learn more. I've decided that I *need to know.*" His voice is icy, and Astrid is growing paler, but as much as I enjoy her discomfort, what has this got to do with us? They're all Lorders.

"You see, dear Astrid, I learned a few things I think I did need to know. Dr. Lysander here—she was a friend of my daughter's, did you know that?—came to me with some very interesting information. She was very *persistent* about getting in to see me, and when she told me about one of your special projects, I could see why. Slating is a legally sanctioned criminal punishment to be applied only according to due process of law, as you well know. Not to orphans under the age of legal responsibility.

"And then we unearthed some information about your *unofficial* training camps. This is two of them?" He gestures at Ben, and Tori's body. "Selected for special abilities, subjected to experimental procedures. Trained and twisted." He shakes his head.

"All within my ambit as JCO," Astrid says.

"I doubt even you believe that. And then we've been piecing some more things together. And worked out some of what you've done to my daughter. And my granddaughter."

Gregory turns. Why is he looking at me? He's blond, of course, though gray-streaked now, but up close I see something I haven't noticed before when I've seen him on TV or in photos: his eyes. Green eyes. The same shade as mine. Everyone is looking at me.

His granddaughter? *Me?* No. It couldn't be.

Could it?

A siren has approached; paramedics enter. At Dr. Lysander's direction, they take Skye and Ben away, and Tori's body. Aiden's arm is broken, but he refuses to leave. They strap his arm to his chest, check Mac's injuries, then leave.

"This is ridiculous," Astrid says. "They are traitors and should be dealt with as such."

"That may be. I'm still deciding. For now, I want to watch this transmission you stopped."

"It's in my camera," I say. I point to it on the floor, where it fell when I tackled Astrid.

Coulson takes it, checks it, and hands it to Gregory. My *grandfather*?!

"Are we ready now? Shall we?" He projects it on the wall.

We all watch it silently; this time, I don't look away. I stare at Florence's eyes just before she dies, standing there, facing them down. Did she feel like I did with Nico at that moment?

All are silent when it ends. Gregory finally turns to Astrid.

"Astrid Connor, your actions have been unacceptable. Further investigations are necessary." He gestures at Coulson. "Take her away, and then leave us."

After they're gone, the door shut behind them, Gregory turns to me. "Can you record on this thing?" he says, holding out the camera in his hand.

"Yes."

He hands it over. "Get ready."

I set it to record, hold up the camera. Hands surprisingly steady.

He begins.

"This is Merton Gregory, your prime minister, head of the Central Coalition Government. I've learned some news that has disturbed me greatly.

"Many of you may know that in the riots over thirty years ago, one of the students who was sentenced to execution was my daughter, Samantha Gregory. At the time I was deputy to then Prime Minister Armstrong; he offered to intervene and pardon her. I didn't allow him to save her, convinced the only way forward from the grip violent chaos had on our country was to apply the law in all cases. This is something I've regretted my entire life, and is part of the reason why I always protected the rule of law at all costs when I became prime minister myself—if I didn't, her loss was meaningless. And I have been willfully blind at times in ways I now regret.

"I have recently learned that my daughter was not executed, but this was not an act of leniency or kindness. There are more details I have yet to unearth as to where she was taken, or if she even still lives.

But I have discovered I have a granddaughter I knew nothing of, a girl whose only crime has been being related to me, the punishment given for this beyond anything the rule of law could condone.

"You're about to watch some very difficult scenes. I'm sorry, but you need to know.

"In light of what you are about to see, I feel I have no choice but to resign as prime minister. The government will be dissolved, and an election called. Change is long overdue. The Lorders served their purpose at the time; their time is over.

"All right, that'll do. I'm done," he says.

I hit stop, lower the camera. My eyes find Aiden's. Is this really happening?

Gregory turns to Mac and Aiden. "Now—can you get this out tonight before I change my mind? And we better use your hijacked system. I'm not sure this would get past the Lorder censors, even with my direct order. They might have me committed."

That evening, Mac does quick checks and repairs the damage to his transmission equipment that Astrid's Lorders inflicted when arresting him and Aiden. Dr. Lysander draws me aside, bandages the cut on my cheek.

"Tell me: How did you find out who I am?"

"Deduction, and guesswork." She sighs. "Really, I'm embarrassed it took me so long."

"Tell me."

"Deduction: I was thinking about everything that has been done and manipulated in your life; the classified DNA set in the system so none could trace it, set by Astrid as it turns out. Who you really were had to be an important part of the puzzle. And guesswork: how I always thought I knew you."

"You said I reminded you of a friend, one who died."

"Not just a friend." She pulls on a chain around her neck, and out of her clothes comes a gold locket. She opens it. "Inside here? A lock of hair. From a girl I loved years ago, who was meant to have been executed in the riots. Gregory's daughter, Samantha. When you cut your leg after your recent visit, on impulse I swabbed the blood you left behind for DNA. Later, feeling foolish for doing so, I compared DNA between that and this lock of hair. However she survived, Sam is your mother."

"And you went to Gregory and told him about me?"

"Just so."

"Where is my mother? Is she still alive?"

"I hope so. Gregory is working on that."

"But how did he link us to Astrid?"

"Thanks to you. Telling me that the orphanage you visited was in Cumbria. It didn't take Gregory long to link first the orphanage, then his daughter's disappearance, to Astrid. She must have seen this opportunity with his daughter, Sam: the ultimate way to discredit Gregory. He was the obvious next prime minister after Armstrong; Astrid wasn't in position to take power yet when she arranged Armstrong's assassination. She was a long-range planner."

"I don't understand. What use was Sam to Astrid?"

"She probably thought at the time that she'd use Sam when she was ready, to make it look as if Gregory broke the law to save his daughter. Then later on, when you appeared, she came up with an even better plan: having Gregory's own granddaughter make a sham of Slating, and to assassinate both him and Armstrong's daughter at the same time. How far back she was putting this in place we do not know; it must have been at least since you were ten, when she arranged through Nico for the AGT to take you."

"If her plans had worked that day, Lorders wouldn't know who might turn—which Slateds were safe or dangerous."

"Astrid's views are notoriously hard-line, and she would have been the obvious next prime minister if Gregory had been killed. She prefers the death penalty to Slating; a clean sweep of existing Slateds wouldn't have troubled her. But you thwarted her plans."

"Because I ran back to save you. I wasn't there, next to Gregory and the others, when they meant to set off the bomb hidden on my Levo."

"Yes. And since then I've learned more from Gregory. That by then Coulson was suspicious of you, who you were: He'd noticed irregularities in your records. When the bomb went off at your house, he took the opportunity to fake your death, to stop any possible AGT interference while he looked into it."

"But how did you find us here today?"

"Gregory has been having Astrid watched. When she came south in force, we knew something big was up. We closed in."

"Just in time."

Dr. Lysander smiles. "Yes. Thankfully, just in time."

I turn it all over in my mind, but keep coming back to two things. I was just a baby when I was taken from a mother I never heard of until today. Where is she? Is she even alive? And then there is Ben.

"What is going to happen to Ben?"

"I don't know. He has committed crimes, though under coercion perhaps."

"Where is he now?"

"He's been taken to the hospital for assessment and observation."

"When can I see him?"

"I'm not sure that is wise. For either of you."

Mac has added Gregory's new introduction to *Need to Know*. It is nine P.M., three hours later than planned, when it hits every television, viewing, and vid screen in this country and others. Can so much really have happened in such a short time?

I stand, awkward and uncertain, next to Aiden while it runs; the pain from his arm is showing on his face, but his eyes are gleaming. "We did it, Kyla. We really did it." He smiles, but his eyes slide from me to Gregory and back again.

When it's over, Gregory glances at Aiden and Mac. "Leave us alone for a moment," he says, in a voice used to being obeyed.

But things have changed. They look to me.

"It's fine. Go," I say, staring at Gregory while they leave. My grandfather; a stranger. Someone I used to hate with every beat of my heart for what he stood for, yet someone who unexpectedly saved my life. Saved us all.

He raises an eyebrow. "Do I pass inspection?"

I shrug. "I don't know. There is good and bad."

"And you're not sure which is the greater."

"Exactly. Are you really resigning?"

"Isn't that what I said? Yet you seem skeptical." He looks pleased.

I shrug. "Maybe this is just a way to get out of blame. Defeat Astrid, blame things on her, rebrand the party and start over again."

"Politics loves a scapegoat." He shrugs. "That'd probably work. You've got a suspicious mind. Maybe you got that from me."

"And?"

"No. I'm done. The country can start over again without me. I'm not proud of things that have been done in my government's name. I'm not proud of things I've done myself. I can't change the past, but I will do what I can now to ease the political changes. But what I really wanted to say to you now is this: I'm sorry."

"What for, specifically? Even if you leave Astrid out of things, it wasn't her who had me Slated, beaten, and threatened. It wasn't her who made kids disappear from my school for no reason. The list is long enough without her; but if you add her in and it gets a whole lot worse, who was in charge of her?"

He flinches. "Don't worry. I don't expect a hugs-and-flowers big family reunion. I don't expect you to forgive and forget. But there is one thing I will do for you. For both of us."

"What is that?" What can he possibly offer to do for me, now, that will mean anything.

"I have a promise to make you. I'll find my daughter, your mother. One way or the other, I'll find her."

He reaches out, grips my hand, and I don't pull away. So many times I've thought, *This is me, I know it all.* And then there is another revelation. But Sam really *is* my mother—DNA doesn't lie. Dr. Lysander doesn't, either. I fight the tears that threaten: not here, not now.

"Where is she?"

"I'll find her."

When I get back to Mac's house, Aiden waits out front. Alone.

"Shouldn't you be on your way to a hospital to get that arm seen to properly?"

"Probably. I had to see you first." He reaches his good hand to my cheek, and I lean against him, into his warmth. So glad he is still alive, that we both are. And suddenly too full of everything that has happened to want to be anywhere else.

Aiden tightens his good arm around me, and murmurs into my hair. "I heard what you said before to Dr. Lysander."

"About what?"

"About Ben. About asking to see him."

I pull away. "I have to."

"After everything he has done?"

"It's not him. They've made him like that. You don't understand."

"Then make me."

"He's fighting what they've done to him."

"How do you know?"

"He saved my life tonight: kicked a knife out of Tori's hand."

"Then I'll thank him for that. But does one good deed wipe out all the others?"

I stare back at Aiden, and I can't answer. Does Gregory's one good deed wipe out all his others? But it's not the same thing. He's had his free will; Ben hasn't.

"Kyla, there is one more thing. The other day, when I said I loved you. I said how can you love somebody when you don't know all of them? And you said, then how could someone who was Slated ever love or be loved."

"And?"

"I do know all of you. And I don't mean every memory you've lost: I know who you are, inside. Despite everything, how you could never deliberately hurt anybody. How brave you are, how fiercely loyal, and all the little insecurities, fears, and stubbornness as well, and I love all of you. Can you say the same about Ben?"

"Yes," I say, but doubt gnaws inside, and Aiden knows it. "I don't have any choice. I can't abandon him; he hasn't got anybody else. Not after everything we were to each other."

His hand touches my shoulder.

"Everything you *were* to each other. That is past tense. Let me know when you're ready for the present, or maybe even the future."

42

EVERYTHING HAPPENS VERY QUICKLY AFTER THE BROADCAST.

Prime Minister Gregory makes his resignation official, as promised. Amid public outcry and international pressure, Parliament is dissolved, and elections called. And it is almost like Aiden always said it would be: Once everyone really knew what went on, they said, *No, no more.* And the Lorders were no more.

Of course it wasn't as easy as that. There were high costs on both sides—pitched battles in some places, like Cumbria, where Astrid's followers refused to accept they weren't in charge anymore—but the cost wasn't as high as living with constant fear under the Lorders. They did it; MIA really did it. DJ, Aiden, and an international council have put a provisional government in place pending elections, and new political parties are forming, setting up candidates.

Gregory is still hunting for Sam, my mother, but now that months have passed I'm starting to accept he may never find her. Mum and Amy are okay; they hadn't been found by Astrid's Lorders, and I'm staying with them for a while back in our newly repaired house. Skye survived and is here, being nursed back to health and spoiled by all three of us. Slating is banned, and Dr. Lysander has been busy removing Levos and brain chips from Slateds, including mine.

But while part of me is rejoicing in the changes that have happened and are yet to come, more is in limbo. Licking my wounds and waiting for this one day.

• • •

Dr. Lysander sits opposite Ben and me at her desk. "There are no guarantees; we don't know who you were before you were Slated."

"I know, I know; Lorders destroyed my records, none have been found," Ben says. He holds my hand tight.

"We don't know who you were, but do we know enough?" I say. "You don't have to do this."

"I want to."

Dr. Lysander goes through her list of cautions, not for the first time. Results of memory adjustment are not predictable; he may have memories he doesn't want and not the ones he does want returned; there is a risk of brain damage, seizures, and death. While simple cases of readjustment have been successful, his case is unpredictable due to the multiple procedures to which he'd been subjected.

"Is that everything?" Ben asks.

"Are you sure you wish to proceed?" she asks.

"Yes. Can Kyla come?"

"I wouldn't recommend it, but if she wishes to do so, it is your choice."

"I'll be there," I say, unwilling to let go of his hand. Despite the things he has done, it was the Lorders—their procedures and manipulations—that led him to betray us. I can't erase the things Ben did: I still wake screaming late at night, visions of Florence and the others dying at All Souls haunting my dreams. And I still can't shake the *if only*s from it all. If only Aiden hadn't brought Ben there; if only I'd tried harder to get through to Ben. If only I'd recognized what was about to happen, and stopped him.

If only.

But it wasn't *Ben* who betrayed us; it was the Lorders' creature.

After all that has happened to me, all the identities that have been forced or taken, I can understand that better than anyone. I can't abandon him while there is any chance of calling him back, no matter how torn I feel. I won't.

They get him ready. He's on one of those beds that hugs you like when I had IMET; they're checking things, monitors, wires, IV drugs, and a scanner all around his head. All the while he grips tight to my hand.

"What if I sneeze?" Ben jokes. He'd found it endlessly funny that the microsurgery goes through his nose.

"You know you can't; you'll be immobilized. Almost paralyzed except for speech."

When the drugs take hold, his hand slackens. "I'm still holding it," I tell him. "Everything is fine." But I'm afraid.

These months have been difficult. Once Ben really understood what had been done to him, how he'd been subjected to procedures and manipulated to be a Lorder agent, he'd been in a dark place. And both of us struggled to come to terms with Tori's role—that she retained her memories, but still chose to act for the Lorders—and her death. Ben only started to come back to life with the hope of this: experimental microsurgery to give him back what was stolen.

Dr. Lysander meets my eyes over a sea of equipment, nods once. "All right then, Ben. Shall we begin?"

"No, I changed my mind. Just kidding! Go for it."

"All right. First I am removing your chip; this is routine." So no chance of anyone activating it to cause him pain, or kill him like Tori was killed, ever again; mine was taken out weeks ago.

Dr. Lysander peers into control screens, remote operates using the scanner and microscopic robotic tools. Time passes slowly; seconds feel like minutes.

"Your chip is removed," she finally says. "Is everything all right?"

"I'm fine, having fun. Carry on," Ben says.

"Now tell me what you experience." She'd explained that different neuronal areas of the brain will be microstimulated as she navigates his memory storage areas, reattaches broken neural connections according to his responses.

"Okay, here goes," Ben says. "Blue, the blue sea. Soft fur—a puppy! It's Skye; I think it is. Fish: I smell fish and chips. A woman, I see a woman. My mother?" he says, and starts describing her, but going by what he says it's not his mum from when he was Slated. Then his voice changes—"Mummy? Mummy?"—a high-pitched note of panic, a child's voice.

"You're okay, Ben," I say. "I'm here."

"Who's Ben? I'm Nate. Mummy?" Then, "Kyla?" he says, back to his voice again. "I remember my mother!"

"One up on me there, then."

"This is good," Dr. Lysander says. "Carry on describing."

He is quiet.

"Ben?" she says.

"I'm still here. Things are zipping through too fast to tell you: people and places. Sometimes like I'm there, sometimes like I'm looking at a photograph."

"Memory can be like that. All right, I am reattaching the final deep links; this is the tricky bit."

"Great to know."

"Describe, Ben."

Words are spilling out; people and places are garbled and quick, and then . . . "Kyla?"

"Yes?"

"At Group. I ran in late, you were sitting there. The new girl. I remember! The first time I saw you, beautiful, gorgeous girl."

And I know he can't feel it or squeeze back, but I'm holding his hand tighter, tears threatening; it's working. He remembers me.

Then he gasps. "Pain, hot pain, in my side."

"Yes, you have a scar, an old knife wound," Dr. Lysander says. "And what else? Ben? Answer me."

"No," he says, his voices changed, angry. "No!"

"Ben?"

"Ben?" she says again.

He is silent.

"Ben?" I try. "Nate? Are you all right?"

"Dandy. I'm dandy, thanks for asking." And with his words I can breathe again, but his accent—was it changed? Into something more London, less country.

"We're nearly done here," Dr. Lysander says.

Before long, the scanner is pulled away, the microtools removed. One tiny drop of blood under his nose is wiped away; that is all.

His eyes are closed, sedation increased; he will sleep now.

"Go home, Kyla," Dr. Lysander says. "He goes into recovery now for monitoring while he sleeps. It will be a day or two before we know how it went."

But I stay. With Ben/Nate—whoever he is, he remembers me now.

EPILOGUE

IT'S LATE SUMMER. I INSISTED ON COMING ALONE, ACROSS the fells. Skye bounds along beside me, still with a limp but it doesn't slow her down. And as I walk, I think. So much of what has motivated me for so long has been trying to find out who I am, where I come from. Each new revelation knocked down walls in my mind, but came at a cost. Will today give any closure?

Everyone is searching for something or somebody. The bit they haven't got to complete them. Why should I be any different?

Mum's son, Robert, hasn't been found, but she is still looking, with the help of MIA—now a government-sanctioned agency, and Mac and Aiden's full-time mission.

Mum refused to run for prime minister, despite all who wanted her to. Gregory, who I see now and then—no matter what he was, he is my grandfather, and so much of how things went better than they could have at the end was down to him—said those suited for power don't want it, and those who want it, aren't. He didn't say which category he was in. Anyhow, some new guy who wanted power is in charge, a whole new government has been voted in, and DJ and his friends are still here to keep an eye on things for a while.

Will everything be all right now? Time will tell, but already I'm not sure everything is good. Like all the new technology flooding in from outside now that the borders are open, all the endless Internet channels, the portable devices and plug-ins so you're always linked in. The traveling curious from other nations rushing to see how quaint we are before we become just like them. Gregory says that is why the world stepped in: not to save anybody, but to have a new market to sell their toys.

With repeal of the YP laws, I'm now sharing a flat in Keswick with Madison. She was in Astrid's slate mine prison like Len thought she might be, and released with all the other illegally held prisoners. Finley had gone into hiding not long after I left Keswick; he came out when it was safe again. Madison's not the same, but with Finley's help, getting better all the time.

I see Stella once or twice a week; a fragile trust is beginning to grow between us. She is slowly coming to terms with all that Astrid did; with Dad not being behind my disappearance. With how much she had it wrong. She's had trouble accepting my refusal to let Dr. Lysander try to return my memories, but they've been mucked around with enough. From now on, nobody but me has any say in what I choose to remember, what I choose to forget.

For now I'm working with Parks as a fell checker. Len is on the list of those missed; he died in the struggle against Astrid's faithful. Being alone in the high places above the world in all weather, the mountains under my feet that have been, are, and will be long after I'm gone, I feel a release never felt anywhere else; it is really why I came back to Keswick, despite Mum and Amy. It is the only place I can think about *anything* and not be overwhelmed.

I still might go back to school myself, then get into teacher training one day and be an art teacher, like Gianelli, but not now. The happy little faces are too much for me, after all the Slated children from

Astrid's orphanage experiment were found: dead. Killed by Astrid's minions to hide what they'd done, but found before the bodies could be destroyed.

At least I know Edie survived, and that Ben never told the Lorders where she was; their house was empty that day because they'd heard what happened at All Souls and bolted in a hurry, gone into hiding. When they reappeared, I went to see them. Edie said I could keep Murray, that I was more alone than she was.

That is one place where I know Ben told the truth after all the lies that followed. He kept up an act long enough to get out of the hospital, and then some of the truth came out. He'd committed crimes worthy of Slating before we'd even met, to add to the ones after at All Souls. He said the only time he was ever happy was when he was Slated.

And then he stole a car and disappeared. No one knows where he has gone. All I know is he doesn't want to be with me. For whatever reason, good or bad, at the end that is the truth.

Should I have seen it coming? I could never really hurt anyone, Slated or not. Ben could, and did; with the Lorders he may have been coerced, manipulated, and escaped legal responsibility because of it, but in the end it was still him who caused and took part in the All Souls massacre. Did that say something about who he was to start with? Dr. Lysander hinted as much; she warned us again and again, but left the choice to Ben.

Sometimes I wonder if he ever really was mine, or was it all illusion from the start. Like Aiden said, how can you truly love somebody when you don't know who they really are?

But most of the time, I know we did. That time and place when we were just what we were then: blank slates. Innocents. Before my memories started to return; before Lorders manipulated and changed him, and Dr. Lysander returned his past. It was real, at least to me. My evidence is the pain left behind.

Seeing how Finley is with Madison tells me it is possible for love to last, to grow. Just not for me, not now. One final lesson the Lorders have taught me is this: There are no second chances. I chose Ben, turned my back on Aiden, and I can't take it back. But Aiden was right, wasn't he? Ben was the past. I don't miss him the way I do Aiden. With Ben it is more grieving for something that *was*. Not something that could have been.

That should have been.

One last climb and I finally reach my destination: Astrid's slate mine prison. She is the only prisoner there now. Behind it are unmarked graves, with flowers and a memorial; a public ceremony today to unveil it. Mum is here, and Stella. Gregory and Dr. Lysander also. There are survivors, women newly released from the prison along with Madison, wearing both the marks of their ordeals and nervous joy at unexpected freedom on their faces. Along with survivors are family and friends, like us, of those who didn't make it.

And one surprise. I almost stop breathing when Aiden walks up to me, gives me a hug. He doesn't say anything, just holds me, and I cling to him, tight.

The ceremony begins. Gregory had been as good as his word; he'd found his daughter. Turns out she died just weeks after I was born—natural causes. If you can call dying of untreated infection after childbirth "natural." Maybe, it was an escape? Though I like to think she would have stayed with me if she could.

I stand with Mum and Stella for the two minutes of silence, but as if that isn't enough, it persists long after the time is marked. *More sinned against than sinning*: I stare at the words carved in the memorial over the graves that include the mother I'll never know, standing between the two that I did.

Afterward, I feel eyes on me—a woman, thin, hunched, skin a papery gray, the determined eyes of a survivor. She draws me aside.

"I was there when you were born. Sam refused to say who was the father, but what options are there in a woman's prison with male guards? I know what your mother named you," she says, then whispers it in my ear as if it can't be said out loud.

It didn't come that day, but on other days, as the sun shines down to melt the ice of another winter, to summon spring wildflowers from the earth; as the sky darkens with sudden, drenching showers before the sun returns, I know that both pain and joy are needed for life to grow. As Skye bounds about my feet, as Aiden comes to walk beside me, against all logic I can almost feel it.

My mother, Sam, must have been an amazing woman. So much circled around her: Gregory's guilt at not having pardoned her made him a rigid Lorder ruler for most of his life. Dr. Lysander's grief at her supposed execution led her to invent Slating—a way to stop execution of underage criminals, yes, but look at all that it led to. And Sam, herself, imprisoned for years by Astrid in that horrible place; I can't imagine what she went through. Yet somehow, she still had it within her to give me a name that reaches out and bridges the years lost between us.

I have both been given and taken so many identities, but at last I am beginning to grow into my one true name. More will come with surviving, and time. With standing on my own feet now; with Aiden and I finding our way together in the future. Because sometimes there *are* second chances.

This was the gift my mother gave to me:

Hope.

ACKNOWLEDGMENTS

WRITING AND PUBLISHING A TRILOGY, A BOOK A YEAR, IS quite a whirlwind!

Special thanks are owed to my agent, Caroline Sheldon: Without her, none of this may have ever happened.

And to everyone at my publishers on both sides of the pond—especially editors Megan Larkin and Rosalind Turner at Orchard Books in the UK, and Nancy Paulsen and Sara Kreger at Nancy Paulsen Books in the US—thank you for everything.

Thanks to Erin Johnson for taking me around Oxford and its colleges, and to the porter at Magdalen College. When I was despairing that you couldn't see into another college's quad from Magdalen Tower, he suggested St. Mary's Church tower and All Souls as an alternative.

Thanks to first readers Amy Butler Greenfield and Jo Wyton, and writing buddies everywhere, especially all my friends at the SCBWI.

And now . . . I've heard that confession is good for the soul.

It is time to come clean: about character names, and where they come from. Some you may know about already. I had a few name-a-character competitions which gave Katran in *Fractured,* and Madison and Finley in *Shattered.*

But what you may not know is many of my other character names come from friends, and that I often hunt them out on my Facebook friends list.

First, the pets. Skye was a real dog! Owned by friend Karen Murray. Sadly, Skye died before *Slated* came out, but the dog's name and character is *so* how I remember her. Sebastian in *Slated* was a real cat—years ago, my parents had two, Damian and Sebastian. The character of the cat in *Slated* was more Damian, and I originally used that name, but somewhere along the way changed it to Sebastian. And in *Shattered*? Pounce was the name of one of my sister's cats.

And now for the people: The real people have nothing in common with the characters beyond the name, unless otherwise stated. Ben came from Benjamin Scott, because he is always smiling. Hatten—Nico's surname as a teacher in *Slated*—came from Caroline Hooten, as the name made me think of owls; the spelling changed somewhere along the way. Nico came from Nick Cross. Kyla's assigned mother, Sandra, came from my sister—and there is more than a little of her in the character. And in *Shattered,* Stella came from Stella Wiseman, and Astrid from Astrid Holm.

And of course, I can't forget Murray: He is my own very sleepy teddy bear!

So there is more than one way to have your name end up in one of my books. My Facebook page is "TeriTerryAuthor": Like it, and you just never know . . .

You can also find me as "TeriTerryWrites" on Twitter and Tumblr, and my website is teriterry.com.

Thanks to Slans—Slated fans—and readers, bloggers and reviewers everywhere, whose support and enthusiasm for the Slated trilogy has been beyond awesome.

And to the most patient and understanding man: Living with a writer can be trying, but Graham is always the calm center of my life.

And finally, to Banrock, Murray, and muses everywhere: cheers!